Shattered Secrets

SHATTERED
BOOK TWO

KARIN WINTER

For my Family,

Please don't read this book.

CHAPTER 1

Ethan

"It's time to reveal the truth," I tell Olive on the phone. "I'll be there to pick you up in a few minutes."

I hang up and call Ayala.

She doesn't answer, and I leave her a voicemail telling her I'm going to be late. "Hey, Bambi, sorry I'll be so late getting home today. I know you're going crazy. There's no progress yet, but I have an idea. You liked it when I took you to Mohonk, right? I think we should go on a trip where no one will find us. What do you say? Miss you."

I never thought I'd be the one to leave these kinds of messages on the phone, but I do miss her.

I stop by Olive's apartment and pick her up. Her parents live in Connecticut, so we have a long drive ahead of us. Olive sits beside me and digs her nails into her thighs. She'll hurt herself at that rate. I grab her hand and place it on my lap.

"Olive, calm down. We're going to talk, not murder someone."

She gives me a sullen look. "Not sure it won't turn into murder after they hear what I have to say. You don't know them."

"We've prepared for every scenario. At worst, they'll kick us out, and I'll help you with anything you need, as I promised. At best, everything will continue as usual. They'll continue to love you and support you."

Her hand on my thigh squeezes gently. "Meeting you was the best thing to happen to me. I hope Ayala appreciates you as much as I do."

I smile. I appreciated the crazy sex last night. "Yes."

"So... what's up with you two? Are you serious? What about this husband of hers?"

"It's complicated. I don't know how to solve this problem yet. But yes, I'm serious about her. I love her, Olive."

Her mouth opens. "Love her? Who is this guy talking about love?"

I laugh. "I don't believe it either. She has magical powers over me. That's what I think." She does. Ayala hasn't left my thoughts since the day I met her. Fate sent her to save me.

I drive through the large entrance gate and turn the car into the long driveway next to the house.

Olive grips my hand when we walk in, where her parents are waiting for us. I don't understand why she's so worried. I wish my parents were a little more like hers.

I inhale when the aroma of the stew reaches my nose. It smells so good. The other dishes arrive one after the other. Surely these dishes were not prepared by Olive's mother, Lisa, as I doubt the woman ever worked in a kitchen a day in her life.

When dessert is served, I nudge Olive under the table with my knee, and she glares at me. If she doesn't say something, I will. It's taken months of persuasion to get to this moment, and I won't let her get out of here without getting this over and done with. If she doesn't gather the courage now, it will never happen. And if she doesn't come clean now that we are officially "breaking up" and the agreement between us is being dissolved, Olive will have to go back to dating other men.

The memory of that horrible moment in bed with her hits me... No, there's no way I will let her go through that again.

"Olive wants to tell you something," I say when she shows no intention of speaking. "Ouch!" I gasp as she steps on my foot with her heel. Damn, those pin heels fucking hurt.

Her parents look at us with interest. Now she has no choice. Perfect.

"Dad, Mom, I wanted to talk to you about something important," Olive says.

They both look up with expressions that say they are ready to listen. They are great parents, and I hope this ends the way I expect it will.

"Ethan and I aren't dating."

Okay. This is not how I would have chosen to start. With a lie. It's better to start with the truth. I watch their reaction closely, ready to jump in to help. Olive looks down at her lap, and her parents glance at each other.

"We're just good friends." She takes a deep breath but still does not raise her face. "I know you were hoping we'd get married soon, but, Mom, Dad. I'm not interested in men. I'm more... I prefer women," she blurts out.

I am so proud of her. She did it! I squeeze her hand under the table.

No one speaks. Lisa's eyes are wide. Larry looks as pale as the wall behind him.

Say something, I beg without words.

"So you're a lesbian?" her father says, breaking the silence.

"Don't say lesbian, Larry." Her mother pokes him with an elbow.

"You can say lesbian." Olive dares to smile a little. "Yes, I'm a lesbian."

"Okay," Lisa says, sounding calm. "So, do you have a girl-friend, then?"

I stifle another smile. Even now, they are pushing her into a relationship.

"Not really, no," Olive says, looking shocked at the fact that the four of us are still sitting here calmly and the ceiling hasn't fallen over our heads, a dragon didn't spit brimstone fire at us, and the hand of God didn't strike us dead.

"I don't understand why you let us believe you were going to marry him." Larry throws an angry scowl at me.

"I never said I was going to marry Ethan, Dad."

It's true. We never said that, but we let the gossip fuel the engagement rumors. We didn't deny it, not even to them.

"So you're not getting married soon?" he continues.

"No. I'm not getting married."

"I need time to digest this." He gets up and paces the room.

Olive watches him with worried glances.

"Will I have grandchildren?" he asks.

"I don't know, Dad. I guess. I want kids someday. Are you mad at me?"

"I'm angry that you tricked us. You let us believe things that aren't true."

"I'm sorry. I was afraid."

Lisa says in a soft voice, "We're your parents and always will be. Why did you think you couldn't tell us something like this?"

"I thought you wouldn't love me anymore if you knew."

I clench my fists under the table. My parents stopped loving me. It's not impossible.

"Oh, honey. I hope you'll find a woman who is at least as nice as this man here." Lisa smiles at me. "I was sure the important announcement was going to be that you two were engaged."

Lisa looks disappointed. Not because Olive wants to date women but because there won't be a wedding soon. It's going better than I thought.

Her father returns to the table, and we finish dessert while talking some more.

"It's getting late." Olive stands, preparing for our departure.

Lisa stands, and comes around the table. "You know, John's daughter is a lesbian. Maybe we can introduce you to her?"

"Mom, I don't need you to arrange my dates."

Ignoring her daughter's protests, Lisa hugs me goodbye. "It was nice to have you here, Ethan. Thank you for watching over my daughter."

I nod. "I'll always look out for her, Lisa. She's a good friend."

Her father nods and shakes my hand before turning to Olive. "We'll continue this conversation later. Give us some time to digest."

As we drive back to Manhattan Olive lets out a loud laugh full of relief.

"I can't believe it." From the sound of her laughter, I think there may be a few tears in there as well.

"What can't you believe?" I glance in her direction but try not to take my eyes off the road.

"That it was so simple. I'm sure they're writhing at home right now, not realizing what happened. But they were okay. No plates were thrown, no blood was shed." Olive looks as if a huge stone has fallen from her heart.

"Thank you, Ethan. Thank you for convincing me to do this, for being there for me, and coming with me. For who you are." She bends toward me and kisses my cheek.

"Whenever you need me, Olive. I told you, friends are forever. I'll always take care of you."

I stop by her apartment and drop her off. She hugs me again.

"I still can't believe that I can go with a woman to the next event. It's amazing." She jumps and skips to the entrance, and I smile widely.

It's amazing. I'm happy for her.

It's already after midnight by the time I get back to our apartment.

Our apartment.

I think of it as ours. I no longer see myself without Ayala. I know I want her to stay.

"Ayala?" I call, but there's no response.

I turn on the lights in the living room. Maybe she already fell asleep. I told her not to wait up for me, and it is quite late.

As I head toward the bedroom, I loosen my tie and take it off. My eyes slowly adjust to the darkness. I notice Ayala is not in bed. I check in the bathroom. Not there either. I frown. Where is she? She knows very well that she mustn't go outside. She can't go anywhere. It's too dangerous.

I put my tie and jacket on the bed and return to the living room, checking each room in the house on my way, trying to understand what's happening here. Then I see it. Her phone is sitting there, on the counter, next to an envelope.

My heart skips a beat.

I take the envelope first and open it carefully. The page inside has the smell of her perfume. God, this can't be good.

My Love,

When I arrived in New York, I hoped to build a new life on my own, but fate had other plans for me. He summoned you to me. The stubborn man who appeared in my life again and again until I couldn't deny you anymore. You taught me what true love is. You taught me I am not damaged, that I am a woman worthy of love. I love you so much.

Even in my wildest dreams, I couldn't imagine you. You have given me so much. Now it's my turn to save you.

Forgive yourself for me because I need you to forgive me too.

I promise to be strong for you.

Always yours,

Ayala

The last words tear my heart from my chest. What have you done, Bambi? What the hell have you done?

With a shaking hand, I pick up her phone and open it. I see she has a new message from me.

She didn't even hear that I left her a message. That was hours ago! She left hours ago while I spent a pleasant evening with Olive.

Ayala left me?

I know she loves me. I'm sure of it. That's indisputable. She wasn't lying to me when she said the words. Love was present in her every movement and gesture, just as it was present in mine.

So why did she go?

I check her phone, looking for clues, and open her recent calls. There are very few calls, and almost all of them are from me. Ryan and Nicky's numbers are also listed here. The last calls are from a confidential number.

I check the time. She must have left after that conversation. The time fits. I sent the message just a little later.

Who is this, and why did she leave?

I promise to be strong for you.

An ominous feeling crawls down my spine. Why do you have to be strong for me, Bambi?

I pick up the phone and call Jess.

"Yes, Wolf," Jess answers in a sleepy voice. It doesn't matter that I've woken him up. When I need him, he always answers at any hour of the day.

"Jess," I shout into the receiver, "I think Summers has taken Ayala."

"Took her from where? Isn't she in your apartment?"

"She was. She's not here now, and she left her phone. I think it's him. There's no other option."

"He broke into the penthouse?"

The building is quite secure. There's a guard, and it's not possible to get to the penthouse without my key. I also hired two undercover security guards and placed them in front of the building to ensure no one entered uninvited.

"No. She must have left the building on her own. There's no sign of a break-in. I don't know what he said to her, but it must have been a serious threat. It's the only logical thing."

"Why do you think so?"

"She wouldn't leave me. And she left a strange letter."

"What does it say?"

I read him the letter.

"She didn't mention Michael Summers in the letter. Are you sure she didn't leave voluntarily?"

"I'm positive."

"Okay. When was that?"

"She has an unidentified call coming in around three o'clock," I report. "I think she left because of that call."

"Okay. I'll try to trace it. But that was nearly ten hours ago. If he indeed took her, she could be anywhere in the world by now, Wolf."

"I know," I say before hanging up.

Why did she leave without talking to me first? I check my phone again to make sure I didn't miss any calls or messages. Nope.

What the hell did he say to her that would make her leave me like this? Without calling me, at least?

I open her device again and go through the latest messages. Fuck. Photos. He sent photos.

I gasp, and my heart skips a beat as I realize what he must have said to her. Fucking hell.

How did he get so close to me? The son of a bitch pointed a gun at my back, and I didn't even notice. I hired security for the building to protect Ayala. I didn't think anyone would come after me. I didn't think I had to defend myself. Shit. I feel the need to hit someone or something.

She went back to the monster because of me.

CHAPTER 2

Ayala

T he noise of the engines mask the pounding in my heart as I fly back to the place I once called home, next to the man I never wanted to see again, the monster in my dreams.

And worst of all, I'm here willingly.

I was innocent and naïve when I got married, but now I know who he is. I know what I'm walking into. I've seen the monster raise its head, and yet, here I am.

The flight attendant offers me water or orange juice with a smile. Michael's hand digs into my waist, hurting me. He makes it clear that I mustn't say a word out of place. But I don't need his warning to remember why I'm here. Ethan needs to live.

I take the water from her, and she continues down the aisle.

"Are you the one who followed Ethan with the gun?" I ask.

Michael grins. "Of course not. I hired someone. Do you think I would take the risk of being caught? I'm not stupid." He pauses. "You know, when I met you, I was sure you would be the perfect match. Beautiful, shy, inexperienced. Religious education. Submissive. You ticked all the boxes. You should have been just right. And how wrong was I, huh? You're just a simple whore. Did you sleep with him?" Michael squeezes my arm, and I wince.

"Yes." I shoot him a look and raise my head in defiance. I'm so scared, almost paralyzed with fear, but I will never regret Ethan.

Michael's face contorts in anger. "On the first opportunity you had, you opened your legs to someone else. After everything I've given you."

"What you gave me?" I almost spit out the words. "What did you give me besides beatings?"

"If you hadn't teased me, that wouldn't have happened."

I can't believe he said that. I was a shadow of a woman. Bent under the rule of fear. I didn't dare speak back then. How dare he say I provoked him? "You're a joke of a man. You don't even know how to have sex with a woman," I taunt, gaining fake courage, taking advantage of the fact that we're on a public flight, and he won't dare hit me here.

A bitter smile appears on his face. "I didn't teach you enough about sex, you say. Don't worry, whore. I'll show you what a man I am."

I was wrong to provoke him. He was cruel before, and he'll be crueler now that I ran away from him. But I promised to be strong. And I promise myself to draw my strength from Ethan's image in my memory.

It will be harder to endure now that I know what a real relationship is supposed to be like, but I'll have the memories to hold on to on hard days. This time, the monster won't break me.

After the long drive, we arrive at an unfamiliar house. Michael forced me to lie on the floor of the car during the drive, so I have no idea where we are. I look around and try to absorb my surroundings. Where are we? In the middle of a forest? I see only trees as far as the eye can see, and the area seems quite isolated. There is no other house within sight.

Damn, this doesn't bode well for me.

Why didn't he take me to our house?

I enter the cabin while Michael takes his luggage out of the rental car.

After six hours of flying, of sitting on the plane with my muscles tight, I'm exhausted. And all I want to do is go to sleep. But sleeping with Michael? I shudder at the thought. There's no way I can close my eyes when I know he's close.

He puts his suitcases down and tosses the keys onto a table at the entrance. Every step he takes makes me cringe more. I want to disappear, but I'm planted in the entrance, debating what to do.

"Why aren't we at home?"

"I arranged a short vacation for you. Aren't you happy?"

I lick my lips.

"You need to be re-educated before I can bring you back into the public eye. Now go upstairs," he orders, and I take my bag and go upstairs, knowing any moment away from him is a blessing. There is only one bedroom, with a bed in the center. I close my eyes and inhale. I should lock myself in the bathroom and never come out.

He'll come right after me, though, and won't hesitate to break down the door.

"If you're thinking of running away, remember that I know where your boyfriend is, and I'll have no problem sending someone to New York."

Yes, I remember. How can I forget?

"How did you know I was at Ethan's?" I ask. How did he find me after two months of me hiding in Ethan's penthouse?

"I have to admit you did a good job of disappearing. I couldn't find you for a very long time. Then I added a cash prize," he says. "People will sell their mother for a nice prize."

Did someone sell me out? Who? I can count on one hand the number of people who knew where I was. Who could have done this?

"Your friend told me that Wolf was courting you, a married woman. It didn't take me long to find out that he had recently purchased an extra phone line for his mistress. My money wasn't enough for you? Were you looking for someone richer? Did he know you were married? That you're an adulterer?"

"Which friend?" Did Nicky tell him where I was?

"Robin, I think she was called."

Robin. I try to digest what he's telling me. Did she hate me that much? I bite my lip. No, she just didn't understand what she was doing. She didn't know he was beating me, raping me, that she was sending me back to hell.

Wait a moment. "What 'she was called?'"

His mouth curves into a half smile, looking more cruel than usual. "Well, she wasn't satisfied with the amount I offered. She asked for a million dollars. Can you believe that? Are you worth a million dollars? There's no pussy in this world worth a million dollars. Too bad she didn't agree to my terms."

"What did you do?" I whisper, my voice shaking.

"What do you think I did? I promised her the money, and after she told me what a whore you are, I made sure she didn't come back asking for more." He marks a line on his neck.

"You killed Robin?" My eyes widen.

"I think the report is she killed herself. Poor thing." He laughs. "It was hard for her to withstand the pressure. It turns out she was in a lot of debt."

My body starts shaking uncontrollably. He murdered Robin. He's a murderer. I'm married to a murderer.

"Lie down on the bed," he commands.

I can't. I can't do it. How can I let him touch me again?

"Now." His tone leaves no room for argument. I have to obey,

13

or he'll hurt me for sure. For a moment, I debate what would be worse, the beatings or the rape.

I lie on my back, and he climbs on top of me. The smell of his sweat rises in my nostrils. I hold back the wave of nausea that hits me and try not to throw up.

I squeeze my eyes closed and try to draw Ethan to me, his pleasant masculine scent mixed with his cologne. The scent that makes my body react. The exact opposite reaction from what I feel right now.

Michael kisses my neck, and his cock rubs against me. I bite the inside of my cheek and try to control my horrified reaction. *Be strong. Relax. Imagine you are with Ethan.* But my body shuts down and contracts, shaking without being able to stop. And I know it's going to hurt again. It always hurts with Michael.

I have to fight.

"I don't care what you do to me," I say with a defiant glare. "You can rape me, but I already know what a real man feels like. I know how a real man makes love, and you will never be a real man!"

Michael roars and bites my shoulder, right where the skin is already scarred, thin and sensitive, a painful bite that has me screaming, and I feel the blood leaking down my shoulder that heralds my skin has been torn.

"Be careful what you wish for. If this re-education doesn't work, I can always announce that we couldn't save you, and you took your life just like Robin did." He puts a sad expression on his face. "Your mental state is so unstable, no one will be surprised."

I push him with all my strength and jump out of bed to stand in a defensive position. He's going to kill me. I know now that I won't get out of here alive.

"Whore! I am your husband. What I do can't be rape because you're mine to do with as I please. Always. You can't refuse me."

He gets up from the bed. "I had a lot of time to think about your punishment. Lots and lots of time..." He grins. "I'll make sure you pay for every day you made me suffer because of your actions. You know I had to talk to the news and explain that I married a crazy woman who has no control over her actions? That I had to hire a team of men to look for my wife? That I had to hear from everyone how worried they were while you were fucking another man?" He speaks in a low voice, with a hidden fury that scares me even more. "Do you have any idea how humiliating that is?"

My legs are shaking, and I'm not sure they can continue to carry me. I'm afraid of this rage. I'm not sure I'll survive it.

He enjoys making me cry, hearing me whimper and seeing me cower. That's what excites him. He doesn't like the new brave me.

He approaches me, and I try to move away, try to kick him, but he dodges quickly. He's not as strong as Ethan, but he's still big, much bigger than me, and I can't hurt him.

A quick punch strikes my cheek, and I hear the horrifying sound of splintering bone. My face. He's broken something in my face.

I'm thrown to the floor. The pain washes through me. A strong metallic taste fills my mouth, my head is pounding, and I think my brain is going to explode.

He approaches me again, and his face is contorted with rage. I curl up in a ball and try to shield my face with my hands. He sends a targeted kick to my ribs, and the air is knocked out of me in one gasp. I choke and try to breathe. The next kick hits my stomach. It's over. I'm going to die now.

More kicks strike my back, and the pain overwhelms me, filling my being. I scream, unable to stand it anymore. It's too much. I want to vomit. Then my vision goes black, and the darkness comes to get me.

I'm sorry, Ethan, I wasn't strong enough. Forgive me.

CHAPTER 3

Ethan

A lion in a cage. That's how I feel right now as I pace back and forth in my apartment, connected to the phone earpiece like it's oxygen. I've been calling anyone I think can help.

"How can I help?" Madeleine turns to me, and I see she's been crying.

Why is she still here? I shake my head. "You need to go home, Madeleine. Your grandchildren are waiting for you."

"I can't go home. I'm too worried about Ayala. I'm worried about you."

I close my eyes. I'm lost. "Maybe make Ryan something to eat, then. He needs his strength."

"You need to eat too. You haven't eaten all day."

"I'm not hungry."

She pushes a sandwich into my hands. "You need to be strong to save her, your beautiful woman. She has a good heart, just like yours. I know it will end well in my heart."

I nod and take a bite. The sandwich tastes like sandpaper. I can't chew, but I do my best to swallow and keep eating.

I'm helpless. Ever since I found Anna dead in the bathtub, I've done everything I could to never feel like this again, to never be in a situation like this again. I even started Savee so no one would have to go through what I did. What Anna did. But lightning strikes twice, and once again, a woman I love needs to be rescued.

And this time, I have to succeed.

We already learned that they boarded a flight to San Francisco, and I even have Michael's home address.

I was shocked at his composure, his audacity to take her to the most obvious place... He doesn't even try to hide her, thinking there's no way anyone can stop him. But he's underestimated me. He doesn't know that I won't give up.

I've been trying to get a hold of someone with rank in the police department all morning. Someone who can give me answers.

Ryan is here with me, making calls, trying to help. But it's difficult to manage the operation from so far away.

I tried asking Paul to send a Savee unit to the house, but without an open call, they can't get in.

Risking a criminal offense is not something I can ask of my employees, only from myself. I groan in frustration, running my hand through my hair over and over. I want to drown myself in a bottle of whiskey, but despite my need to be numb, I hold back. I need clarity to run this operation.

"I need someone from the station in San Francisco to get back to me! Now! It's a case of kidnapping and abuse. It's urgent!" I scream at the police officer who answers my call. The fifth one so far.

I use all my contacts in the police department and all the contacts I've made through my app, but it still takes hours for someone to get back to me. Precious hours wasted. When this crisis is over, I'll need to think about how to improve this situation.

"I need you to send cars to the address I provided. Michael Summers is a psychopath, and the woman there is in danger," I tell the investigator who finally called me back.

"I understand that Mr. Summers is the husband of the woman in question," he says.

"Yes! But he is a psychopath, and he beats her."

"Do you have proof?"

"She told me herself. I saw the bruises on her face."

"Second-hand hearsay is not enough. Can she call us?"

"No! He's kidnapped her. Don't you understand? You need to go and get her out of there."

"I don't understand how she got kidnapped if this is her house. The address you gave me is the residential address of Ayala Summers. That's the woman you mean, right?"

It's like I'm speaking another language, and they just don't understand. No wonder Michael Summers openly took her. The universe works in his favor. "I sent you the pictures he sent her. He threatened my life. How is that not enough?"

"We can't see who's holding the weapon in the photos. Do you have any proof the pictures have anything to do with Mr. Summers?"

He continues to explain that he has no cause to enter the house, but I'm raging and shouting, unable to reach this guy. He doesn't seem to understand how urgent it is.

After a heated conversation, I convince him to send a car there, probably more because of my threats and connections, than anything else, but he agreed, and that's what matters. I ask that they connect me with the officer in the field. I have to talk to him.

"Officer Garrison. What can I help you with?" he says in a rough voice after the connection is made.

"Officer Garrison, Ethan Wolf speaking. I need to warn you,

the man who lives there is dangerous. He kidnapped Ayala, my girlfriend. No matter what he tells you, she's in danger. You have to get her out of there."

"You live in New York, don't you?"

"Yes. He kidnapped her from here."

Garrison sounds surprised. "Kidnapped her? From New York? And why do you think she's with him?"

"He came to New York to take her. Trust me, she's there. He's crazy." I hear voices in the background.

"Wait, are you talking about Mrs. Summers? Mr. Summers' wife?"

"Yes. She's my girlfriend. And she's with him. He took her I know she's there."

"Okay, we're getting to the address."

I hear the critical tone in his voice, and I don't like it. She's his wife on paper, but that's it. And by God, I'll figure out some way to make sure she won't be his wife any longer. I hold back, knowing that yelling at Officer Garrison now won't get me any further.

I wait for long minutes for them to come back to me, to hear her voice, to know she's okay, that they saved her.

When I see the number of the station again on my phone. I stop breathing.

"Did you find her?"

"We found Mr. Summers at the address. His wife is not in the house. He explained to us she had a breakdown and was hospitalized in a private institute."

"Fuck! She's not hospitalized. She's there. Check. You need to force—"

"We checked. He let us in, but she wasn't there. I'm sorry, sir, but she's his legal wife. And he has all the documents of the hospitalization. He's her husband, not you."

I slam the phone against the wall, and it shatters on the floor. "Fuck!" I shout, and Ryan comes running into the room.

"What's happened?"

"I wasted hours on the police, and they tell me she's not there. Everything I set up, everything I've done, years of work, and in the end, I can't save her. I can't..." My voice cracks. I'm going to lose a woman I love again.

Ryan stands silent, his phone clutched in one hand. He's the only one who knows the complete story. Knows why I must succeed. No. He's not the only one. Ayala also knows, and she's still alive. I must not lose hope.

I take a deep breath and try to control myself. Losing my temper won't help. She still needs me. This story is not over yet.

"Ryan. Put me on a flight to San Francisco."

"What are you going to do?"

"What do you think? Put me on a flight now." I go to my bedroom, grab a small suitcase, and start shoving clothes inside.

I hear Ryan on the phone, doing as I asked. Thank God for Ryan. I'm not sure what will happen when I get there, but I have to get into that house and get her out of there, even if it costs me everything I have.

I walk back into the living room, dragging the small suitcase behind me.

"Is everything confirmed?" I growl.

"Already sending you the details." Ryan nods, still busy on the phone.

I look at the smashed phone on the floor. It wasn't the smartest thing on my part. I can't go without a phone. I can't risk Ayala not being able to contact me.

I take Ayala's device and change out the SIM cards. When she comes back to me, I'll buy her a new phone, a better one. Hell, I'll buy her anything she wants.

Could she be hospitalized? Is it possible he put her in a psychiatric hospital like he told the cops?

No. I'm sure he didn't. Ayala told me she never saw the psychiatrist who signed the documents. That it was all fake, and I believe her. He's faking it again.

"I'm going out to the airport," I tell Ryan, already on my way out. There's is no time to waste.

CHAPTER 4

Ayala

I barely open my eyes.

One eye hurts too much and refuses to open. I try a little harder and open it into a slit, hoping to see more clearly. The world around me is blurry. Is this what heaven looks like? Or hell?

I blink, trying to figure out where I am. The door and windows are closed shut, and terrible darkness surrounds me, preventing me from knowing how much time has passed or what time of day or night it is now. The surface under me is soft. I'm on a bed, still in the bedroom. I'm alive.

My arms hurt, and my mouth is heavy and swollen. My face burns with pounding pain. I reach for my face to check my wounds, but my arm doesn't move. I pull harder and startle when I hear a metallic sound. I suddenly realize that both my hands are above my head.

I try to look up to see what's making the sound. It hurts so damn much. I glimpse the silver metal surrounding my wrists.

Handcuffs.

I'm handcuffed to the bed, to its iron frame. I pull again but only get a burning sensation in my joints. I have no way out of this. My heart races, and panic washes over me. He never did such things before. Handcuffs? I don't know him anymore. He murdered Robin. He's a murderer.

This is a nightmare. I can't possibly have married this...thing. This evil thing.

The door opens, and I cringe, trying desperately to disappear, to be transparent, but I'm not. I'm still here, tied to the bed, unable to move.

"Oh, so you're finally awake."

"Let me go, Michael," I say in a soft voice, trying to convince him he's making a mistake, that he's not like this.

"You brought this on yourself, whore. It's too late now."

I try a different approach, even though the thought alone makes me sick to my stomach. "I love you. Let me go."

He furrows his eyebrows. "You love me?"

"Yes. You're my husband. We can go back to the way we were before. I can come home, and we can be together. I'll make you the food you like. Do you remember how we were in the beginning? You liked that."

He comes closer to me and reaches for my crotch. I can't stop my physical reaction and cringe. He smiles. "I thought so."

"Does your father know what you're doing?" I ask, dropping the pretense. "Does he know I'm locked up here? He'll be ashamed of you."

Michael laughs. "Be ashamed of me? Maybe he'll finally be proud of me. He always thought I was too weak. Do you know what I went through after you ran away? Do you have any idea? 'Michael can't even keep his wife. How will he keep my company?'" he says, imitating his father's voice. "I'll prove to him I'm not weak. I'll show him how I taught you a lesson. How I educated you."

I swallow. "He wants to run for governor, right? Isn't that

what you said? He'll never be able to run if they find out what you did to me. You'll ruin his career. He'll never forgive you."

Michael's grin is filled with bitterness. "But no one will find out. As far as the public is concerned, you're in a psychiatric care unit after having a mental breakdown. I have all the documents."

"The police will search for me. Ethan will search for me." Although I didn't tell him why I left, I'm sure Ethan will do the math and figure it out. He'll not give up easily.

"The police have already bought the story I sold them. Piece of cake. And your boyfriend? You can say I'm counting on him coming to my house. I can just see it now." He takes a gun out of his pants and waves it in my face. "Oh my God, come quickly, someone broke into my house. He has a weapon. And I shot him in self-defense." Michael grins wider.

He unzips his pants and rolls them down. My eyes widen. Oh God, please, no.

A sob escapes me against my will. I squirm and thrash, trying to pull my arms, trying to break free. "No, please, no," I shout.

"If you make any noise, I'll have to gag you." He stops what he's doing and shrugs. "There's no one here to hear you, anyway. Save yourself the bother."

But I can't stop, and I'm screaming as loud as I can.

He takes a piece of cloth from the bedside table. "Too bad. But I don't like the noise. It bothers me. So..."

I watch in horror as he approaches me. I try to kick him, but he keeps his distance from my legs and shoves the cloth into my mouth.

I'm suffocating. I have no air.

"Calm down. You can breathe through your nose." He continues to speak in a calm voice and climbs onto the bed. I kick, trying to aim, and hit him between his legs. One of my kicks strikes its target, and Michael recoils in pain.

Yes!

He pulls out a knife. My eyes widen, and I freeze, examining his intentions.

"Are you sure you want to do this? I can bind your legs, too." His eyes narrow, and he brings the knife closer to my neck while resting one knee on my chest. I groan as the air leaves my lungs. I can't breathe. I try to move my head a little, and he presses the knife into my skin.

I recoil at the sharp pain, and warm liquid flows down my neck.

I don't move anymore.

I've lost.

He tears and cuts the clothes from my body and climbs onto me. The heavy weight of his body hurts my bruised ribs. I might have internal bleeding. I'll die here from my injuries with no one knowing. Without Ethan knowing what happened to me.

I whimper as he leans all his weight on a tender area, but I don't dare move, not with the blade still on my neck.

Why can't I be braver? I have to resist him. I'd rather he kill me than what's going to happen.

He rubs himself on my breasts and between my legs. My body reacts with violent tremors that betray the fact that I'm not as brave as I claim.

"I hate you," I try to whisper without success.

He smiles in response.

And then the burning pain of the penetration. I'm as dry as a desert, and even though I know I need to relax so that it hurts less, I can't. The pain is unbearable. The blows I took from him before only increase the intensity of the pain. I want to scream, but even that ability has been denied me.

Tears flood my eyes and wet my cheeks. I try to look away, not to feel, to close myself off from everything. But he presses again with the knife, and I freeze.

"Don't close your eyes. You wanted a real man, right? I want you to see what a real man looks like."

He thrusts into me again and again. The burning sensation increases, and he moans in pleasure. I can't stand it anymore, I can't... And then he pulls out of me and rubs himself until he comes on my chest. I feel contaminated. Violated. Empty.

And still, Michael hasn't had enough. He runs the knife over my body, applying threatening pressure, enough to hurt but not to injure the skin. I close my eyes, ready to die.

But he stops.

"I want to enjoy you a little more. I'm not done with you yet. Let's leave some fun for later," he whispers in my ear, and another wave of nausea comes over me.

He sends a targeted punch to my stomach, and I crumple in pain.

CHAPTER 5

Ethan

It's late when I leave the airport and pick up the rental car. My only dilemma is whether to stop to get a weapon or drive straight to the address I already know by heart. From the news, I remember a man who didn't look particularly strong, but looks can be deceiving. He may also have a weapon.

Fuck, what am I thinking? He has a weapon, for sure. He followed me with a gun. I remember the pictures on Ayala's phone.

Unfortunately, California is not the best place to buy a gun. I don't have time to bother with a license right now, either. Even with all my connections, it will take a few days. And I can't get involved with the black market. Not if I want any of my business left at the end of this ordeal.

I stop at a convenience store that's open twenty-four hours and buy a pocket knife—the only weapon they have—and an energy drink. Let's hope that will be enough.

The road is dark, and only the street lamps light my way. At least the road is empty during these hours, and I will arrive quickly.

I stifle a yawn. After a full day and night of making phone

calls and after a long flight, the lack of sleep is taking its toll. I shake my head and sip my drink, trying to get oxygen into my head and stay awake. I won't be able to help Ayala if I have an accident on the way.

My phone rings, and I press the button to go hands-free.

"Yes, Ryan?"

"Arrived yet?"

"Almost."

"What are you going to do?"

"Get her out of there."

He huffs out a breath. "Perhaps you should take reinforcements with you? You're not a marine, you know. You have no combat training."

It's true, but I don't care. "I can't wait. She's been with him for almost three days. Who knows what he's done to her already..." I can guess what he's done to her.

Pure hatred floods my body. I don't think I've ever felt this way before, not even when Anna died. And toward a person I don't know and never met. I'm ready to kill him. I want to kill him no matter the cost.

"I know you want to save her," Ryan says now, "that you've got it into your head that she's your redemption for what happened. But if you kill yourself in the process, it won't help. Don't go in there alone."

"I love her, Ryan, like you love Maya. What would you be willing to do for Maya?"

He falls silent for a moment. "Just be careful, okay?" he whispers.

My hands tighten on the steering wheel until my knuckles turn white. I know he's worried, but what I need right now is courage, not hesitation. "Don't worry. I'll be careful," I say and disconnect the call.

I have to be prepared for any scenario. I don't know in what condition I'll find her, what she's gone through already.

If she's still alive.

No. She must be alive. I have to believe it. She has to live, and I have to save her. I must succeed this time.

I park in front of a two-story stone house in a prestigious neighborhood in San Francisco. A quiet neighborhood. Neighbors who have no idea what's going on in the house next door. It's late night, and there's not a soul outside. The house windows are dark as well.

It would be best to wait. Michael would leave for work in the morning, and then I could go in and look for her without risk. But I can't wait. A few more hours is a few more hours of hell for Ayala. A few more hours will be on my already shaky conscience. After all, she's here only because of me.

The door opens easily, and I'm once again thankful for my break-in skills. Who knew they would be so useful?

I walk in silence inside the dark house, keeping my steps easy and light. My shoes squeak on the wooden floor, and I stop to listen. I pull out the knife and clench it in my fist.

But I don't hear a thing. The house is still and quiet.

I continue slowly, moving toward the stairs. The house doesn't have a basement, so I assume she's upstairs.

How the hell does he hide what's going on here from all the neighbors?

The stairs are old and require extra attention. I tiptoe, trying desperately not to alert anyone of my presence, to maintain the element of surprise. Surprise is my only advantage.

I check the first room down the hall and find it dark and empty. The bathroom is also empty. The last room is where I head next. I've never done anything like this. I've broken into shops to make a mess, and I broke into Lunis for her, but never into someone's house.

I close my eyes and take a deep breath. Adrenaline floods through me, waking me up. My pulse is high, and my heart pounds hard in my chest. The fatigue has disappeared.

I carefully open the closed door, inch by inch, afraid of what I'm going to find behind it.

The room is pitch black, and the windows are closed. I move in, trying to gage what I see.

CHAPTER 6

Ayala

I wake up again after a few hours of disturbed sleep. I have
no idea how long I've been here. The darkness confuses my
senses. I can't tell if it's day or night. If he comes every five
minutes or every five days. He does it on purpose, as torture. I
stopped counting how many times he was here. I swore he
wouldn't break me, that I would stay strong, but I'm not sure I
can keep my promise. The pain is too severe. I feel a warm liquid
dripping between my legs. Blood, maybe? I'm positive he injured
me the last time. I felt it.

The door clicks open, and I blink to adjust to the light
coming in through the doorway. Light. That means it's daytime.

He carries a tray in his hands, and I can already feel the saliva
building up in my mouth. It's time to feed the animals. I know it's
been a while since the last meal because my stomach is cramping
with hunger. And I'm thirsty. So thirsty. He makes me grateful
for the food I receive and for every bit of humanity he gives me. I
am disgusted by the unwanted feelings that arise inside me.

"I'll release you now so you can eat." He places the tray on the
edge of the bed. "If you do anything stupid, you'll pay for it."

I nod, agreeing to his threat.

He removes the gag from my mouth and releases the restraints on my arms. I rub them with the little strength I have in hopes of returning some blood flow and feeling in my limbs. The skin on my wrists is red and raw from my struggles. My thighs are stained with blood, some dry and some fresh. I swallow an acidic wave of nausea that fills my throat as I take this assessment of myself and glance down at the coagulated sperm on my stomach and chest.

I command my body to relax. Fear has a distinct smell. I notice it now. I stink of fear. It has a bitter and sour scent, a smell of horror and disgust, and I reek of it.

I take the glass with a trembling hand and drink the water in one gulp. Swallowing hurts. My throat hurts beyond my imagination. "Can I have more?"

He smiles. "Please." He doesn't move.

What? Puzzled, I stare at him.

"Say, please." He says, his tone calm yet forceful. "Don't look at me like that. I'm just teaching you your place. You need to understand how to behave, my dear wife."

I bite the inside of my cheek in an effort to control the urge to spit in his face. "Please."

He takes the glass and goes to the adjoining bathroom. I peek at the door. This could be my chance. The door is open, and I'm not restrained. I try to move one of my legs toward the floor and groan in pain. I can stand. My legs are mostly okay. But there's no chance of escaping. I could never escape him in this condition. And where would I run to? To die in the forest? Would I risk Ethan's life only to end this with my death as well?

I can't run away, and even if I could, he would kill Ethan. I know he will. Michael has lost whatever humanity he had. He's become a torturer. A murderer.

I'm the only one who should have to bear the consequences of my choices. The only one who should have to pay for marrying this man.

How was I so wrong? How could I have thought he was a nice man who would take care of me? I thought I had won the lottery when I married him. How did he become this thing, this creature? The ruler of my personal hell?

He places the glass in my hand, and I sip. I examine the plate he's brought me. Potatoes and some meat. No fork. I take a potato from the plate and put it in my mouth, followed by another. I'm careful not to rush so I don't throw up. If I vomit I'll starve. He won't bring me anything else. I know because that's what happened last time.

I take advantage of the faint rays of light coming from the open doorway to examine my surroundings again. The room is simple, with sparse furniture made of dark wood, making the large iron bed in the center of the room outrageous. On both sides are small chests without drawers. The window is bolted closed and covered with a white lace curtain.

White lace.

I blink.

There is nothing here that I can use. If I want to kill him. I have to take the gun from him. I need a plan.

After I finish eating, he takes the tray, puts it outside the room, and returns. He's not done with me yet.

He comes close and sniffs loudly. "You stink."

I remain silent, not daring to raise my head and meet his gaze, afraid to see the cruelty in his eyes. It seems as if his excitement threshold is increasing. He gets a kick out of my suffering.

"Go take a shower."

I look up. Is he suggesting I clean up? I want to wash the disgust and blood off myself, to feel like a human again. But then I understand why he wants this, and I freeze. I'd rather be dirty than have him touch me again.

He takes the gun out of his belt and points it at me. "No nonsense. Get up and get in the shower."

I look at the barrel of the gun and realize I'm no longer afraid. I no longer have a reason to live. No wonder he keeps me weak, with not enough food. No wonder he hits me and breaks my bones. There's no way I could take the gun away from him in my condition.

I try to stand, but my legs refuse to comply. I lean against the bed, moaning.

"Well? I don't have all day."

I want to jump him. Maybe he'll shoot me, and this nightmare will be over. But I limp to the bathroom, hugging my ribs. Every part of my body screams with pain. But the despair is the worst. I can bear the physical pain. I survived rape in the past. But revenge has pulled this beast into another world of cruelty, one that I thought only existed in nightmares.

I used to have hope. I hoped to escape. I had something to live for. What do I have left to live for now? There is no way out of this cycle of torture. And I'd rather die than continue to live this way.

He punches me in the face, and my vision blurs again. I trip and fall to my knees.

"Move already." He grabs my arm and yanks my limp body back into a standing position, drags me into the shower, and turns the tap on full blast. I wince as the cold water hits my body like needles of ice, washing away the evidence of what he's done to me.

I stand there, staring as the trail of blood washes from me. I'm still bleeding. I knew he injured me. But when was the last time I had my period? I don't remember. Well, it doesn't matter whether it's my period or from an injury. Nothing will stop him.

I can feel his eyes wandering over my body. I don't understand how he could possibly be aroused by this, by the signs of violence, the scratches, the bruises, and the blood. But it's clear that he is. His gaze oozes lust. He's a psychopath. I suddenly understand. The thrill was always there, just beneath the surface. During the previous two years in his hell, I'd barely scraped the thin covering and revealed the true monster beneath his facade.

"Enough." Michael's firm voice interrupts my train of thought.

I turn off the water and step outside, trembling, not sure if it's because of the cold, the fear, or both.

He hands me a towel, and I wrap myself in it, hiding behind it as if it were steel armor. The water was indeed freezing, but I've gained a few ounces of energy. Clean and with a full stomach. I feel like a human again.

"How long are you going to keep me here?"

He raises an eyebrow. "Until the interest in you subsides."

There's interest in me? Is someone looking for me? I straighten.

"I don't know what's going through your head, but don't get your hopes up. I'm your legal guardian. No one can take you away from me. I have you, and I have documents that prove you're sick."

The air leaves me in a long breath. I don't know how he does it, how he reads my mind so easily.

He pulls the towel from me. I try to grab it, but it only irritates him, and he pulls harder, knocking me onto the floor.

His eyes light up. He picks me up by my hair, and I scream as the hair threatens to tear from my scalp. The more I scream, the more he pulls. I fall silent, trying to stifle my sobs. I will not give him the satisfaction of subduing me.

"Put me in your mouth," he commands. "Suck it."

He hasn't asked me for it since I got here.

I can bite him. He'll kill me, of course, but it will be a fitting end to my life. I'll die, but he'll be without his d—

"On second thought, get on the bed." He swings me by the hair and throws me on the mattress like a rag doll.

I close my eyes and wait.

CHAPTER 7

Ethan

She's not here.

I do another scan of the house just to be sure. As far as I can tell, there are no secret rooms here. Fuck. She isn't in his house.

I go out to the car and rest my head on the steering wheel. How do we proceed from here? I don't know what to do.

I send a message to Ryan to inform him I'm okay, then call Jess.

"She's not here," I tell him as soon as he answers. "Could she be in that hospital, as he claims?"

"I checked. The documents are from a private center called Naturcare. On the phone, they confirmed that they have a patient under that name but refused to let us talk to her. I sent someone over there as a visitor. He searched the place, and she wasn't there. Whoever works for him is doing a good job. She's disappeared off the face of the earth."

"Find her," I beg. "Please." I'm losing it. Michael Summers had the advantage of more than a few long hours before I discovered she was gone, and he had time to erase any evidence and plan his moves well. Too much time has passed. Who knows what damage he's done to her already? What he's capable of?

"I'm doing everything I can. Summers has no other properties to his name. Perhaps he's rented something, but if he did, he didn't use a credit card. I'm trying to track him down. This guy is good."

"Fuck!" I shout. "Call me immediately when you have something, anything at all."

I rub my temples and close my eyes, trying to overcome the nasty headache. I need to stay focused. There's no time to rest.

An incoming call causes me to jump, and I answer without checking to see who it is. "Jess? You have something for me?"

"This is Paul Sheridan."

Heck, I didn't even check who it was. I have no patience for work now, but I gather what little I can to answer him. "Yes, Paul?"

"I heard about Ayala. I'm sorry."

"Thanks."

"Do you know where she is?" he asks.

"I thought I did, but no. I have no idea where he's hiding her. If he hasn't killed her by now," I mumble.

"Did you contact the police?"

"It's...complex." I pause and decide to tell the truth. Paul will not criticize me. "They're not willing to help because she's legally married to this man."

"Yes. I heard." He stops me. "I guess you know what you're doing, but have you tried using Savee to track her?"

"What? How?" I sit up.

"You know that whoever installs our app agrees to us tracking their device. It gives us a chance to check where their phone is—'

"She didn't take her phone." The air comes right out of me. For a moment there...

"Maybe she didn't take it, but what about the man who kidnapped her?"

"What about him?" I raise an eyebrow.

"I'm sure he has a phone."

"Yeah...."

"If you install our app on his phone, you'll be able to locate him in our systems."

"How the hell can I install something on his phone if I don't know where he is?" I raise my voice.

"Listen for a minute." Paul's firm tone stops my ranting. "You don't need him or the phone. All you need in order to install something remotely is access to his account."

Fucking hell. "Damn. You're right. You are a genius. Thanks, Paul. Excuse me, but I have some calls to make."

I call Jess and ask him to get someone to hack into Michael Summers' account. I'm not sure how he'll get it done, but the only thing in mind right now is saving her. At all costs.

It worked.

I can't believe it worked. Jess was able to install the Savee app remotely, and I have an address.

Well, not exactly an address, but coordinates. It seems to be in the middle of a forest.

This encourages me because it makes sense that he would take her to a secluded place. I think I have the location right. I just hope it's not too late. I wasted an entire day looking for it. Precious time that was lost.

I park the car a distance from the marker, hidden among the trees, and continue on foot. I have no idea what I'll find there. I'm supposed to wait for the reinforcements Jess is sending, but I have no intention of waiting an extra minute. It's getting dark, and it will take time for them to organize and equip themselves, and I'm already here.

The house is revealed as I approach, half hidden among the trees. I see a light in the entranceway, which confirms the presence of people there, but the windows are dark and covered so it's not possible to see what's going on inside. Fuck.

I'll have to enter the house blind. I close my eyes and take a deep breath.

I prepare to use my burglary skills one more time, but as I check the knob it turns out it's not locked at all. I open it slowly, ready to be jumped at any moment, but there's no one.

What does it mean that the door isn't locked? Am I walking into a trap? Cold sweat climbs up my spine. It doesn't matter now. Finding Ayala is all that matters.

I move inside, holding my pocket knife. I find plates with left-over food in the kitchen. Someone is living here. I move toward the stairs, careful to move slowly, clinging to the wall. Upstairs I open a door leading to a dark bedroom and peek inside. My eyes adjust to the darkness, and my heart stops beating.

My Bambi is on the bed, her eyes are closed, and her hands are tied above her head. Her mouth is stuffed with a cloth.

She doesn't move, but I see her chest rise and fall. She's still alive.

She's naked, and her face looks tormented, swollen and beaten, almost beyond recognition. I ease into the room, wondering where Summers is. I need to hurry and get her out of here. I see smears of blood between her thighs and stifle a cry with my fist.

Fuck. I'm about to throw up. I bend down as a spasm of rage in my stomach momentarily subdues me. I can't lose it now. I have to hold on to the fact that she's still alive. I have to get her out of here.

"Ayala?" I whisper.

39

I move closer, swallowing hard and fighting the nausea.

Up close, her condition looks even worse. Bruises cover her beautiful face and mar her ribs. I see a long cut on her neck. Sadistic son of a bitch.

"Ayala?" I whisper again, and now she moves a little but doesn't wake up.

I let out a breath, not even realizing that I'd been holding my breath until now. I reach out to her and lightly shake her shoulders to wake her up. Her broken body is unresponsive. I've arrived too late. I'm too late again.

A rustle behind me makes me turn, and I swing my knife up. A sharp pain drops me to my knees. My shoulder is on fire. Pain screams inside my head.

I stare at my shoulder in disbelief, seeing only the handle of a large kitchen knife protruding from the skin. Michael stands in front of me in a crouched position. I stare at him, but my mind refuses to believe what I'm seeing.

He stabbed me. The son of a bitch stabbed me.

Blood stains my shirt and spreads quickly, dripping onto the floor at an alarming rate. It won't be long before I pass out from blood loss. I need to hurry. I'm the only one who can save her. I'm ready to give my life to save her.

I struggle to my feet and try to swing at him with the pocket knife still in my hand, but I can't move the injured arm. Fuck. I pass the knife to my other hand, ignoring the almost unbearable pain, using the pumping adrenaline to move forward.

He steps back, reaches into the waistband of his pants, and pulls out a gun. I freeze. I won't be able to kill him before he shoots.

"I prefer not to make a lot of noise," he says. "There are campers nearby in the forest. I don't want to startle anyone. But you leave me no choice. I didn't think you would come for this whore. Was she such an excellent fuck, then? I've had better." He tilts his head.

I lunge with a roar, drop all my body weight on him, and knock him to the floor. I shake my head, fighting the darkness threatening to overtake me while struggling for the gun.

In my hazy fragments of consciousness, I slam his hand into the floor.

A loud bang fills the space as the gun goes off. My ears ring, and a moment later, the gun drops onto the floor.

I punch him, trying to knock him out. He's weaker than me, but I'm not in the best shape at the moment. One hand is dangling like a lifeless limb.

I punch him in the face again and hear a scream, not realizing I'm the one making the noise. The son of a bitch has gotten a hold of the knife in my shoulder and is twisting it. I see stars. I can't pass out now. I must stay awake.

With my last bit of strength, I put my elbow on his neck in an attempt to make him lose consciousness. He struggles beneath me, writhing. A black shadow covers my field of vision, but the adrenaline and near-death experience give me supreme power. I have someone to fight for.

I shout and put more weight on his neck, pressing down and holding him in place until I feel him weaken beneath me. His struggles weaken, and his body goes limp. Lifeless.

I lay on him for a few moments more before pulling away, panting.

My shirt is soaked in blood, and I'm dizzy and weak. I need to hurry.

I search his pockets for the keys to the handcuffs and find them. Rising to my feet, I try to steady myself as the world spins around me.

But all I can think about now is Ayala, my Bambi, and all the suffering she's gone through over these days. Torture I can't even imagine.

I approach her, release her hands from the cuffs, and remove the gag from her mouth. She still isn't moving. I lift her upper body and gently gather her into my arms. Her body is lifeless. I take a blanket and cover her.

Please, don't let me be late again. I can't lose her too.

She's dead weight in my embrace, unresponsive. Dizziness hits me again, and I look through the fog at my shirt. Too much blood. I try to steady myself, leaning on the bed.

I close my eyes and see Ayala lying in the tub. Her wrists are cut, and red water pours onto the floor. Too much blood...

Another explosive sound echoes in my ears. I look down.

Bloodstains spread on my shirt.

Fuck.

CHAPTER 8

Ayala

I stroll down the winding path and smile at the sight of the sparkling water of the lake. This is the lake Ethan took me to, the place where I fell in love with him. It will forever be imprinted in my memory. Our first date. I smile and spin around as the trees rustle overhead. I see Ethan smiling back at me, his eyes glinting in the sun, my favorite golden color.

A boat in the lake sails in our direction, and I'm fascinated at the sight. Maybe we'll go sailing?

I hear Ethan talking to me. He's calling my name.

"I'm here," I shout, but he doesn't seem to hear me. Why doesn't he hear?

"Ethan!"

I try to blink. My eyelids are desperate to open. Why does it hurt so much? What's happened? I can't remember. My legs kick instinctively as I feel an unwanted touch, and my thoughts snap back to reality.

I open my eyes in horror. Michael is standing at the foot of the bed. He lifts Ethan's lifeless body off me and throws him to the floor.

Ethan? Ethan! He's here. I try to sit up and find that my hands are free. He's uncuffed me.

But why is Ethan on the floor? What's happening here?

Blinking again, I take in the holes in his shirt and all the blood.

No. Please no. This can't be real. It must just be part of the nightmare I'm in. I'm here to save him. He's not supposed to be here to save me.

Michael now stands with his back to me, unaware that I have woken up. He points the gun at Ethan, planning to finish the job.

"No!" I scream like a wounded animal, and with powers I didn't know existed in me, I leap on Michael's back. We fall to the floor and a gunshot echoes in my ears.

Michael lies under me. He isn't moving. He isn't struggling. I stay still for a moment longer, sprawled over him, trying to calm my rapid breathing. But Ethan is here.

I get up slowly. My legs can barely carry me as they're shaking so hard. I look at myself and touch my body. I'm alive. No gun holes that I can detect. I send a foot to Michael's side, nudging him with the tips of my toes. He doesn't move.

I try again, harder, but he's still lying motionless. I have to check to be sure.

I bite my bottom lip, bend down and push on his shoulder, turning him over. When he rolls onto his back, I jump in panic, stifle a whimper and cover my mouth with my hands.

A bullet hole has opened in his neck, and blood is gushing out with a horrifying sound. I kneel and vomit the contents of my almost empty stomach onto the floor.

As the waves of nausea subside, I turn to Ethan, sprawled on the floor next to me. I call his name, but he doesn't respond.

A large pool of blood has accumulated beneath him. There is a gunshot wound in his stomach, and a knife is stuck in his shoulder. I remember seeing on TV that you should not take out the knife alone. But the blood is everywhere. I have to help him.

I try to stop the blood from the wound in his stomach with my palms. It's like trying to stop a river with a small stone.

"God, Ethan, don't leave me! I'm not letting you go from me!" I scream, no longer aware of my surroundings. I'm not sure if I'm still in a dream or if this is reality. Everything I went through, all this hell, it was all for him.

No, you won't take him from me now, I scream inside. It's not fair. I'm not ready! I sob as I rest my palms on him, trying to put pressure on the wound.

Strong arms surround me and pull me away from Ethan. "No!" I scream. "I need to help him!" I'm kicking, raging, trying to free myself from the unfamiliar people who have suddenly appeared and are trying to keep me from him.

"We'll take care of him," I hear an unfamiliar voice say.

"What are you doing to me? Leave me alone!" I scream. I struggle against them with all my wretched strength without success.

The sensation of a needle's prick surprises me. I try to reach out to the new pain point in my arm, but the hands holding me don't allow me to move.

My thoughts blur and spin, and I sink again into oblivion, but this time the nightmares are also in the dark.

CHAPTER 9

Ayala

BEEP.

B*eep.*
Beep.
A monotonous beeping is constant in the background, a loud, obnoxious sound. I open my eyes a bit, and a bright white light fills my sight. It's so painful that I cringe in pain.

Where is the light switch? I want to turn off this awful light. I try to search for it, but my hands are heavy, so heavy.

"She's waking up!" I hear a familiar voice from the left.

"Mom?" I barely get out on a whisper. My voice is hoarse and muffled. I cough. How did she find me?

"Here's a glass of water. Raise your head a little," she says, and a hand is there behind my head to support me, to help me drink. I take a sip, then another.

I try again to force my eyes to open. My head is heavy, and my eyes sting. I open them into narrow slits.

"Hey, sweetheart." Mom hugs me now, careful not to put weight on me. "You've woken up. You've come back to us." She sounds so...shocked.

"Mom? What happened? Where am I? What am I doing

46

here?" I'm confused, trying to remember what happened, but the world is a blur, just a mix of colors and sounds and pain. It hurts everywhere.

"She doesn't remember," I hear another voice say, and I try to turn my head in his direction.

"Dad?"

"Yes, I'm here," he says, closer to me now. But I can't turn my head.

"Where am I?" My face hurts, and there's something white blocking my field of vision. I try to raise my hand, but there's something on my finger. I try to shake it off me.

"Shh, calm down," Mom says. "You're okay now. You're in the hospital."

But I'm not calm at all. I raise my hand again to touch my face. I feel the bandages on my cheek. My nose is covered as well, and every touch hurts.

My mother puts a hand on me and shares a meaningful glance with my father. "Shh. Relax, sweetheart. Everything will be okay now."

Why don't they tell me what happened? I try to take out all the tubes in me. What is this? What did they do to me? What happened to me?

I struggle to break free, pull out the needle that's stuck in my arm and throw it to the floor. I need to get up and run away. Michael will find me.

"You're hurting yourself." Mom tries to hold my hand to prevent me from getting up. "Calm down."

"I can't go back to him," I groan. "I can't."

"You're okay, Ayala. You're in a hospital," Mom says again. "We're here, watching over you."

I glance at Dad and see tears running down his cheeks. I've never seen him cry before.

A doctor, at least I assume this man is a doctor as he's dressed in green scrubs, enters the room and approaches me. "How are you feeling, Mrs. Summers?"

I cringe at that name. I don't want to hear it ever again. "How did I get here? What happened to me?"

"Why doesn't she remember?" my father asks the doctor.

"It's typical of trauma. The brain represses. Usually, most of the memories return within a few days."

"So we shouldn't tell her what happened?"

"Give her time. Don't push her."

I watch them, talking about me as if I'm not in the room. How did I get here? I have to remember. The shadow of a memory sits right at the edge of my mind, but it's not ready to solidify. It hovers just above the edge of my awareness. Damn it.

The doctor keeps probing my body, and I squirm. "Stop, please," I beg, but he continues.

The examination ends, and I close my eyes. Too tired to continue fighting, I fall back to sleep.

There is no sense of time in this place. When I wake up again, everything looks and sounds the same. The bright light, the beeping...

A vision of Michael restraining me in handcuffs comes to mind, and I feel sick. I pull my arms tight against my body, trying to break free.

"Ayala, calm down. You're in a hospital." I hear my father's voice. "Caroline! Come quick," he shouts, and footsteps approach.

"Ayala." Mom appears beside me and caresses my arm. My body relaxes under her gentle touch. Michael isn't here.

"How long have I been here?"

"Three days," she answers without looking at me.

I squeeze my eyes closed. Three days were taken from my life.

I try to check my condition again. My ribs are sore, and my face is too. But my arms and legs move without restraint.

A hospital worker enters the room and places a lunch tray next to me. Who can eat now? Hunger is far from my thoughts.

"What happened to me?"

"Don't you remember?" My mother's voice breaks, and she can't complete her sentence. "I'm so sorry, sweetie. I'm so sorry I didn't support you. That I thought he was acting in your favor," she cries.

Images of the cabin in the woods jump in front of my eyes. Michael caught me. I was a prisoner. I was his slave.

"Michael. He was there," I cry as the memories hit me. I remember. Every horrible moment of it. Every moment of pain. But how it ended... The ending is blurry. I don't remember how it ended.

"You're safe now," Mom cries next to me. "You survived."

"You were hysterical when they found you," Dad whispers. "And Michael is dead."

I exhale, and my eyes widen. "Dead?"

"Yes. Do you remember what happened?"

I shake my head. Then, images of Michael lying on the floor, blood pouring from his throat. No. It wasn't real. I don't want to believe it.

Images of Ethan float through my mind too. His lifeless body on the floor, blood... Lots of blood. Michael killed him.

I cry out and try to cover my face with my hands, but I'm stopped by the pain. My face is broken.

I remember.

Ethan and Michael are dead.

My mother comes to hug me, tries to comfort me, but when all the memories fall on me at once, I'm overwhelmed and drown under their power.

The sound of someone clearing their throat pulls our attention, and Mom and I break away. She wipes at the tears running down her cheeks. I don't even bother.

A policewoman in uniform stands at the door. I turn my attention to her. Another policeman is standing right behind her.

"Mrs. Summers," she begins, but dad stops her.

"She just woke up, and she's in no condition to answer questions." my father insists and approaches the policewoman in a menacing manner. But the policewoman doesn't seem affected by this at all.

Her steps halt when Dad blocks her way to me. "Mrs. Summers, my name is detective Delfino. I'm a police investigator." She stands with her thumbs in her pockets.

"Not Summers. I don't want to hear that name ever again. My name is Ayala Beckett." I want nothing to do with that monster.

She shakes her head. "Okay, Miss Beckett. Can you answer a few questions for me?"

A doctor pushes his way into the room, followed by the policeman. "I already explained to you she's in no condition to answer questions. Leave this room immediately."

The policewoman waves her hands in surrender and leaves. I know she'll be back soon, but right now, I want to understand from the doctor what's going on.

"I want to go home," I say. "When can I go home?" After I ask, I realize I don't have a home to go to. Where will I go? I swallow the lump that accumulates in my throat.

"Let's have a conversation first, and then we'll see, okay?" he says to me so calmly that it irritates me.

I stare through his glasses into his brown eyes. Everyone wants to ask questions at the same time. But I don't want to answer. They should let me go. I want to be alone. I don't want to see anyone. I don't want to talk to anyone.

"Do you remember what happened to you?" the doctor asks.

"Michael happened to me."

He nods. "Michael was your husband, wasn't he?"

I nod, even though in my eyes, he was my torturer, not my husband. How strange to talk about him in the past tense. Can I not be afraid of him anymore?

"Can I check on you?"

I nod again, and the doctor closes the curtain to give me privacy. "Mom, stay with me." I reach out, and she holds my hand for support.

He approaches my face and checks my nose and my vision, holding a flashlight close to my pupils. I blink in pain.

"We fixed your nose. You'll be just as beautiful as before." He gives me a pitying smile and moves on to check the bandage on my ribs, touching me gently. "You have two broken ribs. It will hurt for a while, but lucky for you, there was no internal damage from the injury."

I bite my lip in pain. I don't think there's a spot on my body that doesn't hurt right now. He lifts the hospital gown and peeks between my legs. I close my eyes.

He straightens. "You're recovering well. We sewed up the tears, but I'm sorry to tell you, you lost the baby. The trauma to the uterus was too great. You suffered from placental abruption."

I gasp and turn my head to mom. She looks down and covers her face with her hands.

"Baby?"

"You didn't know?" he asks. "You were pregnant, the first trimester. I'm sorry, but you lost it. The bleeding was too extensive."

Baby? A pregnancy? Oh my God, I was pregnant? "How far along?" I ask in a shaky voice.

"I estimate around week eight," he says.

"Ethan. It was Ethan's..." I mutter. Probably from that evening when I returned to him, and we weren't careful. The morning-after pill must not have worked... But I lost his baby. Tears accumulate in my eyes. He died, and I lost the only thing I had left of him.

"No!" I scream and shake my arms. "No..."

I can't stand it. I have nothing left.

I cry until I fall back into a dreamless sleep.

When I wake up again and realize where I am, I close my eyes. I don't have the strength to face reality. I lost Ethan's baby. My mother strokes my fingers. I don't want to talk to her. I don't want anything. Please, just let me die.

The detectives are back, entering the room again, and my father blocks them with his body.

I raise a hand to stop him. "It's okay, Dad. I can answer their questions." Let's get this over with already. Nothing matters anymore. There's no point in putting it off. After I'm released, I'll finish everything.

Dad gives me a long and scrutinizing stare. He's trying to decide if I'm able to speak without falling apart, no doubt. I'm not sure myself, but more than anything, I want to understand what happened that day.

Finally, he nods, takes my mother's hand, and they leave the room, closing the door behind them.

I try to pull myself into a sitting position and groan. My entire body feels like a pile of bones that happened to be put together.

"Miss Beckett," the female officer says again, pulling up a chair and sitting beside my bed. "I need to ask some questions."

I nod and watch as she takes out a pad and pen and prepares to write my answers. The policeman standing next to her has stubble. Ethan had stubble, too. I can never touch his face again.

"How long were you and Mr. Summers married?"

"A little over two years."

"Was your relationship ever violent?"

I close my eyes. She's judging me. I hear it in the tone of her voice. "Not at first. It started a few months after the marriage," I explain, "He would throw objects at me in moments of anger, then the hitting started."

"What about rape?"

I blink at the intrusive question and nod.

"Is this yes?" she asks.

"Yes, there were times he raped me." I try to keep my head up, even though my voice is shaking. I remind myself that I have nothing to be ashamed of.

"And you never filed a report with the police?"

"I tried, but Michael had documents saying I was mentally incompetent. He became my legal guardian, so they didn't take me seriously."

"About the documents..." She flips back through her notebook, looking for something. "Mr. Wolf claimed that they were fake?"

"Mr. Wolf?"

"Yes, Ethan Wolf. This is the third person who was in the cabin. You know him, correct?"

I nod.

"He called the police the day before the incident, claimed that your husband kidnapped you and that all the documents were fake. The officers who visited your home in San Francisco found nothing suspicious, and therefore the complaint was closed." She peers into my eyes. "I'm sorry."

If they had kept checking, perhaps Ethan wouldn't have been hurt. He could have been alive now. "Yes, they were fake. I have never been to these doctors."

"It says here that you were staying in New York for a few months?"

I nod again.

"Can you explain to me the sequence of events? How did you get to New York and then from New York back here?"

"I ran away to New York a few months ago because I was afraid of Michael. I believed he was going to kill me. But he tracked me down in New York too." I stop to take a breath. "He killed my friend!" My voice breaks as I remember poor Robin. She wasn't nice to me, but she didn't deserve to die. No one deserved to die but him.

The detective looks up from her notebook. "Killed your friend?"

"Yes. Robin Moyes, who worked with me at Lunis. It's a bar in New York. He admitted it to me. She told him where I was and asked him for money. He staged her suicide. She didn't kill herself. He killed her. He's a murderer."

"Do you have proof?"

I shake my head. "No. But he told me that he did."

She exchanges a look with the police officer next to her, and he starts typing into his phone. "We'll have to check it out."

I nod.

"What is the relationship between you and Ethan Wolf?" She raises her eyes, staring at me.

I glance at my hands, clenched tight on my lap. What can I tell her? That he's the love of my life? My lover? How can I define our relationship?

"Are you intimate?" she continues to ask.

I nod, humiliated. I am an adulterous woman. How does it sound to outsiders?

"Please go on," she gestures with her hand and continues to write my words.

"Michael called me and said that if I didn't come back voluntarily, he would kill Ethan."

"So he threatened to kill Mr. Wolf, and you felt that was a serious threat?" she asks.

"Yes. He sent me pictures."

The detective nods. "We got the pictures from Mr. Wolf."

"He sent you the pictures?"

"Yes, the investigator sent to interview him, similar to what we are doing now, received the photos from him with the threat to his life. But we couldn't confirm that the photos came from Mr. Summers. Are you saying he sent them?"

My heart flutters and almost jumps out of my chest. "Wait, you're saying Ethan sent the pictures *after* what happened in the cabin? Is he alive?" I shout.

She stops writing and lifts her head. "Yes. I'm sorry, I assumed you knew."

He's alive.

Ethan is alive.

My head is empty of thoughts. Ethan is alive.

Is he here at the same hospital? Maybe even in the room next to me? And I didn't know. I didn't go to see him. Why didn't they tell me? Can he speak? Why didn't he call me? "Where is he? What happened to him?" I grab her arm.

She stares at my hand clasped around her wrist but doesn't remove it. She just looks at me with pity. "From what I know, the family asked to fly him to New York for treatment. I haven't been updated on his condition. The statement he gave is all I have. I'm sorry."

He made a statement. That means he's awake. He's talking. Relief washes over me, and I'm filled with renewed strength. I have to talk to him. I have to know he's okay.

I shake off my thoughts when the detective asks for my attention again.

"Can you please tell us what happened after you returned here with Michael?"

"Yes." I remember the horrible days I went through. I hope this will be the last time I have to remember them. I tell her about the time I spent tied to the bed.

The detective listens in silence.

"He had a knife. He threatened me. He enjoyed every minute." I shudder. "I kept thinking that I wouldn't survive this time, that he'd kill me." Tears flow down my cheeks, but I don't bother to wipe them.

I tell her about the rapes, the beatings. I stop as my body shakes violently. "I don't think I can go on."

"Take a deep breath. Just a little longer, Miss Beckett," she says. "Please."

I swallow, and she hands me a handkerchief. I tap my face gently. Every touch hurts.

"Can you give me a mirror?" I ask, realizing that I haven't seen myself since it happened.

"A mirror?"

"Yes. Can you bring me a mirror, please? I want to see what he did to me."

"I don't think it's a good idea." She tries to make me give up the thought.

"A mirror," I insist.

She surrenders and goes to the adjoining bathroom, brings a small hand mirror from there, and holds it in front of my face.

I bite the inside of my cheek until it hurts.

My face is swollen beyond recognition, and my nose is covered with bandages. Black circles surround my eyes. My lips are chapped, and there's a cut on my lower lip covered with several stitches. This is what hurts me when I speak. I touch my bruised face gently, then lower my hand to the large angry cut on my neck. This is where he held the knife. I'm sure the rest of my body looks similar.

I look away. I don't want to see it anymore.

"I wasn't conscious when most of the..." I wonder what word to choose. "The fight happened. I didn't know Ethan came to save me."

"You were conscious when they found you. You must have seen part of what happened."

"When I woke up, I saw Ethan on the floor, and Michael was about to shoot him. I didn't know what to do, so I jumped on him."

"You jumped on him?" She looks surprised, and I wonder why.

"Yes. I jumped on Michael, and we fell to the floor. The gun went off." I remember those moments of horror. "I was sure I was dead. That he shot me. But when I got up, I saw the bullet had hit Michael instead. There was so much blood. Ethan too... I thought they were both dead."

She shakes her head. "Mr. Summers died from his wounds." She looks at me with a serious face. "Are you sure about your version? You jumped on him, and a bullet went off?"

"Yes." I narrow my eyes. "Why?"

"Interesting." She mumbles and exchanges a look with the other policeman.

"I killed him. It was an accident, but I would have killed him on purpose, given the chance. The gun went off as we wrestled on the floor. Am I going to jail?" I ask. I don't mind going to jail. It was worth it. Ethan is alive.

"I don't believe we'll get to that. It sounds like an accident. Or self-defense. Especially after what you've been through. Assuming you're telling the truth and the forensic evidence matches your version."

"Do you think I'm lying? What reason would I have to lie?"

She stands. "I think you have no reason to lie. And that will be enough for now. I'll come again later if I have any more questions for you."

I nod, and she leaves the room. My parents rush in.

"Ayala." My mother rushes to me. "Are you okay?"

I try to stop the tears and nod. "Mom. Mom, she said Ethan is alive. He's in New York. I want a phone. I need to talk to him. I need to tell him I'm okay."

"I'm not sure that's a good idea, Ayala."

What? "Did you know? You knew all along that he was alive, and you didn't tell me?" I wanted to die. I thought I had nothing left to live for, and all this time, they knew.

"You had an affair with him while you were married. Michael thought you were cheating on him. That's why you're in this situation now." I hear the scolding tone in her voice.

An affair. That's what she calls it. What we have is love. It cannot be reduced to a simple affair. I want to hear his voice. I want to talk to him, to know that he's alive and breathing. "He is not to blame for what happened. Michael is," I insist. "Why didn't you tell me Ethan was alive? I want to talk to him!" I cry.

"He doesn't want to talk to you."

I shake my head, despite the pain. "I don't believe it. Let me talk to him!" I shout. I want to hear his voice. I need to hear his voice.

Mom reluctantly hands me her phone. "I don't think it's a good idea."

The phone rings and rings but goes to voicemail. I call again, and still no answer.

I squeeze my fists. I have to talk to him. I try again, and lucky number three.

He answers on the second ring. I didn't think about him not recognizing the number.

"Yes?" His low, husky voice sends a shiver through me. How good it is to hear him.

"Ethan," I whisper into the phone. "It's me."

"Ayala." My name rolling in his mouth is enough to make my whole body wake up.

"Ayala, don't call me anymore. It's over."

The phone is still in my hand, and the monitor is still beeping. I still hear the sounds of the hospital in the background, but the world has stopped.

"What?" I say, thinking I didn't hear correctly. Because there is no other option.

"It's over, Ayala. I'm glad you're okay, but don't call here again." He hangs up, leaving me with the phone in my hand, and I remain sitting in the hospital bed for long minutes as the world collapses around me.

CHAPTER 10

Ethan

My hand drops, and the phone falls to the floor. I
don't care. I don't care that I've been lying on this
couch all day, almost screaming from pain. I don't
care that I have eaten nothing since I discharged myself from the
hospital yesterday. I don't care that I've already drowned myself in
a half bottle of vodka, along with pain pills.

The vodka provides me with a pleasant blur, but I still feel the
emptiness, the vacuum that sucks my insides.

I have nothing left.

My phone rings non-stop. Ryan, Olive, and my parents, more
and more calls, and I hang up on everyone. I guess some of them
have already found out that I left the hospital yesterday against
doctors' orders, and they want to scold me. But I don't want to
hear anyone right now.

When the unknown number called for the third time, I gave
in and answered, thinking that maybe it was something important, but then, the voice on the other end, the one I thought I
would never hear again, knocked me over. God, how good it was
to hear her!

I wanted to ask if she was okay, to ask how she was doing. But I didn't ask anything.

I have to let her go.

I'm not good for her. I couldn't save her from his hands. I let her down, just like I let Anna down.

When I heard her breakdown, I almost regretted it, almost shouted *I love you*. Instead, I said the worst thing I could have said and disconnected.

It's better this way. As her parents told me, I'm to blame for what happened.

I was told to keep my distance. They asked me not to contact her. They told me that her life would be better without me. They're right. I replay the conversation in my head. I'm the one who convinced her to cheat on her husband. Because of me, she returned to him. None of this would have happened if I hadn't insisted that she be mine.

I get up from the couch slowly, holding my bandaged stomach with my healthy hand. The doctors said I was lucky. If the bullet had hit me just a little more to the right, I wouldn't be here today, but somehow, miraculously, the bullet went in and out without hitting any vital organs. Yay, lucky me. As if fate were laughing at me, wanting me to stay alive to watch everyone I love suffer.

I received four blood transfusions just so I could stay alive, and I'm still weak. I have to lean against the wall when I walk. But at least I'm walking by myself. As soon as I could get up on my feet, I wanted out of that hospital.

I snort at myself as I try to make it to the kitchen. One step, and I gasp. What a disaster I am.

My shoulder screams in pain, and I try hard not to move it.

I swallow two more painkillers, even though I was told not to take more than two a day, but I don't care about anything right now. I want the fog of oblivion, the blur. Because if I keep thinking about her, I'll go crazy.

I want to erase her from my memory, the sight of her in that bed of horrors, spread out and bleeding. But neither the pills nor the alcohol helps me with that, and every time I close my eyes, I see her again. I can never sleep again. She will never forgive me. I will never forgive myself.

I return to the sofa, panting from pain and, shortness of breath, and collapse on it, crying, until finally fatigue overwhelms me, and I fall asleep.

I don't know how much time has passed when I wake up to the sound of knocking on the door. It takes me forever to get up from the couch.

Few people have permission to come up to my apartment. Even my parents don't have permission. So I already know who it is.

I half walk, half crawl to the door, unable to stand upright. The pain is killing me. Leaving the hospital early was not my best idea. But my parents were there too. Doctors. Visitors. Poking my body, my mind. I don't want to see anyone. I prefer to be alone.

"Ethan." Ryan storms in, almost knocking me down. I want to yell at him and ask him to go, but I can't form the words. I don't feel so good right now.

I just stand, leaning against the wall, and pant heavily.

"What the hell are you doing? I went to the hospital today, and they told me you checked yourself out against doctors' orders," he says as he starts pacing the floor.

It surprised me he didn't show up here yesterday. Turns out it took a while for the news to reach him.

The room spins, and I surrender to my legs melting beneath me, sinking to a sitting position on the floor and resting my head against the wall.

"Shit, Ethan." Ryan rushes over and squats in front of me. "Don't faint on me. I'm calling an ambulance."

I shake my head. I'm not going back there. "No. I'm fine. Just give me a moment to recover." I try to regulate my breathing. The world revolves around me, but I don't tell him that.

He looks worried, really worried. I probably look as bad as I feel.

"You reek of alcohol."

"I didn't plan on you coming to visit, so I didn't save any for you."

"It's dangerous with the pills you're taking. But you already know that." His mouth twists in anger. "Come on." He bends down and puts his shoulder under my good arm to support me. I moan in pain. Fuck.

Any other person I would have thrown out, but Ryan has seen me in difficult situations before. He helps me get to the bed, and I lie down carefully, trying not to open the stitches.

"I haven't seen you like this since..."

"Since Anna. You can say it." My eyes are closed, and I don't see his reaction. For a moment, I'm tempted to open them just for that. I can't explain to him how both of them have morphed into one woman in my mind. And every time I close my eyes, I see Anna's dead eyes turn into Ayala's blue ones.

"Yes, since Anna. You're falling apart because of this woman, Ethan."

"Yeah, getting stabbed and shot tends to make someone fall apart." I let out a fake laugh.

"You know what I mean, and it's not your physical condition. And by the way, you look awful. You shouldn't have come home like this."

I twist the corner of my mouth into a half smile. "I was naïve to think we could be together. That we could beat the past. I'm a walking disaster. I bring hell to every woman I love. So yeah, a little self-destruction after destroying another woman's life and causing her to be raped doesn't sound so bad to me. I shouldn't have gone out with her in the first place."

"What the hell are you talking about? You didn't get anyone raped." I'm glad I didn't open my eyes now and can't see him.

"She would never have gone back to him if it wasn't for me. It was because of the threat against me. She went back to him because of me. Only because of me." Even her parents said that. They blamed me for everything that happened, and they were right.

"Because she loves you."

"And where did that get her? Back to the monster. I should have never pursued her. Now I've killed another woman I loved." Another death on my black conscience.

"She's not dead, Ethan! You didn't kill her. She survived. And you're not to blame for this any more than you were to blame for what happened to Anna. Ayala knew Michael Summers long before she met you, and she was in an abusive relationship with him long before she met you. You are not the one who got her in trouble. You were just trying to save her."

Now I'm shouting just as loud as Ryan. "You weren't there. You didn't see her. No human can survive something like that without dying. I died a little just looking at her. After that, I can't possibly look her in the eyes again. I just can't."

"You love her, Ethan. You can't just give her up like this." His eyes widen. "She needs you."

"I can. I've already given her up. She'll be better off without me."

"Ethan. She's not Anna," he says, but I seal my heart against his plea and remain silent. There is nothing in the world he can say now that will change my mind. She's better off without me.

Her parents asked me to keep my distance, and that's what I'll do. She doesn't need the destruction I bring with me.

With a little luck, Ayala will recover and start over. Maybe she'll find herself a good guy. I hurt everyone I love. I always knew relationships weren't for me. I have to make sure this never happens again.

"I hope to God it's just the pills and alcohol talking, and after you recover a bit, you'll understand what you're doing. I just hope it won't be too late."

I turn my head to the other side.

Ryan leaves the room and returns after a few minutes, holding a stack of pages.

"Are you still awake? I need to talk to you about something as your lawyer. I'm sorry, but it can't wait."

I turn my face to him and see that he's serious. I try to focus and concentrate, but I'm having a hard time in the fog I'm in.

"Detective Delfino called me today from the San Francisco Police Department. They took a statement from Ayala Beckett."

I narrow my eyes, wondering what he's going to say.

"There's a discrepancy between your versions."

"What?"

"You told me you shot and killed Michael. You signed this affidavit in my presence." He waves the pages.

"Right."

"Ayala stated that at this point, you were unconscious. She says the bullet was ejected during a struggle between her and Michael."

I honestly have no idea how Michael died. I only found out he had been shot and died when I woke up in the hospital, and Ryan updated me on the details. I lost so much blood that I couldn't even save her from him. I'd passed out.

Great help I was.

I pulled out the only logical thing I could say to still try to save

Ayala. I told them I was the one who shot him so she wouldn't stand trial for murder.

"Ethan, it's me. The truth, please. Then we'll think about what to do next."

I close my eyes and open them. I trust him with my life.

"I honestly don't know what happened to him. I was passed out."

"Fuck!" He looks down at the floor, then stares at me again. "This isn't good. Why did you do such a thing?"

"Why do you think? I thought she'd killed him."

"You thought she killed him?" he repeats after me.

"Obviously. Who else could do that? I didn't want her to go to jail. I was going to kill him anyway, but I failed even that."

"Shit, Ethan. Neither of you should have killed him. He should have been in prison for the rest of his life." Ryan tilts his head. "And now you're both in trouble because you lied."

"I'm sorry. I'll tell the police I lied."

"No. It can create even more complications, and it's uncertain they'll believe you at this point in any case."

"So, what am I supposed to do?" I throw up my hands, momentarily forgetting that my arm is in a sling, and grimace in pain.

"Sit quietly, and don't talk to anyone other than me. Not even to the cops. I'll issue a new statement. We'll try to get out of it with the fact that you were dizzy and had lost a lot of blood."

"Will Ayala get in trouble because of me?"

"I don't know," he says and sits on the bed next to me.

Fuck. The last thing I want is for her to get in trouble. "What are you doing?" I straighten up.

"Watching you."

"I don't need supervision. I'm not a child."

"You sure act like a six-year-old."

"I'll be fine. Madeleine will arrive shortly, so I'll have supervision. Go home. Maya needs you more than I do," I lie. I gave Madeleine the day off because I didn't want anyone to be here.

He examines my face. "Okay, I'll go. But call me if you need anything. Okay?"

I nod.

CHAPTER 11

Ethan

T he alarm clock doesn't stop. I raise my hand and throw it against the wall. It makes a faint sound and then stops.

Quiet.

My phone rings. Fuck. Why don't they leave me alone?

I overcome the urge to throw the phone as well and instead silence it. Then put my head under the pillow. I want them all to leave me alone.

A knock sounds on my bedroom door.

"*Kýrios*. Do you want something to eat?" Madeleine asks through the door.

Fuck. What is she doing here? How long has it been? "No! I'm fine. Leave me alone," I shout at the closed door.

"You have to get up and get out of bed. You haven't been out for a long time. When did you last eat?"

I know she's worried, but I can't stand it. Let me stay fucking alone. Is that so hard?

"Leave the food in the fridge for me. Thanks, Madeleine." I try the friendly approach, and she gives up and leaves. It worked.

My shoulder throbs with pain, and so does my head. I try to

get out of bed but move slowly as the attacks of dizziness sometimes hit me by surprise.

I pee and take a few Percocet, then study the half-empty bottle. I'll need to talk to Jess about getting me more since that annoying doctor refused to renew the prescription. Doesn't he understand that I'm in pain?

I struggle to stand up straight and am so nauseous that I crawl back into bed. I just need to lie down for a bit, and I'm sure I'll be okay.

The next thing my foggy brain registers is someone slapping me in the face.

My eyes won't open.

"Ethan! Wake up!" I can hear the voice through the fog, but I can't open my eyes.

"Madeleine, call an ambulance!"

"No, I'll take responsibility for him." I hear Ryan's voice. "No problem. I'll sign whatever's needed."

I open my eyes to narrow slits. Hospital. I'm in the hospital again.

"Oh, I see you decided not to die this time, either." Ryan's cynical voice sounds harsh in my ears.

"I said—" I stop to clear my throat because my voice is so hoarse I hardly recognize it. "I said I didn't want to go to a hospital."

"If you weren't found lying unconscious on the floor of your bedroom, maybe I could have saved you from it. But I'd rather you didn't die," he says sarcastically. "Seriously, Ethan, how many pills did you take? Was it a suicide attempt? You were lucky you threw up. Otherwise, you wouldn't be with us anymore."

I sigh. "I'm in pain, Ryan. Fucking pain. That's all. I didn't try to kill myself. I just needed something for the pain."

"It's not just the physical pain, and you know it. It's been three weeks already. Three weeks of you not functioning."

I go on the offense. "What were you even doing in my house?"

"You were supposed to come to the board meeting today, remember? Your first day at the office. But you didn't answer the phone, and Madeleine said you didn't leave the room, so…"

Ah. So that's why the alarm clock was going off. Everything is so blurry in my head. No thought forms properly. When did all these days pass?

"You told me you were fine, that you were ready to go back to work."

"What do you want me to say?" I shout. "That I'm losing it? That I don't want to live anymore?" How many times can I ask him to save my poor ass?

"Yes. That's exactly what I want you to say. I'm here for you, just like you were there for me whenever I needed you. Have you already forgotten how many times I've cried on your shoulder because Maya didn't want me? And how you supported me after the abortion? And what about that time in high school when they wanted to kick me out, and you took the blame?"

I stay silent.

"You'll have to stay at my house for a while."

"What? No way."

"They want to keep you under supervision. I insisted they release you." He looks at me with reproachful eyes. "But I have to sign that you'll be under my supervision. That makes you my responsibility. Therefore, you're coming home with me until I say otherwise."

"No fucking way."

"I'm a lawyer, Ethan. I'm *your* lawyer. You know I don't sign anything without meaning it, so that's the way it is. A hospital or my home. Deal with it."

CHAPTER 12

One Year Later

AYALA

"**M**om, I found an apartment!" I enter my parents' house and throw my bag at the entrance.

I've been living here since they released me from the hospital, but it's been a year now, and it's time to go back to being independent. The holidays are approaching. Last year I celebrated them at the hospital. This year I want to celebrate in my own home.

Mom doesn't answer. I go into the kitchen to search for her, and indeed she's there, rattling pots and cooking while singing.

I always wondered why she did nothing with her cooking talent, but Mom believes in this traditional relationship, where only the man works, and the woman supports the house.

"What did you say? I didn't hear you," she turns to me.

"I said I found an apartment."

"It's too fast. Don't you think?"

I can never get over what happened. It will always be a part of me. But she can't grasp it. Maybe it's because I never shared with her what happened there. She knows Michael raped me and beat me, I even told her he murdered Robin, even though no proof was found, and I know she believed me. But she has no idea of the extent of his abuse or what Ethan's connection was to the whole story.

I want to tell her how much I love him, how much he helped me, but every time I mention Ethan, she recoils. As far as she's concerned, he was the man I had sex with while married. For her, he is to blame for everything that happened, and I should keep my distance from him. Not that it's a problem since Ethan said he never wanted to hear from me again.

To continue my recovery, I need to be independent again. I want my privacy back. I want to know that when I wake up at night from a nightmare, she's not sitting in her bed worrying about me.

"Mom, I go to therapy twice a week, and I'll continue after I leave. I found a job I like. I'm perfectly fine." As fine as I could be. I stopped hoping for more.

After they released me from the hospital, my parents hovered over me like birds over their chick. They didn't leave me for a moment, making sure I wouldn't be left alone, afraid that as soon as they looked away, I would kill myself.

I won't lie. There were moments when I thought about it. Moments when the black shadows surrounded everything, and I couldn't see a future. I didn't understand how I would ever recover and live again when I had nothing left to live for. Without Ethan, without the baby.

After the call with Ethan, when he told me it was all over, I thought my life was over, too. If he didn't want me anymore, no one would. No one would want the flawed and broken person I am.

But the months passed, and I healed. My body has healed except for a few faint marks that remain and a nose that is now permanently slightly crooked. On the outside, I am completely normal, but on the inside...

My mind will probably never recover, but I've learned to

accept it. I've resigned myself to the fact that the nightmares would likely stay with me forever, that I'll probably never have a normal relationship like other people. But I've come to realize I can be somewhat happy. When I think about it, my psychologist has done well for me.

Three months ago, I started looking for a job again. This time under my real name. It was difficult to show my face outside when some people still remember me from the incident.

I couldn't deny the pitying looks in their eyes, the flickers of recognition and the fluttering gazes searching for the scars, waiting for me to collapse, scream, or do something embarrassing. Although I answered all the questions and passed the interviews with no problem, I wasn't hired. Eventually, I had no choice but to agree to an interview at T.J Publishing, a company belonging to my mother's uncle, Toby Jefferson. At Mom's request, he agreed to give me a chance and hire me, but he still required a preliminary interview.

I was happy to be like everyone else.

I sat across from Uncle Toby and stared back at him. I wasn't going to give him any reason to think I would collapse at any moment. He took no pity on me, and I answered all his questions quickly and efficiently.

When I left with a handshake, I knew the job was mine.

He was looking for a brand manager for their digital fashion magazine. I convinced him that the job was tailor-made for me. He agreed to give me a month to prove myself, even though I arrived with no previous experience.

In the first month, he examined my every move, but now three months later, I manage a team of ten people with a high level of skill. I plan and distribute campaigns on social networks, follow all financial reports, and now I'm immersed in competition research that I conduct to plan our strategy for the future.

This is exactly the type of job I wanted back when I went to study business administration.

Uncle Toby knows I didn't finish my degree, and although he continues to encourage me to go back to school, the degree wasn't important to him when he hired me.

"I see the sparkle in your eyes," he said. "You're hungry for the job." And oh, how right he was.

I love my job.

"I'm ready, Mom. It's been a year already. I can't live here forever." I shrug and sit on a chair by the kitchen counter.

"You can live here as long as you need. You know it. I'll never ask you to go." An expression of guilt washes over her face.

I won't ask again, she means. "I know you still feel guilty about what happened. But I don't blame you." I blame myself. I was the weak and stupid one who believed the man who told me he wanted me. And not once, but twice. Twice I fell into the trap.

I have to endure my parents' expressions of pity every day, along with the guilt they carry, but what they don't know, what they don't understand, is that despite the severe injuries Michael inflicted on my body, the greater damage was done by Ethan. The man I trusted, the man to whom I gave my heart. I was ready to give my life for him, and at the moment of truth, he cut me loose.

She looks over her shoulder at me. "Okay, Ayala. If that's what you want. But you're continuing the treatment, right?"

"Yes, yes." I nod. My parents insisted on continuing to fund my therapy even after I found a job. They want a guarantee I'll continue to go, which I have no problem promising because I have no intention of stopping. The sessions help me.

I go up to my room and lie down on the bed, shoes and all, and look up at the shining stars stuck to the ceiling of my room. I think I was seven years old when I convinced my father to tape them up for me.

I love my job. I work overtime every day, even though I don't get paid for it. Not because I don't get the job done in a normal eight-hour day or because I'm not up to it, but because work helps me forget. The work fulfills me. I'm as busy as a bee collecting honey, constantly hovering over tasks, and supervising my employees. It fills all my time and all my attention, leaving no time for other thoughts to invade.

But as soon as I get home, reality checks in at the door and hits me full force.

I can no longer sleep without sleeping pills. My nightmares have changed. At first, I would dream about what happened, Michael on top of me, the smell of his sweat in my nose, and the intense pain, and I would run to the bathroom to throw up.

Now it's worse. The dreams are worse.

I dream of Ethan. We make love by the lake. The sun warms our skin, the golden glint of desire in his eyes. I can hear the branches in the wind, like that day we lay on the blanket together. I feel him. I feel his heat. Then the setting changes. The trees disappear and become a black and menacing shadow. The sun disappears, and Ethan's face becomes Michael's. And then I scream...

Sometimes I see Michael standing in front of me, his gun pointed at Ethan, and I just stand there, watching the circle of blood spreading on Ethan's shirt, while I can't move. My limbs are glued to the floor. I can't reach him, can't help him. I stand there and watch him wither and die before my eyes.

There are brief moments when I'm sorry he's not dead. Maybe if I'd lost him to death, it would be final, and the grief would be final. It would be hard, but not as hard as the rejection. And then I'm horrified by my terrible thoughts.

I've had a hard time explaining to my psychologist what happened with Ethan. Why I can't get over it. How could it be that the man I loved, a man who gave me my body back, also took it from me with one short phone call?

I can't understand what happened there, can't wrap my head around it. How could it be that he came to save me but didn't stay to see that I survived? How could I have thought we were in love, given my life for him, only to find out it was all a lie?

A huge fat lie that consumes worlds.

I'm getting over Michael's trauma and seeing the light at the end of the tunnel, but I don't think I'll ever be able to get over Ethan.

CHAPTER 13

Ethan

I watch the presentation put on by the managers of Lemon Games and try to show interest in the numbers, but my thoughts wander to other places.

I bought the company a little before the "event"—that's what I call that terrible day now—but wasn't into it in the following months.

Well, let's not embellish reality. I was stoned about ninety percent of the time.

The alcohol and pills were the only things that blurred the picture that dominated my thoughts. Luckily Ryan insisted on taking me to his house and putting me through accelerated rehab. He and Olive pulled me out of it before it was too late.

Since I returned to the office a few months ago, I've tried getting back to operating my little empire, but my interest level is so low as to be practically non-existent. I can't seem to revive my drive. Even Savee doesn't interest me like it used to, and I leave Paul to manage without me. What good is the entire operation I set up if, at the moment of truth, I couldn't even save the woman I love?

After months of being away, I don't understand what I'm

doing here at all. Everything worked perfectly without me. I have excellent managers who know their job. They don't need me here.

I nod in the right places and say the right things, but nothing moves me. From the outside, life is back on track. I conduct myself in the world as usual, but nothing is as usual.

I feel numb. I feel...off.

On the outside, I am perfectly fine. The injuries have healed, although I still do physical therapy every night to improve the condition of my shoulder. I'm eating regularly, I'm functioning normally, and I've even confirmed attendance at the children's fundraiser next week. Although I'd rather get stabbed again than smile at everyone. I've confirmed without a plus one.

After the presentation and meetings are over, I sit alone in my office and open the weekly report from Jess.

No one knows I'm still following her, still checking on her.

Ryan would go crazy if he knew.

But I can't stay away. I have to see her, even from afar and know she's okay. It's the only bright spot in my week.

I open the email with shaky hands. He's sent pictures. I wait a bit for them to download to the device and open it.

I take a deep breath.

Her figure, so familiar to me, walks down the street, wearing a knee-length black pencil skirt and a tight yellow blouse that high-lights her breasts. She's wearing heels with a bag tucked under her arm. Her hair, lighter and longer now, flutters in the wind, and she reaches to tuck the bothersome strands behind her ear.

I can't see her eyes from the distance the photo was taken, but I remember how blue they are.

She looks amazing.

She looks like a woman who has moved on.

She still works at the magazine and seems to excel in the job. I always knew she would be amazing. I'd offered her a job once. She had that fire I was looking for and a sharp mind. But she refused my offer, and I wonder now if the situation would have been different if she hadn't still been working at the bar but instead had been working for me when he started looking for her.

I'm glad to see how well she looks, how alive. Not like Anna. Ayala is stronger than Anna and always has been.

Turning from the photos, I continue reading the update. It seems she's rented an apartment in the suburbs. Well done, Bambi. You go, girl.

I wonder if she had forgotten me or if she has already gotten over me. Because I don't think I will ever get over her.

My office door opens, and Ryan walks in. I dim the phone screen so he doesn't see what I'm looking at. "Don't you ever knock?"

"Since when do I have to knock?" He sits down in the chair in front of me. "Or were you planning to fuck someone here?" He looks around as if looking for where I hid a woman. "It will do you good to start fucking again. It's been a long time."

"Concentrate on your own fucking."

"Don't worry about me. The pregnancy makes Maya so horny." He smirks, and I frown in mock disgust.

But truly, I'm happy for him. I was afraid that the miscarriage would destroy them. Those were difficult days. But Maya got pregnant again easily, and their relationship is everything one could hope for. For a moment, I thought it could happen to me too, but I realize now that those were false hopes. Such happiness is not my destiny.

But Ryan's right. I need to get back to business. Getting laid will give me some interest in life. The fun I'm missing.

"Okay, let's get to the point," Ryan says, interrupting my train of thought. "Today, I received an official letter from the police in San Francisco that they're closing the case." He smiles. "There's no evidence that the death was caused by anything other than an unfortunate accident."

I allow myself to smile. It's a relief to know Ayala is finally free. And me too. My business took a hit when the whole story came out. Being a suspect in a murder case, even if no indictment had been filed, isn't good for business. I'm glad that part will finally be behind me.

I wonder if she received the news as well. I wonder if she was as happy as I am. If she was worried or didn't care. I wonder if she thinks about me.

"Earth to Ethan."

Fuck, I didn't listen again.

"What's wrong with you? You're not focused."

"I have a lot on my mind, Ryan. Leave me alone," I mutter. "What else do you want?"

We sit for a few minutes and discuss updates on some burning legal issues, yet, I struggle to stay focused. When we finish, I feel nothing but relief.

I'd pour a glass of whiskey right now, but I know Ryan wouldn't take it well. Not after what I've put him through these past few months, so I hold off.

I stare at myself in the rearview mirror and try to straighten my bow tie. Why the hell did I agree to come to this event?

I put on a fake smile and go inside. My first appearance at a public fundraiser since the "event," and it turns out that the interest has not died down. The photographers chase me, snap pictures, and ask for a response.

I just keep the smile plastered on my face and keep walking. Publicity is always good.

"Maya, you look great," I say, greeting my friends, who approach me near the entrance. Her belly is huge. When's her due date again? I don't remember, but it seems like any moment.

"I know, I look like an elephant. But thanks for lying to me." She gives me a dazzling smile, happiness reflected in her eyes as she turns to Ryan. That lucky son of a bitch. I take her arm and lead her inside.

This is the first time in a while that I've gone to an event alone, and the rumors have spread their wings. People are whispering about me, thinking I can't hear them.

It doesn't bother me, though. I don't care what people think of me. I glance around, looking for someone who seems interesting. It's time to break the dry spell. Many eyes are on me. This is going to be easier than I expected.

Shit. My parents.

I take a glass of champagne from a passing waiter, and Ryan gives me a scolding look.

"I'm fine." I glare back. I wasn't planning on drowning myself today, but I need some alcohol to survive this evening if my parents are here.

I see how my mother's gaze locates me in the crowd. She walks toward me.

Ryan follows my gaze, grabs Maya, and they walk away, leaving me alone in the lion's den.

"Ethan." My mother's voice is soft.

"Mom." I tilt my head and sip the champagne. Too bad it's not whiskey.

"Ethan, it's been months." I see the tears in her eyes. "You got hurt, and you didn't even let me come visit." She reaches for my arm, and I take a step back. Pain flashes in her eyes. "Are you okay?"

"Yes. Fine." I'm not in a cooperative mood.

"You're our son. Please don't cut us off. I want to know what's going on with you. We love you."

"You might, but Dad is another story." I turn my gaze to him, standing a few steps behind her, keeping a safe distance. Maybe he's worried I'll cause a scene.

"No. He just worries about you, like me. Will you come to dinner? So we can talk?"

I don't feel like going through that again, but they did try to save me from all the mess I made in the past. I still feel indebted to them. "Fine."

She tries to come closer for a hug.

I take another step back, and she stops, looking at me with disappointment. I said I would come. Right now, that's all I can give them. I move away and sit down at a table.

It's amazing what a famous murder case does to a girl's libido. All evening they approach me, touch me, and do more or less everything except take my pants off. I should be happy, that's what I wanted, but instead, I'm uncomfortable.

I have to get out of here with a woman. Ryan is right. Too much time has passed. I'm not sure if my cock is still working.

The blonde at the side table has been examining me for several minutes. She looks good. I smile and raise a glass at her. Yes. Bingo.

I get up and go to her. "Shall we dance?"

She stands, and I place my hand on her back, leading her to the floor.

Tomorrow our picture will be on all the gossip sites. Let's hope I chose well.

Fuck, the sun is blinding. What's the time? I glance at the phone next to the bed and read the message on the screen.

Ryan
Well, did you break the dry spell?

I call him.

"Are you living your life through me now? Go fuck yourself.'

"I'm fucking just fine, thanks. The question is, are you?"

Ahhh... He just won't give up. What shall I say? That it was horrible? She was not Ayala. She didn't have Ayala's big blue eyes. She didn't moan like Ayala did. I almost couldn't get it up. Luckily, she didn't notice. It could have been a disaster.

"Of course I fucked her."

"Hope you let her come at least twice. But why did you have to choose Richard's daughter?"

"Richard?" The name means nothing to me.

"Richard Castle."

"Fuck."

"Yes. Hope you didn't upset her. Otherwise, there'll be an increase in the rent."

She came. I'm sure. I went down on her for hours until she came. My jaw still hurts.

"Okay, Ryan, why are you waking me up in the morning for this nonsense? It's Saturday. Let me sleep."

"You don't run anymore?" There's a note of surprise in his voice.

"What?"

"You're not running? I never woke you up at eight in the morning before. I thought you'd be back from your run already."

"Uh... I changed the hours a bit. I don't run outside because of the nosey gossips." Half true. I no longer have the commitment like before. I don't run every day like I used to. "Anything else, or shall we talk later?"

After a few more meaningless comments, he lets me go. And just as I lie down again, there's a knock on the door. Fuck, what do people want from me today?

"Hey, Olive." She storms into the apartment as I open the door, waving her phone. "Good morning to you, too," I mumble.

"Why did you do this? Why with Lena?"

"Huh?"

The phone is waved in front of my eyes again. I see a picture from last night's party of Lena Castle and me.

"Oh."

"Why did you sleep with her, Ethan? This woman will only bring trouble."

"What are you all doing interfering with my sex life today?" I press the button on the coffee machine. "Do you want coffee?" I don't wait for an answer and pull out a second cup for her.

"You don't interfere with mine because there's nothing to interfere with. Jenny and I broke up months ago. Why did you do this?"

"Why not? You know, I'm a man. I like sex." She's crossing the line here.

"You love Ayala."

"Not anymore."

"Ethan, she'll see these pictures. Don't you care that you're hurting her?"

Fuck. She's right. If Jess sent me a picture of her with another man, I would go ballistic. "We're not together."

"I still don't understand why not. You obviously still love her. And the way you did it... I still can't believe you did that to her." Olive's sitting on a stool at the kitchen island and straightens her long legs before taking a sip of her coffee. "You have to talk about what happened with someone. It doesn't have to be me, but you have to talk to someone. You don't act like yourself anymore. I worry about you. It's like you're turned off."

Wow, that's a pretty accurate description of how I feel. Turned off. I didn't think it was that noticeable. "I don't enjoy you meddling in my business." I turn and go to stand at the window.

First Ryan, now Olive. I'm sure they coordinated this intervention.

No one knows what happened there, nothing but what the media has put out, and I'm not going to tell them. I don't feel like going back and picking my brain with psychologists again. They didn't help me when I was seventeen, and they won't help me now. But maybe she's right. Maybe I'm not as capable of handling this alone as I thought. I guess I've failed again.

CHAPTER 14

Ayala

"Hey, Olive." I plug in the headset and answer the phone while walking at a fast pace. I don't want to be late for the office. "What's going on?"

"Sorry I didn't get to call last week. I was busy with the new store."

"And how is the store doing?" I cross the road, and a speeding car honks at me.

"Work in progress. There are some crises because it seems it's impossible to do without them." She laughs. "But we'll open on time."

"That's amazing! I can't believe it's going to happen."

"Would you come? I realize it's in New York, and it's far and all, but I want you to be there. I can buy you a ticket, and you can sleep at my place."

"Hmmm." I don't know what to say. "I'm not sure I can get away from work." Can I fly to New York?

"You don't need to stay for very long. You can get back the next day. Please be with me at the opening. All your pep talks and ideas over the last few months have been an integral part of the store, and you just have to see it all in person. How the wallpaper you chose turned out and everything else."

"I think you're confused. You're the one who encouraged me, not the other way around." I laugh. She's been by my side all this time, from the moment she found out that Ethan dumped me, even though she didn't have to be there. After all, we barely knew each other.

"Okay, I'll make an effort to come. And there's no need for you to buy me a ticket. I have a job now."

"I know, very important lady. Say, in connection with that, perhaps there's a small, tiny, microscopic chance that your magazine will cover the opening?"

I bite my lip. "I'll see what I can do. But I can't promise anything, okay? I don't want you to be disappointed." I'd love to help her out, but I'm not the one who decides what to cover.

"I know. So, how are you?"

Olive and I sink into our usual conversation until I get to the office, then say our goodbyes.

I knock on the door of Uncle Toby's office. "Can I come in?" He gestures with his hand, and I go in and sit in front of him.

"I have an idea for an article or spread in the magazine. A new designer store in New York is opening in two weeks. I know the designer, and she's amazing."

"In New York? What's special about this store? Why should we review it in particular, and more precisely, in New York?"

"The designer is something special. She's a rising social network star, and she has a crazy buzz. More than a million followers on social networks. The opening is going to be a blast for sure. Lots of celebrities will come. We should be there."

"A million followers, you say? Okay, that sounds more interesting. And how will you get an invitation?"

"I already have one." I smile. "The designer is a friend of mine."

"Can you write the article? Maybe we'd better send Liz."

I shake my head. "It's important to her that I be there. I can write a piece, but if you prefer, Liz and I can fly together." I'm not a journalist, but I can cover an event.

He considers my words. "All right. But you'll have to take a photographer with you. We'll need photos."

I nod. "Yeah, sure."

"Okay, so send me dates and book flights for you and Claire."

I almost skip out of the room. It worked out great. And this will be an excellent feature in the magazine. Claire is one of our best photographers and also fun to work with.

I send Olive a message.

> I'm coming to New York! And I'm also bringing a photographer with me. You're in. Okay?

> **Olive**
> Yes! You're amazing. And, of course, the photographer is welcome. I'm so excited!

I return to my desk, send the information to Claire, and book flights and a hotel for both of us.

Only when the excitement subsides, do I realize what I've done. Olive is my friend. We've talked almost every day since what happened. But she is also a close friend of Ethan's.

Ethan was involved in this store from the beginning. There's no way he won't make it to this opening.

I try to stop the vibrations that attack me. How am I supposed to face him? I can't. I'll cancel the trip. But Olive... I already promised her. I'll have to let Liz go in my place like Toby suggested.

My breathing is fast and shallow. I try to inhale deeply to stop the onset of the anxiety attack. Maybe Ethan won't be there at all? I Google his name daily, and nothing comes up except for a few articles about his businesses. After the incident, he disappeared from society. He doesn't appear in public.

And as if to annoy me, when I type his name now, a picture from yesterday comes up.

Of course. Of course, there would be a new picture of him right when I'm on the verge of having a panic attack. He's still beautiful, still looks amazing. Still makes my body crave him. But on re-examination, I see that something has changed. The intensity I used to see in him is missing, that playful mischief. I open the next picture, and my heart hurts as if he's hit me. I'm horrified to see that there is a blonde hanging on his arm. I wonder if she's important to him. If they are in love like we were.

My nails dig so hard into my thighs that they leave marks. I remind myself that Ethan can date whoever he wants. We're not together. Just because I can't get over him, that doesn't mean he didn't succeed in getting over me.

I engage myself at work and fill my head with numbers and campaigns. There's nothing like being busy to distract myself.

It's been a long time since I've been so tense before a session with my psychologist, but today I feel like I did nearly a year ago. I remember the first few times I went to him when the wounds were still fresh and open. It's like I've once again returned to the days of the beginning, to the paralyzing fear, to a place I thought I was no longer in. Turns out I still have a long way to go.

I slump on the gray sofa in front of Dr. Sullivan.

"The dancer is really beautiful." I point to the statue in the corner of the room.

"I love it, too. But it was also here the previous times you visited. What's bothering you, Ayala?" His brown eyes study me through his glasses, but there's no judgment in them. That's why I don't mind coming here. No judgment, just help.

I nod and try to get out the words. "Olive asked me to come to her grand opening party."

"That's great. It's nice that you keep in touch from a distance. I understand she's important to you. Are you planning to go?"

"I meant to. I even arranged for her to receive a PR spread in the magazine. The travel plans have already been made for me and also for the photographer the magazine plans to send."

He waits for me to continue, watching me in silence.

"Then I remembered Ethan would be there."

"Ethan Wolf?"

"Yes. There's no way he won't be there. He's Olive's close friend. He's very involved in the business."

"And what do you think of that?"

"I think I'm going to pass out."

"I understand you're afraid of seeing him again."

"Yes. It's too soon. I'm still... Still..."

"Do you still have feelings for him?"

"Yes."

"And what do you think will happen if you see him?"

"I'll fall apart."

"I think you're stronger than what you believe. But only you can judge if the situation will set you back. You need to decide."

We continue the conversation, and I leave with a decision. It's too early for me. I can't attend the launch. I'll have to see Olive and the store another time.

CHAPTER 13

Ethan

Ryan
Mom's birthday party is at eight.

I close my eyes and sigh. He doesn't even bother to ask if I'm coming because there's no other option. I have to go to Jennifer's party. I would normally have no problem attending. I'm close to Ryan's parents, but I'm just so exhausted. I'm tired of the pretense, tired of the fake smiles.

But this is Jennifer. The person who gave me a place when I felt like I didn't belong. When my parents ignored me. I remember how all my friends abandoned me on the advice of their parents. *"You shouldn't be seen next to the wayward son, the one who dropped out of school and makes trouble."* It might be contagious. Only Ryan stayed by my side. And his mother never made me feel unwelcome in their home. On the contrary, she was always happy to see me as if I were her own. During my tough year, I was a guest in my house and a family member in theirs. I didn't realize then how much she sacrificed to provide me with that safe place. How our community pushed them aside just for being close to me.

I send a message to Olive.

> Can you come with me to a party tonight at eight?

I sit and hope for a positive answer. I need her by my side today. She'll make sure I don't do or say anything stupid that I'll regret later, and she'll smile even when I'm not able to.

Olive
For you, always.

"You look amazing." I congratulate Jennifer and kiss her cheek. "Did you do something?"

"Hyaluronic acid," she whispers in my ear. "It's the new hit now. But don't tell anyone. I want everyone to think I simply look good for my age."

"You look great for your age." I squeeze her arms and examine her. Her slim figure is wrapped in a long wine-colored dress. It's hard to believe she's turning sixty-three. "Why does it say fifty-nine on the signs?"

She raises a shaped eyebrow. "Why do you think?"

"I brought you something." I hand her the bag with Olive's new brand logo, the orchid flower engraved in delicate gold.

"You know you don't have to bring me gifts." A blush rises on her cheeks.

"I designed the dress, especially for you," Olive says with a smile. "It's one of a kind." Jennifer's eyes light up.

We have known each other for over twenty years, and it still embarrasses Jennifer to receive gifts from me. The truth is I didn't know what to bring. Then Olive offered to give her a new piece she designed, and I jumped at the opportunity. Olivia's original and unique designs are a gift that any woman would want, and I'm happy to let Jennifer show one of them off. I do everything I can to make her proud of who I am today, much of it thanks to her.

We go inside, and I spot my parents. Fuck. I rush to team up with Ryan and Maya, using them as human shields.

"No dress fits me," Maya complains. "Everything is ugly. When will you open a line for maternity clothes?" she asks, turning to Olive.

"Let me open the shop first. Then we'll see. And you're about to give birth. So you can buy from me soon." Olive winks at Maya. "I'll design you something special."

Ryan snorts. "It will be great when I no longer have to go out in the middle of the night anymore to buy ice cream and corn."

"Corn?" I raise an eyebrow.

"Don't ask." He laughs.

Maya punches his shoulder. "You have no right to complain, rich boy. You're not carrying a bowling ball that contorts your entire body, and you will not be pushing a watermelon through your v—"

"Ahhhh..." I stop her before unpleasant images appear in front of my eyes. "Too much detail. I'm going to get a drink. Does anyone want anything?"

"Water for me," Maya says, and I see how happy she is in her pregnancy.

"Can you get me some red wine, please?" Olive asks, and with a nod, I go to the bar and order.

"Ethan."

I take a deep breath before turning to her. "Mom." I glance around, and thankfully, Dad is nowhere to be seen. Seems he's keeping his distance from me. Excellent.

"I saw you came with Olivia."

"Right."

"Are you back together?"

I let out a laugh. "No. We're just friends."

She looks disappointed. "So there's no one special in your life?"

I cringe. There was. But I almost caused her death. "No." I take the whiskey I ordered and drink it in one gulp, welcoming the burning in my throat.

"Will you come to dinner? Tomorrow?"

"I can't tomorrow," I lie.

"Next week?"

"Maybe."

She shakes her head. "Please don't cut us out. You promised you would come. You talk more to Jennifer Blake than to me."

Maybe because she talked to me when you just sent me to psychologists without exchanging a word? "I'll come when I can."

"Ethan Wolf."

The firm voice coming from behind me startles me. "Martin Nightingale." I shake his outstretched hand. We haven't spoken in a long time, and I know they were angry that I fired their son last year. I hope he doesn't mean to make a scene. The last thing I want is to embarrass Jennifer at her birthday party. I didn't publicize the reason for the dismissal. I didn't want to shame the family.

"I was sorry to hear about what happened to you. I hope you've fully recovered."

I nod. "Yes, everything is fine, thanks." I wait for him to get to the point.

"I'd be happy if we could set up a meeting to talk about PlayMaker."

I tilt my head. "That's a company you own, right?"

"Very true." He seems pleased. "I understand you've been investing in gaming companies lately, and we're looking for new investors."

Okay. Not the point I expected, but... On second thought, considering their son's betrayal, I'm not sure I want to do business with them. A son with questionable morals can certainly testify against his parents. At least he didn't come to yell at me.

"You're welcome to make an appointment through the office."

"What are you doing, Dad?" Clifford suddenly appears at his father's side.

Shit. Just when I thought he must not be here tonight. Why is he here? I didn't think he'd want to show his face at a Blake event. How is he not ashamed?

"What do you think I'm doing?" Martin says in a low voice.

"Sucking up to Wolf. Again. I don't understand what your business is with them, Dad. They're not the royal family. Do you really admire them that much? Want to kiss their feet?"

Martin's eyes narrow, and he grabs his son's arm and pulls him aside. I see them whispering, and Clifford's face contorts in anger.

I have no idea what's happening here right now, but I'm happy for the rescue, and I quickly make my getaway.

My happiness is premature, however. Clifford breaks away from his father and approaches me once again.

"Don't you dare make an appointment with my father," he says in a low voice, but the rage drips from him like poison.

"Why not?"

"I'll be damned if I let our businesses go to your family."

"My family is as good as anyone else's." I always suspected he had something personal against me, but I didn't know what. This could be my chance to understand.

His mouth stretches into a thin line. "For some unknown reason, Dad adores the Wolf family. 'Clifford, why can't you be more like Ethan? Look how he excels and how well his businesses are doing. Look how many companies he started all by himself.'"

he mocks. "I don't want to hear another word. Even after your sister was raped, you got in trouble and didn't graduate from high school, and he still thinks you're perfect. The perfect son. Can you believe that shit? I graduated with honors, and you screwed up your entire senior year, and yet you're still better than me." He finishes his tirade by smashing his finger into my chest.

"I'm not perfect." I wish my father had thought even some of these things about me.

"Damn right, you're not. You're nothing but trash, like your whole family. And my father's company will go to me. I'm not ready for him to sell it, and certainly not to you. I don't care what he thinks."

"And what is he thinking, Clifford?"

"He thinks I'm not capable of leading the company, that I couldn't even hold a job. But I'll be the one who manages it. Not you."

I don't want his company or the meeting with his father. But I don't like threats. "I'll decide about that."

"If you interfere, you'll pay for it."

"Do you want me to go public with the reason I fired you? Shall I embarrass you and your family that way?"

He narrows his eyes but doesn't respond. I take a deep breath. "I suggest you keep your distance from me from now on. If you threaten me again, you'll bear the consequences." I take the wine and water and return to my friends.

CHAPTER 16

Ayala

Good luck tomorrow!

I send Olive the message and receive a heart emoji back. Unbelievable how quickly the date has come. I enter the offices and go find Liz and Claire to give them a final briefing.

I find Claire in her office, examining camera lenses, and slump into the chair next to her desk. "Everything ready?"

Claire looks up. "I'm debating which lens to take." She waves two large lenses that seem the same to me.

"Both of them?" I raise my hands, and she exhales. "When is the flight?"

"I don't remember exactly, but not until this evening, so you have a full day yet. Several network influencers are expected to be in attendance. You'll want to get photos of them, preferably with a quote. I made you a list of who's important to photograph." I hand her a sheet of paper, and she takes it and skims over the names.

"You also attached pictures." She smiles.

"I didn't know if you would be able to identify them just by the names."

"This is excellent. I might have easily missed someone otherwise." She puts the page in her handbag.

"Where's Liz? I wanted to talk to her too."

"She hasn't arrived yet." Claire balances the lenses in her hands as if weighing them on scales. "Why don't you come with us? I understand this is your friend's opening?"

"Yes, and I'd love to be there for her. But there's a history for me in New York, and I prefer not to open old wounds," I mutter.

"Is it related to...?"

I nod, and she shuts up. A year has passed, and still, no one can talk to me about it. They're afraid to bring up the subject. This is the closest anyone has come so far. Dr. Sullivan thinks it will help me talk about what happened with other people. That I will see that the world will not collapse in on me and that life will go on. But what if he's wrong?

I go back to my office and start working on organizing the social media budget for next month. I add a section for Olive. She should join our influencer campaign and I plan to ask her about it. It's perfect for her. I'll update her with the details after she gets through the stressful opening. I'm sure she'll agree.

As I lift my head from my laptop and look around, I realize it's lunchtime, and I still haven't seen Liz today or had a chance to give her my last-minute tips about the trip. I'm on my way to the cafeteria to search for her when Toby stops me.

"Can you come into my office for a moment?"

I nod and follow him.

"Liz didn't come in today," he informs me as soon as we enter. "She contacted her manager this morning, letting him know that she's sick and wouldn't be able to make the trip."

"What? But she'll probably be fine by tomorrow, right?"

There are only a few hours left until the flight. This is so last-minute.

"I don't know. She says she won't, and I can't take the risk. We have to send someone else. Are you sure you don't want to fly in her place? It was your idea."

I shake my head. I can't ask Olive to uninvite him, and I'm just not ready. "Can Carol replace her?"

"Carol needs to finish another article for next week's magazine. I need her here."

"How about Samantha?"

"You can try."

I smile and leave his office, hurrying to find Samantha. There's little time for me to convince her. I find her in the cafeteria, along with several other reporters. I don't like to interrupt, but I have no choice.

"Hey." I stand in front of her.

She smiles at me with a surprised look on her face. She knows who I am, but I haven't had a chance to really get to know her until now. I get straight to the point.

"I'm looking for someone to replace Liz for tomorrow's event. She's sick."

Samantha looks interested. "What's the article?"

"Olivia Danske's store opening. She's expanding into evening gowns and opening her own shop."

Samantha's eyes light up. "Danske? The famous wedding dress designer?"

I nod.

"Sounds great. Tomorrow you said? What's the address?"

"The opening is in New York. There is a flight booked for this evening."

She shrinks. "Oh. Sorry. But no thanks."

"What? But a moment ago, you said you were interested."

"That was before I realized I would have to fly. I don't fly."

"What? Why not?"

"I'm not entering those tight tin cans that are supposed to hold me in the air. Sorry, but you'd have to kill me to get me on a plane."

Damn it. She seemed really excited. I glance around at the other reporters sitting at the table, pleading them with my eyes. They don't look back at me.

"Jerry?"

"Sorry. I can't fly on such short notice. I can't leave my wife with the children like that. She would be furious."

I bite my lip. "Okay, thanks." I leave and hurry back to Toby's office. What should I do? I can't cancel. I can't do that to Olive. This is not just an anonymous designer. This is a friend. A friend who supported me throughout the last year. And Claire is already waiting for the flight today. I knock on Toby's door, and he invites me in.

"Well? Did you ask her?"

"She's not willing to fly." I twist my mouth in displeasure. "And neither can Jerry."

"Look, I can't force you to go. But we've already paid for the trip. Everything is set for tomorrow, and again, this was your idea." He raises an eyebrow. "You were supposed to be the one going if you'll remember."

I understand very well what he's saying between the lines. He wants me to take the story. And I guess if he didn't know me, I'd be fired for refusing after I'd asked to go and convinced him this whole thing would be great for the magazine. I can tell him why I don't want to go there, but it would sound like nothing more than an excuse. Ethan is just a man who didn't want me anymore. What will it look like not taking a job because of my ex? Especially after I declared that the entire episode was behind me and promised it would never interfere with my job?

I close my eyes and inhale deeply. "Okay. You're right. I'll go."

I can do it. I went through hell and survived. I can handle one man who doesn't love me anymore. Even if his name is Ethan Wolf.

CHAPTER 17

Ethan

"Olive." I try to stop her from her endless fussing and bustling through the store. "Enough. You're making me dizzy. Everything looks great."

"It has to be perfect," she says and continues to fuss with a display, arranging the balloons and the tables at just the right angles. The place is decorated in elegant white and silver, in coordination with the fact that most of the store is aimed at brides.

"I'm going outside," I report, though she doesn't seem to notice my existence at the moment. It's fun to see her so excited. It even makes me a little excited, which I haven't felt in a long time.

I sit on the steps outside and take a deep breath. Too bad I don't smoke. I can't drink because soon dozens of people will fill this place, and I need a clear head. Olive will need my support, but I have a few minutes to enjoy the last moments of the calm before the storm.

A good storm, of course. Many reporters expressed interest, and a number of celebrities will be in attendance. The preliminary marketing we did was excellent, and I have no doubt the launch will be successful. I'm sure of it.

I go back inside to find Olive still running around like a hurricane.

I try again to stop her. "You need to get dressed. You only have forty minutes left."

Her eyes widen. "Forty minutes? Why didn't you tell me before? How the hell do I get ready in forty minutes? Ethan!" She punches my shoulder.

"Ouch!" I grunt. "Don't hit me. It's not my fault you weren't paying attention to the time."

I go to the inner office to put on my suit before people arrive, bringing Olive with me.

I stand with my back to her as she dresses behind me.

"Ethan," she calls, and I turn around, still buttoning up my shirt. "Help me with the zipper, please."

"Shit," she blurts out, looking at my chest.

I look down, trying to figure out what I did wrong. "What? Did I get a stain on my shirt?"

She bites her lower lip. "Your scars."

I close the other buttons. "I'm safe and sound. It's nothing." I sometimes forget my new look shocks other people. I like my scars. The ugliness of it fits how I feel.

The dress she chose for the event is a striking red, long and flowy, but with a sexy split that reaches almost to the crotch and straps that close behind her neck, emphasizing her bare shoulders.

I close her zipper and whistle. "You look amazing. Everyone will want to buy this dress to look just like you."

"I'm counting on that." She smiles. "I made several copies of it to sell."

"That's my Olive." I kiss the top of her head, and she reaches to adjust my silver-gray tie.

We head downstairs just in time to see Ryan and Maya arrive. It's impossible not to smile when I see all my friends hugging, and all in one place. I'm lucky to have them.

The place fills up at a dizzying pace, and I have to make sure that the event runs properly, the alcohol is flowing, and the food is generous. I'm called several times to confirm entry for guests who are not on the list. The place is full.

I smile and straighten when I'm photographed with Olive, my hand resting on her back. I'm so proud of her. She did it. She started her own business.

Another smile for the cameras.

In the corner of my eye, I catch my parents coming in, turning their heads, examining the place, or maybe looking for me. My fists clench instinctively, and I put a hand in my pocket.

They'll beg me for the dinner I promised them. I'll go eventually, but I can't help postponing as long as possible. I don't want to spend another difficult evening in their company.

As soon as the photographers finish, I grab a shot of vodka from the bar and down it in one gulp.

Then I turn and my mind goes blank when I notice her. What the fuck is she doing here?

She's supposed to be in San Francisco. She can't be here in New York.

It's the woman I see in my dreams and my nightmares. A vision in a silver dress that highlights every curve, every amazing curve I know with intimate detail, and she's walking straight into a hug with Olive.

And Olive... She doesn't look surprised at all to see Ayala. Olive knew she was coming. And I call her a friend.

They say their hellos and happily chatter with each other. I didn't even know they kept in touch.

I can't move. I'm frozen in place and staring. The rage rises inside me and fills me, washing through me. What the hell is she doing here? How dare she?

Four big steps are all it takes for me to reach her, and I grab her arm firmly.

A look of shock takes over her face, and the pupils in her crystal blue eyes widen. She didn't expect me to accost her, and I take advantage of that by pulling her after me into the office before she can resist. Before the photographers notice us.

As soon as we walk in, she shakes her arm free of my hold. My fingerprints appear in red marks on her white skin. Fuck. I didn't mean to hold her so tightly.

"What do you think you're doing?" She puts a distance between us and takes an aggressive posture.

God, she is so beautiful. More beautiful than I remember. The mounds of her breasts rise and fall rapidly with her breaths. I can't think. What was I going to say? "What are you doing here?"

"Olive invited me to cover the event."

"Why? You're not a writer or photographer."

"How do you know what I am?" Her eyes narrow to thin, blue slits.

Shit, she caught me.

"You have no right to be here." And to look like that, like the angel in my dreams.

"What? I have the same right as anyone else. I have an invitation from Olive. It's her business, and she can invite whomever she wants. I can't believe what audacity you have. And to think that I was afraid to come here because of you."

Her angry speech wakes up my cock. Damn it.

"Get out of here now."

She gasps. "I'm not going anywhere. Olive wanted me to be here, and I came here for her."

"Go, or..."

"Or what?" Her chin rises in defiance, and that's all I need to break down.

She's in my arms, and I stroke her mouth. Forcing her to open her lips and accept me as I kiss her violently. She's perfect. Totally perfect. I'm the damaged one, the broken one, but I have no control. I have to have her mouth, have to taste her.

And God, she's so delicious I can't stop. She doesn't stop me, either, but even if she tried, I'm not sure I could survive it. I draw her into me. Her body fits mine exactly. Every curve and arch merges with the hard lines of my body.

My cock is hard like a rock now, after months of barely being able to get it up, and I know she feels it against her stomach. I hold her tighter, closer—I have to be inside her now. Nothing else is enough. Nothing else comes close to it.

It's like someone woke me up from a deep sleep, and now, now I can't get enough.

CHAPTER 13

Ayala

H is tongue circles inside my mouth. What is he doing? My body knows him and reacts instantly. I melt into him. Shit, this is not what I meant to happen.

On the advice of my psychologist, I was supposed to take advantage of today's event to deal with Ethan to understand that he is only a man. An ordinary man and human. Not the god I made him out to be in my imagination. But right now, he sure feels divine.

I prepared for this moment in a guided imagery session, but at no point did this happen. At no point did Ethan kiss me.

I know I should stop him, keep him away from me, but I don't want to. His mouth, the taste of alcohol, his cock hard against my body. He feels too good. Too right. Too arousing.

His hand is under my skirt, moving up my thigh. An involuntary sigh escapes me. What the hell am I doing? I come to my senses and push him away.

He's standing there, panting, his eyes wild and dark with desire. He's thinner than I remember, much thinner. But still looks like a god, and damn, he still holds my heart. I haven't gotten over him at all.

I want to reach out to him, to touch him, to check his body for wounds, to see that he's healthy and whole right here in front of me, but I can't.

"I need you." His voice is hoarse and low.

"The hell with you!" I shout. "By what right? When I needed you the most, you dumped me. You threw me to the dogs. You have no right to come to me now. And for what? Just sex? Go sleep with one of the girls chasing you." I shout my pain, everything that's inside me coming out with each word.

It's as if all the air went out of him at once, the straight shoulders now hunched. He runs a hand through his hair.

"You're right," he says in such a weak voice that I have to strain to hear him.

I remain silent, and he turns and leaves, leaving me standing there alone on shaky legs.

I sit on the chair, trying to control myself. Trying to stop the uncontrollable shaking for long minutes. It was a mistake coming here. I wasn't ready for this at all, and I knew it. I want to lock the office door and stay here, away from everyone. But I promised Olive a story. I can't let her down.

I close my eyes and inhale deeply before walking back out into the crowd.

The event is amazing. Models in wedding dresses walk among the guests, gigantic screens project interviews with Olive, and fashion shows of the dresses. I recognize a lot of familiar faces, celebrities, and influencers.

I need to interview them. I have a story to prepare. Damn, I was so shocked I forgot I had work to do. Where is Claire?

I find her immersed in photo shoots of the models. At least she does her job properly.

I call her to come with me and approach one of the TikTok stars I recognize.

"Libby! Libby!" I call after her, and she turns to me with a fake smile.

"Yes?"

"I'm Ayala Beckett, from the magazine *Style in Class*. Do you mind answering a few questions?" She looks impressed. They are always thirsty for more attention and more publicity.

I ask her some questions about the event, what she thinks about the designer, her favorite dress and so on. The standard. I'm not looking to make waves, just to give some publicity to Olive.

We move on, but I feel Ethan's eyes burning a hole in my back the entire time, following me everywhere I step. But I don't look.

During our third interview, Claire whispers in my ear, "There's a man staring at you."

I nod. "I know."

"Do you know him?"

I just nod. Know him? I am connected to him with the seams of my soul.

"Wait a moment. Is this? Is that the man...?" She doesn't finish the sentence.

I bite my lip and nod again. I knew it would be hard to come here and see him, but his horrible behavior earlier reinforces my anger. And anger is good. I know how to deal with anger.

"What does he want from you?" She's still whispering as if he can hear us over the noise of the party.

"I don't know, and I don't care." He made his choice.

There is a curious look on her face. No one knows what happened there and what Ethan Wolf had to do with it. There were a lot of rumors, some of them quite crazy, such as that he was a hired assassin who got caught or that he and Michael were a couple. Some of them are close to the truth about him being my lover, but I never talked about it with anyone.

"Why didn't you want to come?" Claire asks. "I mean, can he do anything to you? He looks scary."

"No. Everything is fine. Don't worry." I turn to glance at him, and his gaze catches my eye.

He looks scary, following me like a shadow. His eyes are missing the golden glint I used to love, as now they are dark and moody. But he will never scare me. Only the strength of my feelings for him scares me now.

We continue to seek out people to interview for the story, and after I think we have enough material, I send Claire to take more photos without me.

Claire pulls away, and instantly Ethan clings to me from behind, startling me, and I jump. He takes a step back.

"We need to talk."

"No." I walk away from him with quick steps. He won't pull me in again. I came for Olive.

He wraps a hand around my arm again, then lets me go when he realizes we're attracting unnecessary attention.

"Please. Let's talk in private."

"Why? So you can lure me into sleeping with you, then tell me on the phone that it's over? No thanks."

He runs his hand through his hair again, sighs, and walks away from me.

It's hard for me to breathe. It would have been a lot easier if I didn't love him still, but I won't let him bring me down again.

I repeat in my head the mantra that gives me strength.

I am strong; I control my life; I deserve true love.

The number of guests thins out as the hours pass, and Claire yawns in front of me.

"I think you can go back to the hotel," I say. "We have more than enough material for the article. Don't you think?"

"What about you? Are you coming?"

"No, I came to support Olive. I'll stay until the end. But you can go." We hug, and she leaves.

I stand aside, trying not to attract attention. Some time has passed since the incident, and the interest of the media has faded and disappeared, but still, at any moment, a curious reporter could spot Ethan and me in the same room and turn it into an item.

I only relax when I see there are just a few guests left, and Ryan approaches me to say goodbye.

"Ayala." He hugs me. "We didn't get to talk. Will you be here tomorrow, too?"

"No. My flight leaves at noon tomorrow. Won't you stay a little longer?"

"Maya is tired. She's due soon. It's a little difficult for her. I want her to rest."

"Yes, of course." I glance at his wife sitting at the table, her hands on her stomach. She looks exhausted. We hug again, and he and Maya leave.

Finally, everyone left seems to be filing out. Olive turns to start cleaning up the mess, and I go over to help.

Ethan is standing near the entrance. Next to him is an older couple, probably his parents. I never met them, but I remember the woman from the event where I served.

He looks angry or frustrated. I'm not sure, but I'm curious, so I get a little closer and try to hear the fragments of the conversation.

"I said I would come, so I will." He raises his voice, making it easier for me to eavesdrop.

"Leave him alone, Laura," I hear the man say. "You know what he's like. Never willing to compromise, always in the shoes of the tormented."

"Because you're the only one suffering here, right? Only you lost her! It shouldn't bother me at all?" Ethan looks furious. His eyes flash with anger.

I watch them out of the corner of my eye. He trusted me and told me what had happened to his sister. I know how much he's suffered and still suffers because of it. They just don't understand. I want to hug him. Support him and comfort him. Then I surprise myself and do exactly that.

"Hello." I approach and introduce myself to them. "Ayala Beckett."

They seem shocked. For a moment, they even forget to speak. I love those moments when people understand who I am, and they're embarrassed and can't find the words. It just shows me how far I've come and how strong I am now. I survived hell. No one will make me feel uncomfortable.

Their embarrassment is even worse than others because their son was involved. I wonder if he told them what happened and what exactly he did there, but from the conversation I just heard, I assume not.

Ethan glares at me. Like he would burn me if he could. But I completely ignore him.

"Hello, Mr. and Mrs. Wolf," I say in a calm voice. "I'm sorry to interrupt, but I have to tell you something."

Everyone looks at me with wide eyes. I continue. "I know you mean well, but you did a terrible job with Ethan. He never got over what happened to Anna. A young boy finds his sister in a terrible state, and all you did was send him to a psychologist. Did either of you even talk to him? Tell him he's not to blame for what happened? That he couldn't have expected what would happen? You are to blame for what happened, not Ethan. You left a thirteen-year-old girl alone at home." I feel the anger intensifying in me now. My parents supported me all this time in everything I needed after Michael died. Once they realized how wrong they were with Michael, they were on my side. I don't think I could have done it alone. And Ethan was all alone.

Ethan grabs my arm for the third time tonight and pulls me outside, away from the store and his parents, before they say a word.

His nostrils flare with anger. "What the hell are you doing?"

"Telling your parents what I think of them."

"Why?" The intensity of the pain in his gaze makes it difficult for me to look at him.

"Because they need to know. Because I love you, and I can't watch you continue to deal with something that was never your fault."

He's silent, and for a moment, I think he's going to turn around and walk away from me. I shiver, and he takes off his jacket and puts it around my shoulders.

"Why did you say you love me?"

"Because I do." I have no problem admitting it. "You are the one who decided that what was between us was over. I never stopped loving you. It's not a switch I can just turn off."

"Fuck!" he shouts, the emotions changing on his face, and he turns his back to me. I stand and watch, wondering what he's going to do.

"I can't do this anymore. I can't," he turns to me and mumbles.

What? What is he talking about?

"I can't let you go. Not when you're here in front of me, telling me things like that."

I don't understand what he wants. "What are you talking about?"

He takes a step forward and is now dangerously close to me. "Come with me."

I can feel the tension emanating from his body. I can smell it. My defenses start to collapse one by one when he gives me those looks that tell me he wants me. But he was very clear that what was between us was over. I'm not supposed to go anywhere with him. I need to close this chapter in my life. Nothing good can come of it.

His lips brush against mine, almost touching. "Please."

I tilt my head up, and his lips capture mine, tasting.

His taste is divine, of coffee and alcohol and mint mixed with the familiar taste of Ethan Wolf.

He feels amazing, like I never left, and I have no doubt that I belong here, in this moment.

CHAPTER 15

Ethan

Her hand is in mine, and that's the only thing I feel right now, the only thing I'm capable of feeling. I take her to the car, to my house.

It's easy to tell myself that she's better off without me when she's in San Francisco. It's a completely different story when she's here next to me and when she tells me she still loves me so easily.

Her blue eyes penetrate my soul and see through me. How can I stay away?

We are both silent on the way to my penthouse. I'm afraid to say something out of place. It's hard for me to believe that she's really here next to me, right here with me. I can touch her, and not just in my dreams.

She's better off without me, but if it was hard to say goodbye to her when she was so far away, how could I possibly manage it when she's close.

She enters my apartment but is hesitant, her eyes scanning the familiar place.

I walk into the kitchen and pour myself a whiskey. "Want some?"

She nods, and I take out another glass.

"I behaved terribly," I say. "I have no excuse. I knew I was hurting you, but I thought it would be better for you that way. That it would be for the better if I stayed away from you."

"Leaving me in a hospital, after everything that happened, broken and injured, when I needed you the most, and telling me on the phone?" she sobs. "Telling me on the fucking phone that you don't want me anymore? That was for the best? How is it for the best?" She surprises me with her outburst. She's damn well furious.

Shit, she is so right. And there is no way in the world she will understand why I did that.

"I only went with him for you!" she shouts.

"And that's exactly why I left!" I shout back.

She's silent, a confused look filling her eyes.

"I fail to protect the women I love. Not Anna, and not you." I swallow. "They all end up getting hurt because of me. I destroy everyone I come close to. Your parents think so, too."

"You talked to my parents?"

"Yes. They called me in the hospital several days after... They wanted to know about the nature of our relationship, and they made it very clear that what happened was my fault. They insisted that I not contact you again, and they were right."

"My parents said that?" She looks shocked. It's apparent they didn't tell her about our conversation.

Ayala begins to pace, then turns back to face me. "He would have hurt me, anyway. That's who he is. Or was," she corrects.

"But you wouldn't have left here if he hadn't sent those pictures, right?"

"Did you see them?"

I nod. "Yes. And when I couldn't get the police to do anything about it, I flew there to search for you myself."

"When I woke up and saw you injured on the floor, I thought

you were..." Tears flow down her cheeks. "I thought you were dead."

I shake my head and try to shove the memory away. "For a moment, I thought so too."

"When they told me you were alive, which they didn't tell me until that day I called you, by the way, the only thing I wanted was for you to be okay. I wanted to know you were safe. You were everything to me... And all you had to say was, it's over between us. You broke me, Ethan. It was you who broke me," she cries. "Michael couldn't break me, but you did."

Hell. I want to gather her in and comfort her. I step forward, but she flinches.

"I'm sorry. I thought it was better that way. That you would get over me and move on. Choose someone who deserves you."

"You don't get to decide for me who deserves or doesn't deserve me. You didn't even give me a chance, Ethan."

"I couldn't. I couldn't look you in the eyes and know that I caused it. Not after I saw.. " I shiver from the image of her broken body that comes before my eyes.

"So I disgust you." She looks down.

I close the distance between us and raise her face to me. "No, never. You are the most amazing, strongest woman I know."

"You moved on quickly enough."

I frown, trying to understand.

"The blonde in the picture."

Ah shit. The picture. An unfortunate mistake. "No. Just my desperate attempt to show everyone that everything is fine with me when in fact, I'm completely broken." I smile sadly. "How can it be, I'm the one who fell apart, and you're so whole? How are you so strong?"

"Oh, I fell apart. But I put myself back together. Do you know why? Because I promised you I would. Because I swore he'd kill me before he broke me." She lets out a hollow laugh. "But I broke in the end anyway. But do you know when? When I real-ized you weren't coming back to me."

I squeeze my eyes closed, trying to hold back the tears. Then I look at her and try to make her understand. "I was stupid. I am stupid. I still love you. I never stopped loving you and wanting you. Please, let me fix this. Give me a chance." I wrap her in an embrace, and she feels so good in my arms, but she pulls away from me.

"I'm sorry, Ethan. I can't. I just can't." Her gaze is fixed on mine, and her blue eyes glisten with tears. "I love you. I don't think I could ever stop loving you. But when I needed you most, you weren't there for me."

And just like that, she disappears, leaving me alone again.

Sadness, shock, rage and shame. All the emotions are mixed in my head right now. But at least I'm finally feeling something again. I feel alive. She brought me back to life.

And now I know what I have to do.

I have to win her back.

CHAPTER 20

Ayala

"...**I** told him I couldn't trust him anymore." I say as I lay on my psychologist's couch. "I know I did what I had to do to take care of myself. So why does it feel so bad?"

"Because you still have feelings for him. And that's natural. But you did what was best for your recovery."

"I don't feel like I'm making progress. I wanted to stay with him."

"But you didn't act on those feelings. You acted on your decision. This is progress. That's what we want. Progress."

I'm still not so convinced. My heart is heavy, but at least since I returned to San Francisco, the nightmares have gotten better. Ethan no longer dies every time in front of my eyes. I still have nightmares, but Ethan doesn't appear in them anymore. That's a colossal relief.

"I think you should start spending time with some girl-friends," the doctor tells me. "You're young. I want you to spend time with girls your age. Have fun."

I shake my head. "No. I'm not ready, and besides, I have no friends here."

"That's part of the problem. You've shut yourself off. You don't open up to new friends. You told me when you were in New York, you would go out together to parties and have a good time."

"That was a different time. Michael—"

"Michael is dead. He won't chase you anymore. Let me give you a task. Before our next meeting, you're to go out with a friend. Agreed?"

I nod.

Go out in the evening and hang out with a friend. That's something I haven't done in such a long time. I don't have that many friends here, not true friends, and I can understand why. It's hard to connect with someone whose past is so complicated and scary. Who needs such a history on their head?

I send Claire a message. We didn't become friends during that trip, exactly, but we had a nice evening in New York. Maybe she would agree.

> There's a party on Friday at the Fantasy Club.
> Would you like to join me?

She takes a while to answer. I stare at the phone when I see the three dots that show she's typing a reply and almost crash into a poll. Oops.

> **Claire**
> Yes, sure. Can I bring another friend?

She's probably afraid to be alone with me. That's okay. It will be less embarrassing for me that way too.

> Yes, of course.

Mission accomplished. I'm going out with a friend on Friday, and it wasn't even as hard as I thought. I arrive home, happy with my quick success, and look for the keys in my bag. Where did they go?

"Ayala Beckett?"

The voice behind me surprises me, and I drop my handbag on the sidewalk in a panic. My heart pounds in my chest. "Yes?"

"Sorry, I didn't mean to startle you. You've been served." The guy with the helmet hands me a big envelope, gets on the motorcycle, and disappears.

I pick up my handbag and study the envelope.

I go inside, put my bag in the entryway, kick off my heels, and rip open the seal.

What the hell?

I'm being sued. Michael's fucking parents are suing me. Fifteen million dollars in compensation for the death of their son. Hysterical laughter bursts out of me. I can't stop laughing.

Fifteen. Million.

They know I don't have it. Where do they think I'd get this amount? Ridiculous. They can't be serious.

My mood goes from happy to depressed with the wave of a hand. Or an envelope.

A new text message pops up on my phone. It's from Ethan and surprises me. Where did he get my number? Well, he was always good at spying.

Ethan
Michael's parents filed a lawsuit.

Are they suing you too?

I look at the forms again. How did I miss it? His name is written next to mine. They are suing us both. Now everything becomes clear to me. They hope to get the money out of Ethan.

> **Ethan**
> Do you have a good lawyer?

> No. And I don't have a bad lawyer, either.

I answer jokingly, but I'm sure Ethan isn't kidding. That's a huge amount.

> **Ethan**
> Ryan can practice in California too and he'll be representing me, but he can't represent both of us, so I'm sending you the number of an excellent attorney. Talk to him. Don't worry about payment.

> Why would you pay for a lawyer for me?

> **Ethan**
> Completely selfish reasons. We're both part of this lawsuit. I don't want to lose.

Shit. Because of me, they've dragged him into this whole mess and now into this lawsuit.

> Okay.

I open and save the new contact he sends me.

The music in the Fantasy Club pounds in my ears, the bass shakes the floor, and I have to shout to Claire and Jenny to be heard. "I'm going to the bathroom!"

After an hour of dancing and a few drinks, the sweat drips from me, and I need a moment to freshen up.

The dancers are dressed in the most revealing clothes I have ever seen. To the same extent, they could dance naked. I'm on my way to the bathroom and can't help but stare.

The club is decorated in reds and greens, like Christmas decorations, but on a huge scale. It's cool.

The bar presents a special drink menu for the evening, and they serve an eggnog drink bursting with bourbon and a hot buttered rum that tastes amazing. The rest of the drinks were also given red and green colors, in the spirit of the holiday, and are decorated with small candies on a stick and miniature Christmas trees. After tasting a few of these drinks, my bladder presses down on me, and my head spins.

While in line for the bathroom, I lean against the wall in the hallway, shifting my weight from one foot to the other, trying to ease the pain from the particularly high heels I wore today.

"Can I help you?" a voice behind me whispers in my ear. A low and familiar voice.

I turn so fast that my head spins, and I find Ethan, his eyes dark in the low light.

"What are you doing here?"

"I moved here."

My mouth falls open in surprise. "Moved here?"

"Only for the foreseeable future. Because of the lawsuit and the upcoming hearing. It will be more convenient for me to conduct myself from here."

"But what are you doing here?" I insist, pointing toward the floor. "In the club?"

"I followed you."

I inhale quickly. Not exactly the response I was expecting. "You're following me?"

"Yes. I won't give up. I know I hurt you, Ayala. I know I was a shit. I can't blame you for not agreeing to stay in New York and give me a chance, but I'll do everything I can to change your mind."

I shouldn't like it that much, but I do. I like his determination.

"The dress you're wearing... I would be happy if you would wear it for me and then take it off for me too."

He examines the generous cleavage of the short black dress I chose for the evening. His husky voice sends shivers of anticipation through me. Then he moves away.

Leaving the bathroom, I look for him, but he's nowhere to be seen. Could it be that he has already gone?

I return to the girls and find them by the dance floor with drinks in hand. Claire serves me tequila in a green glass.

"Cheers!" We raise our glasses, and the tequila slides down my throat and warms me.

"There was a man here looking for you," Jenny bends down to me and shouts in my ear so I can hear.

"Yes, he found me," I answer, and she looks at me with interest. Now is not the time to explain who he is. I don't want to scare them with my past.

We return to the floor, and I feel Ethan's eyes on me. It's like a tingling that starts in my stomach and goes down.

I turn around, and he's there. Watching me. He closes the distance between us in a few quick steps, and before I know it, he's standing right next to me, body to body, his arms resting on my back, and he's dancing with me. I feel his erection pressed against my stomach. His black button-down shirt is open a little at the top, and my gaze wanders to this exposed spot of skin. The lights, the music, the darkness, everything increases the erotic sensation of this moment.

I see how his gaze descends to my stiff nipples, which stand out through the fabric. There's an animalistic hunger in that look as the shadows flicker across his face, and it's so sexy.

He brings his face close to mine, so close I can smell him. My breathing quickens as my entire body wakes up to him. Always ready for him. I can't stop my physical reaction. I never could. I remember how he feels over me, beneath me, inside me.

His body moves to the rhythm of the music. I surrender to the feeling as he pushes me further and further to the edge of the cliff.

Our lips are almost touching. God, how I want him now.

"I love you," he whispers to my ear, his lips brushing against my cheek now, and then his hands leave me. He pulls away and out of my line of sight, leaving me standing there, stunned. My whole body fills in unfulfilled anticipation.

Claire comes over and grasps my arm. "What. The. Hell. Was That?"

"It was the sexiest dance I've ever seen," Jenny adds. "God, I could come just from watching the two of you. Do you know each other?"

I nod.

"What is he doing here?" Claire asks me.

"I didn't know he was here. And we're not together."

"So, can I have him? He looks so good. I want to lick him all over." Jenny looks like she's ready to undress right now on the floor. I don't know her well enough to know if it's the alcohol talking or if that's how she always acts, but her words cause my stomach to clench. He's not mine, but I can't see him with someone else, either.

Claire laughs. "You think? Do you have eyes? You saw them dancing? He wouldn't look at you even if you were naked, Jenny. And besides, you don't even know who he is."

"What does it matter who he is? You saw what he looks like. I'm ready for a man like him to fuck me however he wants, whenever he wants," Jenny moans. Her voice is a little slurred, and I guess she's pretty drunk.

I still haven't decided what I think about her, especially with this lightness that doesn't come naturally to me. But this is what my psychologist wanted for me. He wanted me to spend time with girls my age and experience real and uncomplicated life. So why do I feel like I don't belong? My life *is* complicated. I can't just erase everything I've been through.

"It's Ethan Wolf," Claire tells Jenny, and she glances around as if his name would make everyone stare at us, but no one hears. It's too noisy in here.

"Ethan Wolf?" she whispers back, and it makes me laugh. You'd be lucky to hear someone scream in here unless they were standing right next to you.

"It's a long story," I say. "And right now, I prefer to dance."

She gives up and nods, and I drag her back to the dance floor.

CHAPTER 22

Ethan

A lthough this lawsuit is bad news, it's also given me the perfect excuse to come to San Francisco to pursue her. I intend to do everything I can so Ayala understands that we are meant to be together.

I hired someone, so I could see what she was doing at all times. Yes, it's creepy. Yes, it's a little crazy. But I have to know she's safe, and I have to find a way to fit into her daily plans.

When her tracker sent me an update yesterday that she went out to a club, the first thing I did was go there myself. I didn't want to disturb her at work, and I couldn't disturb her at the psychologist's office. But at a club? Sure. It's the perfect place to show my presence. I want her to know I'm here.

The dancing was a slight drift on my part. I planned to watch from a distance and exchange a few words, but I just can't control myself when she's so near.

I want to take her on a date. A real one.

I hesitate before pressing the Call button. I have never been so afraid of rejection.

"Hey," I say as she answers the phone.

"Ethan?"

"Yes."

"What do you want?"

"I want you to know that I still love you."

"Why did you come to the club yesterday?"

"So you'd realize I'm here, and I'm waiting for you."

"But you left."

Does she sound disappointed, or are my hopes giving me false illusions?

"I didn't leave. I'm here. I'll be here and wait until you're ready."

"I love you too." I hear a sigh from her side. "But that's not enough."

"I know. I messed up badly. Please let me prove myself again. Prove that I'll never betray your trust again."

She doesn't respond.

"I wanted to ask you on a date with me. A first date."

"A first date?" I can almost hear her smiling through the screen.

"Yes. Let's start from the beginning."

"I don't think that's a good idea."

"Ayala, we just met," I say with a smile. "Give me a chance to get to know you."

She's silent for a long moment. "Okay. I expect you to take me on an expensive date. And you're paying."

I laugh because I know she doesn't care about money. But she agreed. She said yes.

"Tomorrow at seven?"

"Okay. I live on Bul—" she stops. "Actually, I forgot you were following me, stranger. So you already know where I live."

"Bye, beautiful." I hang up.

I try five flower shops until I find one that is open at such an hour. They're closing, but a generous payment convinces the owner to make one last delivery for the day.

I feel like sending her the world. Flowers, chocolates, diamonds. I want to impress her, but that's not the way to Ayala's heart. I know her better than that. And I need to take it slowly.

I have no idea where to take her on this date. We're not in New York, and this is not my kingdom. I'm not familiar with the surroundings.

I lift the phone to write to my assistant to find me a place, but I stop. I have to do it myself. I'm the one who should invest in this relationship, not transfer roles to my assistants.

Google it is.

After going through all the restaurants at the top of the lists on all the websites, despair hits me. This is not what I was looking for. It's true that she said she wanted a luxurious date, but that was just a joke. I know her well. What I want is uniqueness, romance, and privacy. All these restaurants are...just restaurants.

I rub my face, and then it hits me. I know where to take her. It will require some legwork and a lot of preparation in advance, but it can work.

Ayala
What should I wear?

> Jeans and a t-shirt.

Ayala
Jeans and a t-shirt for a date? Hmm. Now I'm curious. Where are we going? Hiking in nature again?

> It's a surprise.

It makes me happy that she's curious. I hope she likes what I have planned. It's a gamble, which can go either way. But we're not actually on our first date, so I think I know what she'll like.

———

Exactly at seven, I stand at the door of her apartment. She's dressed in light-colored jeans and a delicate white knit blouse that hugs her body. She answers the door barefoot and studies me with those captivating blue eyes.

"What shoes should I wear?" she asks.

"Sneakers will do." I shrug and wait while she sits down and pulls on a pair of white Sketchers.

"You sent me lots of flowers."

"It's not a lot. It's what was left in the store."

She laughs, and it's amazing to my ears. "Not a lot? Look at my apartment. There are flowers everywhere, in the kitchen, in the living room, even in the bathroom." She glances up at me. "I know I told you I wanted an expensive date, but I didn't mean it. I don't want you to buy me expensive things or quantities of flowers."

"I know. I tend to get carried away with gestures." She takes my extended arm. "But I'm trying."

When we reach our destination, she looks confused.

"There's nothing here." She looks at me questioningly, waving her arm toward the perfectly ordinary street.

"But there is." I take her hand and step forward. The dark building does not reveal what's inside.

Her gasp of surprise when we walk through the doors, and she realizes where we are, is exactly what I was going for. I'm still not sure if she'll like it, but at least I didn't choose something banal.

"Pottery?" A glint of excitement fills her eyes.

I move closer to her ear to whisper, "Just think of the soft wet clay when you press and caress it under your hands and sculpt it into a shape you want. I can't think of anything sexier than that." Shit, it is sexy. I straighten to my full height and tug on my pants. "But first, let's eat because I promised you food, and I don't want you to be hungry."

When making these arrangements, I asked the owner of the place to prepare a table for us and leave us alone for the first hour while we enjoyed our meal. I found someone who prepares fresh homemade food, and I asked her to bring her best dishes. Now all that remains is to see if I succeeded in all the plans.

Ayala sits down, and I sit across from her. A pot filled with beef stew is already on the table, with fresh bread next to it. The food smells great.

The bottle of red wine opens easily, and I pour it into our glasses.

"To the first date of many." I raise the glass and watch her. She taps my glass lightly and drinks. She eats with little sounds of pleasure. She must be mine. She must. I tried life without her, and it didn't work.

Jane walks in just as we finish, and Ayala looks at her with interest, listening carefully to the explanations.

"I'll show you how to work on the pottery wheel. We start the work by centering the clay, so it won't be wobbly. This is also the hardest part. After this stage, you can start opening the clay and raising the wall for the form of your choice. Shall we begin?"

We nod, put on large nylon aprons to protect our clothes, and sit side by side on the wheels. Jane brings each of us a bowl of water, a sponge, and a large lump of gray clay.

Ayala looks at it with suspicion as if it's about to attack her, and I smile.

We both place our hands on the material, and Jane stands by, explaining how to operate the device, how to control the speed, and how to press the clay so that it stops moving like a funny lump.

After completing the first step, with a little help, she shows us several options. I choose a bowl and Ayala a vase. Then we both start working according to the demonstration.

Her lump collapses, and giggling, she starts again. Both of our hands are full of wet clay. She raises a hand to wipe her forehead and smears a streak of clay across her cheek.

God, how beautiful she is.

"I'll give you some time to practice alone." Jane catches my expression and leaves. I jump at the opportunity and go to stand behind Ayala. "Need help?"

Ayala looks up at me and nods with a playful smile.

My hands are on hers, and I apply some pressure, guiding the clay to the center. The wetness of the material and the faint touch of body on body is enough to arouse me. Something in this material, maybe the noise it makes, the wet suction, the pressure... Whatever it is, it all concentrates my thoughts in one place. I must be out of my mind. There's no other explanation for why I'm horny because of fucking mud.

I inhale the scent of her skin. It was a mistake to choose this place when I know I can't get what I want. It was a fatal mistake that will cost me a lot of hand cream.

Ayala's breathing is picking up, too. I'm sure of it. It doesn't affect only me.

My lips pass over her neck, nearly touching the sensitive skin. I exhale and watch how her body shivers. She turns her face to me, and I don't hold back anymore and kiss her.

I maintain restraint, but she doesn't stop, and her tongue tastes me, asking to enter my mouth. The kiss turns heavy and needy. She lets go of the clay, and her hand goes to my face. I don't even notice as she smears the mud on my cheeks.

We pull apart, gasping for breath. When Jane comes back into the room to check our progress, our faces are dirty. Ayala's lump is not even close to being a vase, but a smile is plastered on both our faces.

Jane looks at me with a half smile and a raised eyebrow asking if she should disappear again, but I think we should stop here before I lay her on the floor of the studio.

I go back to my wheel, and Jane helps Ayala finish her vase while I finish my bowl. It was more fun than I thought, much more.

Jane informs us she will send us the creations after burning them, and we leave the studio smiling.

"I enjoyed it," Ayala tells me after we get into the rental car. "It wasn't what I expected."

"What did you expect?" I'm interested to hear. Maybe I'll learn what to do next time.

"Not that. I thought you'd take me to a restaurant or a bar. You know, something typical." She puts her hands on the air conditioner outlets to warm up. It's freezing today.

Without holding back, I reach out and rub her hands with mine. She doesn't flinch from my touch.

"You're not an ordinary woman. I didn't want to do anything ordinary. I wanted you to remember this evening."

"I would remember every evening with you. Even if it's just a restaurant. Ordinary was never our problem."

"I know," I agree. "I've tried life without you, Ayala, and it doesn't work for me. Right now, I want you so bad, I'm going out of my mind."

"I'm not ready for that yet." She shakes her head. "I've done nothing like that since... I thought about it a lot. Wondering if I could ever go back to living a normal life. If I could ever have sex again, or if it was lost for me. You always make me feel like anything is possible. I feel awake with you. You give me hope I might live again."

"You're the only one in the world for me." A stab of pain hits me when I think about how much she suffered. I can't stop thinking about how good it was to feel her, to be inside her. All I want is to experience that again with her. I know where I need to be and what I need to do, but she still needs time.

"I'm not sure I'll ever be ready," she admits.

"I'm willing to wait for you until the end of my life."

Ayala

S tanding in court is something I never thought I would have to go through. But still, here I am. My lawyer wants to file a counterclaim, but I'm still hoping the lawsuit will go away. Today's hearing is on our motion to dismiss.

"I can't believe their audacity to sue us after everything he did to you," Ethan murmurs beside me. "I'm not willing to lose this case. It's a matter of principle, not money."

The worry eats at me. It's true that I was physically and mentally abused, but Ethan broke into the house. And he has money. Michael's parents know what they're doing.

I interlace my fingers with Ethan's, trying to gather courage. He glances at me in surprise and squeezes my hand in encouragement. At least we got a closed-door discussion, and the courtroom is empty, with the exception of the parties involved. The media will not be able to gorge on our blood. At least not today.

Their lawyer begins, and my mind disconnects from the situation. I try to escape to an alternate reality.

Then one sentence penetrates the layer of fog I'm in.

"Mr. Wolf admitted he shot Michael Summers at his home—"

I jump from my chair. "That's a lie!"

"Sit down, Mrs. Summers," the judge scolds me.

"But that's not true! Ethan did no such thing."

"Sit now, or I will charge you with contempt." The judge bangs his gavel on the desk, and I fall silent.

Ethan tugs me down, and I sink back into my chair.

"How does he allow them to keep lying like this?" Rage fills me.

Ethan doesn't respond. His face is blank and pale. Something strange is happening here. "Ethan?"

"Because it's true," he whispers. "I stated I shot him."

Did I hear right? "What?"

"Shhh." The lawyers scold us, and I have to stay with my thoughts until the hearing is over. I have no idea what they decided. I can't concentrate on anything. I remember the detective at the hospital. She was surprised to hear my version... I have to talk to Ethan alone. Now.

As soon as the hearing is done, I rush out, pulling Ethan by his arm to a side corner, completely ignoring my lawyer's call to stop. There's time to catch up later. Right now, I need to hear what the hell happened there.

I glare at Ethan as we find a quiet corner in the hallway. "Ethan? Why did he say you admitted to shooting Michael?"

"Because I did. When they took a statement from me in the hospital, I said that I was the one who shot Michael and killed him."

"Why would you do such a thing? You weren't even conscious when it happened."

"Because I thought you did."

"What? I'm confused. What do you mean?"

"I knew Michael was dead, and I knew he'd been shot. Ryan updated me at the hospital. When the cop came to take a statement from me... Well, I just assumed you'd shot him." He's wringing his hands. "I didn't know what happened."

"So you meant to put the blame on yourself?" My mouth falls open.

"Yes," he says simply.

"I can't believe it." I raise my hands to my mouth, unable to digest it. "I can't believe you did that for me." My heart beats fast. This is the most amazing and crazy thing anyone has ever done for me. "So what are we going to do? How do you get out of this mess?"

"I don't know. The judge continued to hearing, and we have until after the holidays before we have to come back. The lawyers will have time to file their pleadings in the meantime, so they'll have to think of something by then."

Oh. "But the police closed the case against us. Why isn't that enough?"

"It helps, but this is a civil lawsuit. It's an entirely different story." He turns his head, and I follow his gaze and see Ryan and my lawyer waiting impatiently for us. "We need to get back to them."

He lied for me. He was ready to take the blame. The dissonance between the sense of betrayal from the hard breakup on the phone and what I just discovered he did for me makes me dizzy. How do I continue from here?

Ethan follows me to my apartment and waits for me to get inside. But I'm not ready to say goodbye to him yet. "Do you want to come in?"

"I don't know if that's a good idea," he says.

"Please? I want you to stay with me."

He turns off the engine and gets out of the car. Neither of us dressed well for being outside, and we rush inside to the heat.

"I'm so confused by you," I say as soon as we're inside. "How could you be so cruel to me on the phone and be willing to go to jail for me at the same time?"

He plops down on the couch, looking defeated. "I couldn't stand myself at that moment. I think that best sums up the situation."

I can't read the expression in his eyes.

After a brief silence, he goes on. "I couldn't live with the thought that everything that happened to you was because of me, and I couldn't save you. The sight of you on that bed haunted me for months. Honestly, it still does. In the end, you saved yourself again. I thought you'd be better off without me."

"How could you think that? When you knew I loved you? And after everything that happened between us?"

"I wasn't worthy of your love."

I shake my head. "It wasn't your decision to make, Ethan. It was mine."

"I understand it now. It took me a long time to get out of the black hole that sucked me in, but after seeing you again, I realized that my future doesn't exist without you. So here I am, ready to convince you to choose me again."

Tears flood my eyes, and one runs down my cheek. I move closer to the sofa, then I sit next to him, holding his face so I can look into his eyes. "I choose you again."

The golden sparks in his eyes flicker now as he tries to stay in control of his emotions. But I see the flashes of those emotions on his face: wonder, hope, and love.

What happened between us that day, the way he broke up with me when I was at my weakest, I'm not sure I'll ever be able to forgive it. But now I'm close to understanding. I want to put it behind me, behind us, and try again.

He puts his hands on the hem of my shirt and pulls it up. I raise my hands and allow him to take it off me.

He stops and looks at my recent addition, the one that wasn't there before. Right on my scar, the words now engraved are "progress, not perfection."

His fingers flutter over my tattoo, and his gaze meets mine with a questioning look.

"A reminder to myself," I answer without him asking. "To always move forward, and not to strive for perfection."

He kisses my scar, runs his tongue over the words, and I shiver.

"In my eyes, you are already perfect." His mouth claims mine, demanding. His hands cup my breasts, squeezing and crushing.

"God, how I missed you," he whispers and looks up at me "Do you want me? Stop me now if you don't."

I can only nod. But how will it be now? After the physical and mental injuries both of us hold? The scars on our bodies serve as evidence of everything that happened. And I'm afraid but also excited. I'm not sure I can take this all the way yet, but I think I'm willing to try with him.

When I don't stop him, Ethan's mouth is already tasting my neck, then the hills of my breasts above the bra.

"Hold me," he says and puts my hands on his shoulders. Then he wraps his arms around me and rises, swinging me in the air.

I wrap my legs around him and lock my heels behind his back so as not to fall, but he shows no difficulty in carrying me.

"Which direction?" he half moans, half whispers, and I remember he has never been inside my apartment.

I just point to the bedroom door because my mouth demands to kiss the pleasant hollow between his ear and jaw.

He drops me onto the bed, pulls my pants down impatiently, and then stops. A heavy shadow passes through his eyes. He says nothing. But I see the hesitation.

"Does this bother you? Are you disgusted with me?" I suddenly feel like taking the blanket and wrapping myself in it. I try to move away from him and sit up, but the weight of his body doesn't allow me. I suddenly feel trapped.

He senses my panic and gently clasps his hands around my forearms.

"No! I'm not disgusted by you. Far from it." He rubs his pelvis against my underwear so I can feel him. "I just remembered how you were when I found you, and it hurts. It hurts to even think about it."

I stop my attempts to escape from him and close my eyes. He saw me in the worst place of my life.

"But you survived." He brings his face closer to mine and kisses me, then he moves down and kisses my neck, my stomach... "You are so strong. You can never disgust me."

I want to feel him too, and eagerly send my hands to the collar of his shirt to pull it off. When he realizes what I'm doing, he gets up and takes off his shirt and pants, leaving only his boxers.

Now it's my turn to exhale. The scars on his body are severe. I automatically send my hand to the jagged scar on his shoulder and caress it with my fingertips, hesitating to touch it.

His eyes follow my palm. "It doesn't hurt anymore." He takes my hand and places it on his skin, demanding that I touch him, and I comply. My hand wanders over him as if of its own accord, cherishing the body I once knew. He's different now, much thinner than before, and the muscles are more prominent. I reach the scar on the side of his stomach and caress it, too. We both carry on our bodies testimony of the horror.

"You're too skinny."

"I had no appetite."

It hurts me to hear that he suffered. We both suffered. "I'll take care of you from now on." My hand continues its journey south, under the band of his underwear, and I find him awake and ready for me. He groans when I surround him with my hand, then stroke from bottom to tip and back again.

"I want to taste you. I've missed your taste so much." He spreads my legs and positions himself between them, asking for my approval before removing my underwear.

I'm not wet, and he notices it right away.

"Ayala?" A worried look rises on his face. "Do you want me to stop?"

"No. Don't stop." The last thing I want now is to stop. It has to work. If it doesn't work with Ethan, it won't work with anyone. He is the only one with the power to heal me.

He understands immediately, without words, without explanations. I feel relieved to be with someone who understands. Who knows. And he continues, his tongue now licking my thigh. The skin there is more sensitive, and it feels good. I concentrate on the sensations of his tongue, trying to stay in the here and now and not let my thoughts wander.

When his tongue circles my clit, I soften. Little by little, he frees me. He sucks hard, sucks me in, and it's good! I want more of him and my back arches, expressing my desire. My body begs him to continue, the arousal rising inside me. It's working.

"Yes," I moan as I feel myself climbing. The mountain is high, but I'm going up. I'm almost there.

He raises his face and looks at me, then kisses me, and I taste myself on his lips. "God, how I missed you," he whispers and immediately sends a finger to continue the work.

"I want you inside me now," I demand.

"No. You're not ready. It will hurt you."

"I'm ready," I moan. "I'm about to come." I reach between my legs to lift his face to me.

"No," he insists. "I'll decide when." There's a promise in his voice. My toes curl in anticipation.

"Oh my God!" His mouth does amazing things to me. I climb up, reaching the edge, screaming out loud as my body convulses. Nothing feels like the pleasure he gives me.

I'm lying on the bed. My body feels like butter. I think I've lost consciousness because I see stars.

He rises, his face in front of mine, his eyes sparkling.

"I don't remember you being so loud." He smiles. "I love it."

His body is so hot on mine, burning. Mine too, I'm sure, as I'm on fire.

I was so afraid that what was between us was gone that I was broken forever. But my head still wants him, and my body remembers it well. The attraction works between us, just like before.

Ethan is already moving to the next stage, and his mouth is on my nipple. "I'm ready to live here," he says, and his tongue licks around the mounds of my breasts. He sucks hard, and my stomach tightens again. Yes, I'm ready to continue.

"I love it when you do that."

"Do what? This?" He sucks my nipple again, and this time, his hand is on my clit.

"Yessss..." I say with a half moan, losing my words, "just like that."

He puts one finger inside me, and I wince. He stops and waits for me. I force myself to relax and let go. "Let's do it slowly. Like the first time."

His finger moves inside me again, and now it's so pleasant my pelvis moves to meet him.

"Yes, just like that," he whispers. "Be with me. It's just the two of us here."

He pauses for a moment and pulls off his underwear, freeing himself.

I can't help but admire his body and the way he moves, the flexibility of his muscles.

I clasp his butt tightly and pull him to me. Enough with the games. I'm as ready as can be.

He rises from me, and I grab his arm. Is he leaving me now? "What's wrong?"

"Condom," he growls.

"No need. I'm protected." It's not like I can get pregnant again. Not after what happened.

He narrows his eyes. "Without?"

I nod.

As his mouth and tongue explore mine without breaking contact for even a moment, he places his tip at my opening and thrusts inside.

I flinch as he pushes in all the way. It shouldn't be painful. The injuries I had have healed, and they removed all the stitches long ago, but it still stings and surprises me. An unwanted tear emerges.

"You're so tight." He mumbles through clenched teeth, then looks up and flinches as if startled.

"Am I hurting you? Fuck, I'm hurting you." He pulls out immediately, startling me, too.

"No. No, it's good. I'm fine." I try to pull him back to me.

"You're crying. You're not okay."

"I'm not crying. It doesn't hurt. It's just tension. It passed right away." I convince him to continue.

He slowly pushes into me again, a look of concentration on his face as he tries to control the pace. This time it doesn't hurt at all, and I breathe a sigh of relief. I try to encourage him with movements of my pelvis until he responds and starts at his own pace.

He lifts my legs and places them over his shoulders. The new position presses on a sensitive spot inside me, and my eyes fly open. Oh shit. "Faster," I encourage him and grasp his butt. "Yes, harder."

The knot in my stomach grows. I contract my muscles, try to stop myself and delay the end. I want to feel him come inside me first, but I can't hold back. The pace is fast, and I climb higher and higher until I reach my peak, seizing him inside me, my limbs twisting and shaking under him.

He sinks on top of me, the weight of his body on mine, and he comes inside me with a loud moan of pleasure. For a long moment, we just lie there on top of each other.

When he leaves me, the emptiness is overwhelming. He's here next to me, but I already miss him. "Stay with me?"

He pulls the blanket over us, clings to me in an embrace, and closes his eyes.

"Want to take a shower?" I ask, but he doesn't take his hands off me.

"Later. I want my smell on you, just for a little longer." He breathes me in.

Ugh. Why does he have to be so sexy?

CHAPTER 23

Ethan

C uddled with Ayala, all I can think is, *this* is the way to wake up. This was also the first night I slept without nightmares. Her skin is warm and pleasant against mine, and I take a moment to smell the scent in her hair.

She has been through so much, but still, she is here with me, trusting me.

Ryan once told me that the universe sent her to me to show me I was forgiven. Sometimes I think he's right.

I kiss her neck, and her blue eyes flutter as she wakes up.

I don't think there is a part of her I don't like, but there is no doubt I love those huge eyes the most for all the intensity of the emotions that lie in them.

If I didn't think she would run away screaming, I would propose to her right now.

Yes, I'm ready. The realization hits me like a hammer in the head. I wasn't myself when we broke up. Everyone told me that, and I didn't want to listen. She makes me feel alive. If anyone knew what I was thinking, they would laugh at me. It's the thoughts of someone deeply in love. I never thought that would be me.

145

I want her to be my wife. Now I just have to convince her she wants it too.

She stretches under me. My cock, which was already half-erect, is fully erect now, and I rub myself a little on her thigh.

It scared me yesterday when she wasn't wet. I thought she didn't want me, that the trauma was too severe, and that it wouldn't work. But her body just needed a little encouragement to get back to itself. It was hard for me, too. The images from that terrible day keep coming up. I had to focus my thoughts on the present several times and kept telling myself that she's safe and sound. But as soon as she started responding to me, I forgot about everything and immersed myself in the moment.

She moans as she feels me on top of her, and I continue to kiss her, sending my hands to her heaven. This time it goes easily. She is wet in seconds, and I turn her around, press her back against me, and slowly slide into her.

Yes, I'm ready to wake up like this every morning.

After we shower, and while Ayala is getting dressed and ready for the office, I'm in the kitchen, trying to make her coffee. I open all the cupboards in search of a spoon and sugar and make two cups of hot coffee, ready the minute she arrives in the kitchen. She studies me while drying her hair with a towel. She's wearing a pencil skirt and a tight button-up shirt. The fabric of the shirt is stretched against her breasts, and I can't take my eyes off the way they move as she moves her hands with the towel.

I don't believe it, but I want to fuck her again. I tug at the front of my pants, and her gaze is drawn there.

"I feel like a teenager next to you. Everything you do makes me horny." I try to lighten the atmosphere that has suddenly grown thick.

She smiles. "You let me come a few times, and you only came once. So it makes sense."

"Yes, but I'm a man. We can't come in succession like women. And I'm not that young anymore."

"Of course, you're young. You're only thirty. And you're capable of more." She winks. "I'd help you with that little problem, but I have to go to work."

"Little? Nothing is little here," I object. "You shouldn't say such things to a man."

"Sorry, my giant." She laughs, then approaches and kisses me, the taste of coffee on her tongue, demanding that I give my all.

Fucking hell, I need a cold shower now.

I sit down across from her. "So, what day do you want me to book our flight to New York?"

"What flight?"

"Now that we're together, I thought you'd come back to New York with me. I understand if you need some time to get organized, but I'd like us to go back soon."

She stops and puts the coffee on the table. "I'm not moving to New York."

I think I didn't hear her correctly. "What?"

"I'm not moving to New York. My home is here. I have a career that I enjoy. I've built a life here. A real life."

"Your life is not with me? I thought you said you were choosing me again, that you were giving us a chance." I raise my voice without meaning to.

"Yes. But I'm not going to leave everything I've achieved. Maybe you could move here?"

"Ayala, all my businesses are in New York. I can't stay here. Be reasonable."

"Am I unreasonable? You think I should give up my career?" She stands, and her posture tells me she's angry.

"What career? You started only a few months ago. What do you have here that you can't start over?"

"I can't believe you just said that."

I don't understand what's happening. How did we go from an amazing morning to this? "You can have the same role in one of my companies. Choose whichever role you want. Hell, you can even take my place."

"I don't want to work for you! I thought we had this covered already. I want to build my own life. I don't want anyone to think I got something the easy way."

"What do I care what people think? I know what you're worth." I stop to think for a moment. "I can buy the magazine you work for and move it to New York."

"Don't you dare!" Her cheeks turn red. "Don't you dare do anything that concerns my job."

"Wait, wait. I didn't do anything. I learned from last time. We're just discussing this."

The situation is deteriorating rapidly, and I don't know what to do. "I think I'll go back to the hotel and let you calm down a bit. We'll talk this evening." I get up and collect my things.

"You're running away again."

"I'm not running away. I don't know what to do, and I don't want to fight. Maybe it's better if we calm down first and talk later."

"If you leave me again when I need you here, don't bother coming back."

Wow. That escalated quickly. "I'm not leaving," I say, trying to talk some sense into her. "You're not making sense. I'll come back in the evening after you've calmed down, and we can talk like two grown people." I collect the keys and go outside.

I pound my hands on the steering wheel hard. Fuck.

What happened there? Did we just break up? I have no idea, and it's not what I meant to happen. After yesterday, I was sure that everything was working out and falling into place. She'll come live with me, and we'll get married. We'll grow old together. It's something I never thought I'd have, and now I want nothing else.

Was I wrong when I asked her to come back with me? I thought it was obvious when she agreed to give us a chance. After all, she knows where I live and where my businesses are.

I drive back to the hotel and log in to all the Zoom meetings that were already planned for today while repeatedly looking at the phone.

She sends nothing. Fucking hell. I was sure she would calm down.

I look up from the phone when I realize that someone is asking for my attention in the meeting.

"Wolf, what do you say about the campaign we proposed?" one manager asks, and I don't know what he's talking about.

"Can you go back to the numbers, please?" I ask him. You can always understand what you need from the numbers.

I go through the presentation and ask for a few changes. When all the details are closed and approved, we end the meeting, and I return to the phone. My heart skips a beat when I see the message.

Ayala
I need some time apart. We jumped in too fast.

This is a nightmare. Just another one of my nightmares. Must be. Because our night together was perfect. She can't possibly want to break up the day after.

I'm on edge, waiting for the next meeting to end. Then I grab the car keys and hurry to her. I won't let her throw away what's between us so easily. I promised I would be here for her, that I would wait, and I intend to keep my promise.

CHAPTER 24

Ayala

As the hours pass, I am more and more convinced that I made a mistake with Ethan. I shouldn't have jumped into bed with him. I let the romantic in me take over. The horrible day I'm having at work certainly does not contribute to my mood. Nothing goes right.

The photos for the campaign I ordered turned out horrible, and I had to order new photos. One of our editors wrote a Facebook post against surrogacy that was blown out of proportion, requiring full damage control. When I asked him to write an apology post, a loud argument started. Toby came in and forced me out of the room. The big boss needs to solve problems for me? Not good.

When we finally leave for a late lunch break, I head to the cafeteria by myself. I buy a cinnamon cake instead of the expected. There is nothing like sugar to improve my mood.

I don't know what I want. I love him, but we are running too fast. I am drawn into his vortex when I don't know myself well enough yet. After what happened, I'm not in a hurry. I want to be sure.

My phone rings, and on the line is the only person who can give me advice about Ethan.

"Hi, Olive," I say between bites.

"Ayala! The article you did about the store is crazy. You don't know how many followers it added for me. And everything here is insane. We sold all the dresses, and I'm sure it's mostly thanks to you."

"Awesome! I'm so happy for you. This is amazing."

"Right? I'm crazy busy. I thought it would take me two years to recoup the investment, and now it looks like it's going to happen in a few months! Can you believe it?"

"I knew you would do awesome. Ethan invested in you. He knows a good thing when he sees it."

"Speaking of the devil, Ethan texted me that he's in San Francisco. Does that mean you're back together?" she asks in a voice full of hope.

"Hmm... Do you have time for a story?" I finish eating the cake.

"Sounds like I should have time for a story, so yes."

I tell her what happened between us, keeping it brief. "He runs away every time there's an obstacle."

"That doesn't sound like Ethan. He's very loyal to the ones he loves. He isn't a man who runs away at the sight of trouble. He's the one who convinced me to come out of the closet, accompanied me to confront my parents, and convinced me to open the business. The man is not afraid of anything."

I ponder what she says. "This is a serious obstacle, Olive. I don't want to throw away everything I started here to be the little woman in New York."

"Is that what he said? He asked you to stop working?"

"No. He wanted me to come work for him. But I love my job. I'm good at it."

"Okay, and wouldn't you be good at a role in Ethan's company too? I would jump at the chance if I was suitable."

"You don't understand. All my life, I have always depended on someone. First my parents, then Michael. And now, I'm taking baby steps in the real world. I don't want to depend on someone again."

Olive is silent for a moment. "Explain it to him. Try to reach a solution. Your love is genuine. Not something you find every day. Don't give up on it. He's not Michael. You can make it work."

"I wanted to talk to him this morning. But he ran away. Again."

"From what you told me, he was just taking time to cool down, and he wants to talk. You may not like it, but it's not a crime."

I laugh. "No, it's not a crime. I'll talk to him. Thanks, Olive. You always know exactly what to say."

"I have to say that I have a special interest here. If you come back to New York, I can see you every day."

"I miss you too, even though we saw each other recently. And even if my relationship with Ethan doesn't last, I got to know you, so it was worth everything."

"You're exaggerating. Enough, enough, but continue." She laughs. "I love you too."

We say our goodbyes, and I go back to the office and immerse myself in my million projects.

I look up from the computer and realize that it is already seven o'clock. I rush out and arrive at the house exhausted, spotting Ethan's rental car parked in front of the house.

Damn. I've had a long day. I don't think I have the strength to deal with him now. I don't want to fight again. But I'm also glad he's here. That he's not giving up this time.

I approach the car, and my mouth curves into a smile when I

notice him. His head is slumped on the back of the seat, and his hands are on the steering wheel. He's sleeping.

I raise my finger to knock on the window but hold off, taking a moment to just look at him.

His hair is wild, crushed in the places he leans on it, and his skin is stretched over his cheekbones, emphasizing how thin he is. I don't like that he is so skinny. He doesn't look relaxed like I would expect from a sleeping person. He looks haunted.

I bite my lip without realizing it, take a deep breath, and knock on the window.

There is panic in his eyes as he wakes up, not expecting to see me standing there. But when his eyes brighten, the most beautiful smile in the world appears on his face, and a wave of warmth floods me from the inside. When I look at him, at this moment, a gentle and unexpected moment, I suddenly have my answer.

He gets out of the car, and I see in his eyes that he's ready for battle, about to drop the speech on me. I'm sure he's been thinking about it for hours.

Before he can say a word, I throw my arms around his shoulders and kiss him like there's no tomorrow, pulling him into me.

I break away from him, short of breath. "I don't want to fight."

"Me neither." He takes my hand, and we go inside.

I make some hot tea, and we both settle in. "Before we talk, I want to explain something." I sit down next to him on the sofa after placing the pot of hot tea on the table. "When I met Michael, I thought he was perfect."

Ethan frowns.

"He was charming, rich, and he gave me all his attention. I felt on top of the world. He was the most wanted man on campus, and he chose me. Throughout my time with Michael, I believed I was the one to blame. That if I was better, more successful, more beautiful, maybe none of this would be happening to me. He reminded me daily how bad I was at everything."

Ethan remains silent, and I know he's listening, that he's hearing me, and that gives me the fortitude to go on.

"As time passed, he cut me off from everything I knew. He did it slowly, almost without me noticing. At first from friends, then from work, and finally from classes. Until I was left with nothing, and I had no one to turn to."

"Ayala—"

I put my hand on Ethan's thigh to stop him. "I know this is not what you want. I understand that. But to leave what I have achieved, and move to New York, to disconnect from the familiar and the known, the feeling, is the same."

He sighs and rests his forehead on mine. "I don't know how to solve this. I want you next to me."

I know it's unreasonable to ask him to give up his entire business empire. All the offices are in New York, with hundreds of employees. He can try to manage remotely, but it will never be the same. I'm the one who has to decide.

"Come with me to dinner with my parents," I ask, surprising even myself. My parents don't like him. I mean, they don't know him, but they don't like the idea of his existence in my life. They don't like that there is someone with whom their beloved daughter cheated on her husband. Even though Michael was a piece of shit, and they realize that now too. Ethan told me they asked him to stay away from me. If I decide to leave, I want to work it out with them first. Maybe if they love him as much as I do, the decision will be easier.

He nods. "Okay. Whatever you want." He thinks for a moment. "Can we just sit together and watch a movie now?" he asks.

There is nothing I want more. I nod and go to the kitchen. "Do you like popcorn?" I ask, taking a packet out of the cupboard. "Because if not, we should say goodbye right now. I'm addicted."

His rolling laugh ties pleasant knots in my stomach, and I put the popcorn in the microwave.

"How about an addition of hot chocolate to accompany this popcorn?" He grins. "Because otherwise, we really have nothing to look forward to together."

"I would never turn down a hot chocolate in the winter."

We sit in front of the TV, and I bring out a big blanket from the bedroom to snuggle under. He raises his arm, allowing me to lean on him. This feels so right as if we've been doing this forever. All the pieces are exactly in place.

I sip loudly from my cup of chocolate.

He looks at me in wonder. "What is that noise?"

I giggle. "I was just checking to see how you would react." I send him a beaming smile, and he lowers his face to kiss me. The chocolate in his mouth tastes better than what's in my cup.

He laughs. "I'll kiss you until you stop. A good enough response?"

"Then I better make some more noise." I sip again, making the same noise, and pucker my lips for a kiss.

He willingly responds to my call, and we drift into each other until I mutter, "We didn't choose a movie."

"I've already chosen," he murmurs into my mouth. "*The Ring*."

"Isn't that a horror movie?" I break away from him to see his face.

"Oh, yes." He winks at me.

"I'm not a fan of horror movies," I say with wide eyes. "They scare me."

"I'm counting on it." He smiles a sly smile.

We sink onto the couch, and I place the popcorn between us, take some for myself, then put some in Ethan's mouth as he watches the movie with interest. Watching him is more interesting for me than the movie.

When the scary parts start, I cringe and bury my face in his chest. "Tell me when it's over."

He laughs. "It's over."

I lift my head just when a rotting corpse appears on the screen. "Yuck!" I squeal, hitting him on the shoulder. "Why did you tell me it was over?"

He bites his lower lip. "Because you're charming when you're scared. And I think it's making you horny."

"And does it make *you* horny?" I tilt my head toward him.

"Honestly, I don't think I need a movie to be horny. And you?" He takes my hand and places it on his crotch.

"No, I don't think I need a movie," I mutter as he kisses me again, his hand reaching for me.

CHAPTER 25

Ethan

I feel like a gorilla in a cage being thrown bananas over the bars. Ayala's parents stare at me during the entire meal, and these are not admiring looks.

I try all my tricks, but nothing seems to work. The game is rigged. I don't see what I did wrong. I'm usually quite successful with parents. They usually love me. I behave politely. I'm rich and good-looking. What more could a parent want for their daughter? But they approved of Michael, so maybe the problem isn't with me.

I smile widely at Ayala's mother as she serves the potatoes.

"So, how did you and Ayala meet?" Ayala's father asks, trying to get information out of me. I'm not entirely sure what he's trying to catch me at and why they're not happy with me for showing up in California, especially considering that I did everything possible to save their daughter when they didn't.

"I went to the bar where she worked with a good friend of mine, and she fascinated me."

Her parents' surprised faces tell me I messed up somewhere. Fuck, I should have gone over topics for conversation with Ayala before I got here. It's like I'm walking on eggshells and making a terrible omelet out of them.

Michelle turns to Ayala. "You didn't tell us you worked in a bar."

Okay, I guess I shouldn't have said that.

"I had to earn money, Mom." Ayala shoots back. "I had to run away when no one believed me and no one else would give me a job."

"Ayala, you know that I... That your father and I are deeply sorry for what happened that day you came to us. But he had documents. It sounded real."

"I know, Mom. But you knew *me*. You should have believed your daughter over him." Ayala stabs the food on her plate with her fork.

"They thought they were helping you," I say, jumping in. "The documents looked real," I add, hoping to get the point across. After all, I also initially fell for Michael's scam.

Her parents glance at me in surprise, obviously not understanding why I came to their aid.

"Mom, I'd been gone for months, and you didn't even search for me."

"But we *were* searching for you! At first, we didn't understand what was happening. Michael said you were in treatment and getting better. After two weeks, when we insisted on seeing you, he suddenly told us you had run away, and he didn't know where you were. We wanted to contact the police, and he said we shouldn't. He said he was using all of his resources and that he would find you. That we shouldn't go to the police because it would just scare you off."

"And you believed him?"

"Yes," Tom replies. "We fell into the trap he laid for us. Only when two months passed, and I realized nothing was progressing, did I tell him I was contacting the police no matter what he said. At that point, he addressed the public on television himself."

"He wanted to be the worried husband..." Ayala mumbles.

I find it strange that more than a year has passed, and they never talked about this. Looks like they have been walking on eggshells, too. And seeing the love and concern in her parents' eyes, I think it's time to open it all up.

"So you initiated the search?"

Ayala looks surprised at my eagerness to lead the discussion.

"Not exactly," Tom explains. "I wanted to contact the police and said I would. But Michael suggested doing it himself and asking for the public's help. It sounded like a great idea, so I agreed. I thought it would be better if it came from him. He also had a lot more resources than we did. At no point did I think he wasn't sincere."

Ayala and I exchange looks, and I squeeze her hand under the table.

"It had to happen. Without it, you could never have lived as yourself."

"What do you mean?" Tom asks me.

I bite my lip, glancing at Ayala, wondering how much she's willing to let me tell them because she seems to have left her parents in the dark.

When she doesn't say anything, I answer. "When I met your daughter, she called herself Hope. I realized it wasn't her real name, but I couldn't find out anything about her." I take another peek at Ayala, her blue eyes studying me with interest. I never told her about the background checks I did. "After I saw Michael on TV, everything became clear. I tried to protect her and failed. You know what happened next."

"So you didn't know she was married?" Michelle asks me.

"No. I didn't even know her real name. She did an excellent job hiding. Even my investigator couldn't find anything on her."

Her parents exchange looks. Something is happening here now.

"Ayala didn't tell us what happened in New York. We only knew that she had run away and started a new life there. We knew she met you and that she went back to Michael after he threatened you."

I glance at Ayala, who has continued to remain silent. She's put me in the lion's den without warning, letting them assume I took her, knowing she was a married woman. And from what she told me, they are very conservative. And on top of that, she let them think I let her go back to Michael to save myself. No wonder they wanted me to keep my distance from her.

I wonder if she was trying to burn me on purpose.

By the end of the meal, they are joking with me like we're old friends.

When we finally leave, I have a hard time holding back my anger.

"Why did you do that?"

"Do what?"

"You let them believe I knew you were married, that I willingly let you go to Michael to save myself, that I was responsible for what happened."

"I didn't mean it that way. I just didn't share the whole story with them."

"You knew very well that's how they would interpret it." I slam the car door behind me and turn on the heater. "What did you think to accomplish tonight by bringing me here? That you would make them hate me so it would be easier for you to leave me?"

"No!" she cries out, but I don't believe her. I won't let her leave me. She's mine. My lips are on hers. I bite and lick. It's painful and arousing at the same time, and I'm taking what I want. My tongue invades her mouth without asking permission. I know it's too much. She was traumatized. But the anger takes over me, acting on my behalf.

She grabs my hair and pulls me to her, and I moan into the kiss.

My cock is so hard it hurts.

She reaches between my legs, but instead of touching me, she moves my chair back. I stop the kiss, and she takes the opportunity and climbs on top of me.

Damn, the friction in the front of my pants is too much. I growl.

"Ayala, we are on your parents' lawn. They will see us."

Her eyes lift, and she gazes into mine. In her blue depths, I see torment, hunger and need. This evening seems to have affected us both.

"I'll park in a more private place." I barely exhale the words, start the car, and drive a few blocks out of the neighborhood, glancing at the seat next to me. Ayala's squirming, trying to remove her underwear from under the dress she's wearing. Fucking hell. Where can I park?

The nearby commercial area is closed at this time of night, so I park on the side of the road. I'm hoping that no one will pay attention to us here. I've been involved in enough scandals lately, but I can't wait another minute. I have to feel her, her sweet warmth wrapping around my cock.

She seems to understand my sense of urgency, too, because she doesn't wait another moment to climb on top of me again, her hands hurrying to undo the waistband of my pants. I pull my cock out, and I run my hands over her while she studies me.

"I need you."

She doesn't wait. Ayala lifts her pelvis and takes me inside her paradise.

"Fuck, you're flooded," I moan. There's no better feeling than that.

I lift my pelvis and push myself in until I'm balls deep. Now she's the one moaning.

It's not enough for me, though. I need it harder. Stronger. I need control. I take her off me and push the front seats down as far as they'll go. When I rented a large car, I didn't think it would be so useful.

"On your knees," I command. Her eyes widen, but she obeys, trusting me.

I grasp her shoulders and pull her body to me, thrusting myself into her hard.

The pace increases rapidly, and our sighs and the sounds of thrusting limbs fill the interior of the car. There is no other thought in my mind now. I want her to come hard. I thrust myself into her from behind over and over.

The sweat drips down my back. I grab her hair and pull, lifting her up and pinning her against me, then bite her neck.

"Yes!" she shouts, and I feel her walls closing in on me. She's close. I release her, pull myself out, and pinch her clit.

She screams and comes hard on my hand with violent contractions. I hold her shaking body and thrust myself inside her again, riding the waves of her orgasm, feeling her internal muscles squeezing me, bringing me closer to my climax.

I reach out and caress her anus, then insert a finger. She flinches, but her body shows me she's enjoying it. I fuck her ass with my finger while pounding her vagina with my cock. I feel my balls filling up, ready to give her everything I've got.

"Ayala!" I shout while my cock expands and convulses inside of her.

I lean against her and take a moment to regain control of my breath, then pull myself out.

She remains on all fours, still shaking from the waves of her second orgasm, and I can't help but stare at my seed dripping out of her, marking her mine.

She takes almost a full minute to come to her senses, then she straightens her dress, panting. "Wow."

I agree. I've had rough sex before, usually rougher than this, but I'm feeling very satisfied.

"How screwed up am I that I got horny because you're mad at me?"

I laugh. "Make-up sex is the most fun."

"Michael was angry all the time, and it wasn't—"

"Because you were afraid of him. He wanted to hurt you. I don't want to hurt you. When you trust your partner, when you know he won't push you beyond your limit, rough sex can be insanely exciting."

I can see the thoughts going through her head. "I loved it."

I blow out a breath. "Me too."

CHAPTER 26

Ayala

I can't believe I said that. I regretted it as soon as the words came out of me.

No. I don't regret it. What we had, those feelings, I want it again. I always thought it would remind me of Michael. But it turns out that with the right person, I like it. I can lose my inhibitions with Ethan. I can discover myself with him.

He was right about my parents. I expected them to say he was not good for me, to say I should keep away from him. I almost hoped they would convince me I shouldn't move to New York with him. But somehow, he came out on top, and now they like him too.

I have no more excuses.

My heart and head mutually decided. "Ethan?"

"Mmm?" he mutters without taking his eyes off the road.

"I want to move to New York with you."

Now his head turns to me. "Really?"

"Yes. I want to be with you. I'll find a new career in New York, but not in one of your companies," I clarify.

"I'll help with whatever you want. But you'll have to ask. I'm

afraid to do something that will cause you to take my head off."
He's smiling now.

Ugh. It's hard for me to resist that smile, a smile that melts my body. "Help me find an apartment?"

"An apartment? Are you serious?"

"Yes. You didn't think I'd go back to living in that storage room, did you?"

"No. I thought you would move in with me."

"You want to live together? It..." It feels too fast.

His face falls. "Would you at least be willing to live in my building?"

I want to say no, but the look on his face makes me reconsider. "I won't be able to afford the expenses of an apartment in the most expensive part of Manhattan, even with my new job."

"It's my building. So no expenses. There's a tenant who has a contract ending at the end of next month, and I haven't yet signed a lease with anyone else. Consider this, please?"

I hesitate.

"That way, you'll have the privacy you want, and you'll still be close enough to me."

"Okay." I nod. It's a reasonable compromise. I can live with that.

He parks in front of my apartment and quickly gets out of the car.

"I'd love for us to fly back before Christmas." He looks at me as I open the door. "I'll understand if you prefer to stay with your parents and come later, but it would be nice if you flew with me. I'm going back in two days."

"In two days?"

"We got that extension from the court, and I want to use the time to return to the offices before the holiday. Several subjects are waiting for me."

It's too fast, too stressful. I have to quit my job. Say goodbye to my parents. "I can't leave that fast. I can't leave with just two days' notice to my boss. And I have a lot to sort out first. But perhaps I'll join you for the holidays?"

He leans in to kiss me. "I'd love that."

I wake up in a panic. I try to understand where I am and realize that I'm in my bed. What woke me up? Then it happens again.

Ethan is in bed next to me, squirming, the blankets tangled around his body. He's sweating, and his facial expression is tormented.

"No!" he shouts. "Leave me alone. Let me go. I need to save her!" He kicks at the blankets, but they only get more tangled around him. I hurry to turn on the light in the room, then rush back to the bed and try to wake him up.

"Ethan, wake up. You're dreaming."

He thrashes about in bed, and I'm careful not to get in the way of his fists.

"Ethan!" I shout, succeeding in shaking him. His eyes barely open, and he blinks at me. I notice how obscurity turns into painful recognition.

"Ayala," he whispers, burying his face in my neck. "You're here."

"Yes, I'm here."

"Fuck! Did I hurt you?" He looks frightened.

"No. I'm fine. I was just scared. What did you dream about?"

"Nothing. I don't remember. I'm sorry I woke you." His arms wrap around me.

I know he remembers what the dream was about, but I don't press because I also know how it feels to share your tormented soul with another person. When you're trying to show the world that you're okay, that you've recovered. When inside your head, you're still living that day, and you're still broken.

Ethan is used to pretending since mourning for Anna. No one was there to tell him he was allowed to break, that he could also be weak. It's easy to ignore the problem when you're alone with yourself when no one knows. But when Mom woke up every night from my screams, I knew I had no choice. I had to talk about it. Ethan is not at that stage yet, but he'll get there.

Two days later, we say our goodbyes before his flight back. I know we'll see each other again soon, but that doesn't help the feeling of longing that starts even before he's gone.

"Are you flying in a private plane? Like Christian Grey?" The question pops into my head.

"Christian Grey?"

"Yes... You know, from *Fifty Shades of Grey*. The handsome, rich man every woman dreams of."

"I'd like to be that rich man every woman dreams of," he says with a laugh. "But no. I have enough money, but I don't have planes or helicopters if that's what you were hoping for. I don't understand the need for it, I prefer to spend my money on other things. I hope you dream about *me* at night and not of Christian Grey."

"I'll miss you."

"Me too."

I go to the office after he leaves for the airport, knowing these are my last days here. Yesterday, I submitted my resignation letter to Toby.

In a week, I'll pack and fly to New York. I planned to give two weeks' notice, but the holiday issue is ready, and with Christmas coming, Toby thinks there's no need for me to stay.

I feel the eyes on me before I see them. I look at the surrounding tables. Everyone is looking at their screens, trying not to show any signs of their curiosity. But I notice the sudden movement in every room I pass through, the whispering.

What am I missing?

Maybe I have something on my face? I glance at myself through the glass of the conference room. No, everything looks fine.

Claire. I need to find Claire. The closest to a friend I have here. She'll tell me what's up. I enter her office, and she hurries to bury her face in the screen when she sees me approaching, and I realize I was right. Something happened.

"Claire." I land on the chair next to her desk, and she raises her head as if she hadn't noticed my existence until that moment.

"Oh, hi, Ayala."

"Spill it."

"What?"

"Whatever it is, that has everyone looking at me, and why you're also afraid to look me in the eye."

"I... I don't understand what you're talking about?"

I gaze at her. "Now."

She holds my gaze, then makes a few clicks with the mouse and turns the screen to me.

My heart stops.

A large image fills the screen. An enlarged image of my face smashed and broken, with dried blood on my lips. It's the picture the police took of me after the incident. I take the mouse and scroll down, unable to stop my inclination to run. I cover my face with my hands. They published the picture of Michael's body. It's blurry but still shocking.

Where did they get it? These were confidential! And why now?

I don't know what to do with myself. I don't want Claire and everyone in the office to see me lose it. I run to the bathroom, enter one of the stalls, and lock the door.

The tears are already breaking out. I open the story on my phone, trying to read through the tears what they wrote about me.

The shocking affair at the Summers family home refuses to fade away.

The Summers claim that the other man who was in the apartment, Ethan Wolf, a New York businessman, was Ayala Summers' lover while she and Michael Summers were married.

Michael Summers surprised them during the act at their lovers' cabin. The incident became heated, and Mr. Wolf struck and killed Michael.

The family has filed a civil lawsuit against Ayala Summers and Ethan Wolf:

"We are ashamed to say that this adulteress was our son's wife. He died because of her. Ethan Wolf used his money and resources to bribe the police, and they're not pressing charges. We will not accept it, and we will not allow them to get away with it without punishment," said Michael Summers's mother.

My hands are shaking, and I almost drop my phone.

The rest of the story contains difficult-to-view photos taken by the police.

I click on the blurred pictures, and a wave of nausea washes over me. These are pictures of Michael and me. Everyone can see my battered body, my injuries. I lean over and throw up into the toilet.

No. I can't believe this is happening. I can't breathe.

The sobs come out of me in force. I'm panting so much that my head spins. I have to get it under control. Inhale... Exhale...

How did they get the pictures? Why? All the memories of that day float over me and rise. The pain, the fear...

Just as the incident is starting to fade and my life is finally returning to normal. I can't stop shaking, can't face the people outside.

My phone rings non-stop. Numbers I don't recognize. Likely news reporters celebrating on my blood. I turn it off.

Hours pass as I sit in the bathroom stall with my head between my knees, hyperventilating. My whole body hurts, but I dare not leave here.

Someone enters the bathroom and calls my name. I put my legs up on the toilet seat and remain silent, waiting for them to leave. I want to disappear. I want the earth to open up and swallow me because I don't know how I can continue to live after everyone has seen those pictures.

I'll wait until the evening, when I know no one is around, and then sneak out.

CHAPTER 27

Ethan

I arrive home tired after the flight. My muscles ache from sitting for so long. But none of that matters. I'm happy because, in a week, Ayala will be with me in New York.

When I arrive at the entrance to the building, I understand that something is wrong. Journalists surround the entrance.

I put a blank expression on my face and enter through the parking garage, aware of the flashes of the cameras. When the gate closes behind me, I allow myself to relax.

What the hell?

I rush upstairs and call Ryan. "What did I miss?" I shout as soon as he answers. "What's happened?"

"Ethan, did you land? Are you okay?"

"Yes, tell me what's happened. Why are there reporters at the house?"

"Michael's parents have accused you of murder, and they released the photos to the press."

"What? What photos?" I completely ignore the first sentence.

"Michael's and Ayala's."

"What photos of Ayala, Ryan?"

"All of them."

"Fuck! I told you not to publish anything."

"I didn't do that! Do you think I would go to the press behind your back? I only talked to Summers' lawyer about a settlement. They got angry. They said the only thing they want is to destroy you."

"And you didn't think to warn me?"

"I thought it was just a threat."

"Post a response."

I hang up. I can't believe Summers posted the pictures just to hurt me. I saw Ayala's photos from the police investigation. Hell, I saw Ayala herself that evening. It was awful. I need to check the extent of the damage.

I open my phone and click on the story.

I shout when I look at the pictures. Her broken body, the terrible pain. Did she survive hell only to get to this moment?

They'll never let her be. Fuck, she's alone. All alone. How did it get published at the same time I flew here? I have a feeling the timing is not a coincidence.

I call her, but she's turned off her phone, so I call her parents. "Where's Ayala?" I ask, hoping she's with them.

"We don't know. We can't find her. She went to the office this morning, and no one has seen her since. Someone looked for her in the offices. But she's not there."

"We have to find her. She can't be alone now. Call everyone she knows. You should also talk to her psychologist. Please make sure she's not alone." I wish I had never left. "I'm in New York. I'll try to fly to you as soon as I can."

I hang up and call Jess. "Did you see?"

"Yes. What do you want to do?"

"Take those pictures off the net. I want to sue their asses."

"You know that once it's published, it's out there."

"I know, but do what you can. And they'll pay for this. The next one will think twice about posting. And I want you to find me everything you can about Summers, all the dirt. If they want to bring me down, they'll go down with me." Money makes the world go round, and I'm willing to invest everything I've got to make them pay.

"Oh, and Jess?" I say before hanging up, "Find out who told them I was flying home today."

Being far from her and not knowing where she is or if she's all right is driving me crazy. I have to fly back there. Now. I need to support her, to be by her side. Not like last time. I must not make the same mistake again.

I pick up my suitcase and head right back out as I never got the chance to unpack.

Why did I leave her? What was so important that I couldn't wait until she was ready to travel?

I'm willing to throw away all my businesses just to make sure she's okay.

I check my phone every few minutes, hoping for a message saying they've found her, that she's okay. The fear of the worst fills me and overwhelms me. But when I board the long six-hour flight, there is still no sign of life from her.

CHAPTER 28

Ayala

I t's dark outside. I don't know what time it is, nor do I care, as I walk through the empty corridors on my way out. I waited a few hours past the end of the workday to make sure that no one would be here.

I try to control the shaking as I drive home. It wasn't a good idea to drive like this, but what choice did I have. My eyes are so swollen I can barely see. The tears are no longer flowing. I think I'm cried out.

"Ayala." The familiar voice calls my name as I get out of the car.

"Mom!" I run into her arms, looking for the comfort I need now. It's hard for me to breathe. The universe is closing in on me.

"Everyone saw," I moan into her shoulder.

"Shh..." Her soothing voice relaxes me. "It'll be all right. Everything will be all right."

My father squeezes my hand gently, leading me inside my small apartment.

They look at me as if I'm going to break. As if, at any moment, I'll shatter into pieces all over the living room.

Maybe it wouldn't be so bad to let myself fall apart. To stop trying to hold on, and let myself shatter all over the floor, and allow someone else to do the cleanup. I can imagine them standing there, sweeping parts into a nice pile in the middle of the room.

"Ayala, I want you to meet with Dr. Sullivan." Mom's voice is soft when she speaks like she's afraid to wake up the demons. But it's too late. They're already here, floating in space and surrounding me. "We're worried about you. And you've come so far." She exchanges glances with my father.

I know I need to meet with him. He helped me a lot in the last few months, and he'll probably help me again. He'll put things in proportion for me. The proportion I need so much and that I don't have today. But I just can't see anyone right now. I can't talk. I don't want to talk. I just want to be left alone.

"Tomorrow, Mom." I go to the shower and lock the door. The white tiles are clean and polished. I feel contaminated and dirty. The same stained feeling I had after they released me from the hospital.

I turn on the hot water and undress in front of the mirror. My body is covered in blue marks, bruises, and scratches.

I know it's not real. My mind imagines it and takes me back there to those first few days. But the feeling is real. I stroke my tattoo with my fingers, trying to draw strength from it.

I open the cabinet above the sink and take out the bottle of pills, placing it on the white counter in front of me.

Dr. Sullivan prescribed me sleeping pills to help with the nightmares. I haven't taken them in some time now. I thought I had reached a good place. But the emotions are just lurking under the surface, like lava waiting to erupt. My shell is thin. It didn't have time to harden. So a minor setback is enough to open everything up.

I open the lid with the child lock and peer inside. There's about half a bottle. What will happen if I take them all? It will never end. It will never go away. Improvement is an illusion. At any moment, a stone can shatter the thin glass that I glued so carefully. Will I ever be able to live with this trauma? Or will it forever raise its head?

"Ayala, are you okay?" Mom asks beyond the door.

"Just taking a shower," I answer and turn the water on full blast until it's steaming hot. I take a step and go under the stream. The water burns my skin, and I accept the pain with joy, watching as my skin turns red. I stay as long as I can tolerate it before the pain gets too bad, then I shut the water off and sink to the floor, creating a puddle underneath me.

"Ayala, open the door." My mother's voice sounds hysterical.

"Almost done," I call, getting up slowly, wrapping myself in a robe, and binding it around my waist, making sure no one will see the redness of my skin. The pills call to me from the counter, and I put the bottle in the pocket of my robe.

Inhale...

I open the door to find Mom waiting just beyond.

"Ayala, are you okay? You were in there for such a long time," she says, but I can't talk to her right now.

"I'm going to sleep. I'm tired." I walk to my room, ignoring all their mutterings. They're worried and scared, but I can't handle anything but myself right now.

In bed, under the covers, I fight the urge to swallow the entire bottle.

Don't make life-changing decisions in a moment of difficulty.

I repeat the mantra I memorized in therapy over and over. I take out two pills because one won't be enough in this situation and swallow them. The peace of dreamless sleep is what I need.

The door opens and closes every few minutes. My parents peek in with worried looks on their faces. I pull the blanket over my head. *Let me sleep. Please, just let me sleep.*

I don't know how many hours I've slept when the door opens

again. Jeez, I thought they'd let me be. The pills make my head feel fuzzy, but even under their influence, I can still hear the footsteps.

The blanket is lifted from my face.

"Let me sleep," I mumble, hoping they'll see I'm fine and leave me, then I try to pull the blanket back over me, but I'm met with resistance.

The rustle of the pill bottle has me opening my eyes a little. The room is completely dark.

"Ayala, how many did you take?" It's just my imagination playing tricks on me. Weird, but I didn't have hallucinations when I took them before. Maybe it wasn't a good idea to take two.

"Mmm..." I try to tug on the blanket again, but muscular hands shake me, forcing me to focus.

"Ayala, how many did you take? Answer me!"

"Two," I say. The morning will come soon and force me to face reality. Give me a few hours of peace.

Sigh. And then the noise of a belt, the whooshing sound of clothes. The bed next to me sinks, and I'm cuddled into Ethan's warm body. *These pills create realistic dreams.*

I adapt myself to his embrace.

CHAPTER 29

Ayala

I wake up from the light outside streaming in through the blinds. I'm not sure what time it is, but I think it's late in the morning. Trying to move reveals that I have a weight on me. I have an arm on me. I try to shake off the cobwebs of sleep and turnover to discover Ethan in my bed.

What is he doing here? What happened last night? Wasn't it a dream?

I was sure that what I felt was my mind's desperate attempt to calm me down, but the sleeping man next to me seems completely real. I reach out to touch him.

His skin is warm and pleasant under my hand, and my touch involves a sigh, and he moves. He's here.

My hand wanders over him, and when I look up at him, I see that he's awake and looking at me. Not a muscle on his face moves.

"Ethan," I whisper. "Are you really here, or am I crazy?"

"I'm here, beautiful," he whispers back. "I promised I wouldn't betray your trust again."

He still doesn't move, letting me feel his skin under my hands, giving me time to be convinced that he's real.

"But you left yesterday morning. You flew to New York."

"As soon as I got to New York, I heard what happened, and I flew back. I tried to call you, but your phone was off. I called your parents, and they didn't know where you were. It was the longest flight of my life. I was afraid you'd done something..." His voice breaks.

I know he's remembering what happened with his sister.

"Where were you?" he asks.

"I hid in the bathroom at the office until everyone left. They were all staring at me," I confess. "I couldn't..." My face crumples. "Why did this happen?" Tears flood my eyes again as all the emotions surface.

"Michael's parents decided to destroy me. Us. Apparently, they'll stop at nothing. They're the ones who published the pictures." He strokes my hair. "I'm so sorry I wasn't here with you yesterday, and you had to go through it alone."

"But you came back."

"Not fast enough. When I saw the pills by your bed yesterday, I almost lost it." He bites his lower lip.

"I thought about it," I admit. "How can I ever go out again after everyone saw...?" My tears wet his bare chest.

"We'll get through this together. We'll be fine. I'm here with you."

This is the first time I have him to support me, the first time I'm not alone. The situation is unfamiliar to me. I'm not used to leaning on someone. Can I trust him? He has let me down before. But he came back from New York for me.

"Where are my parents?"

"I sent them home to rest after I arrived. They were very frightened."

"Ethan, everyone saw!"

"What did they see? That he hurt you? What that maniac did to you? His parents are the ones who should be ashamed, not you.

You should be proud. Not only did you survive, but you're stronger than he ever was."

"They're saying you killed him because we were in love."

"I know."

"What if they reopen the criminal case? What if they accuse you of murder?" I'm not sure I could stand something like that.

"Don't think about it. We know it's not true, and we'll prove it. I'll take care of it." He lifts my head so I can look into his eyes. "Nothing will happen to me."

I stay in his embrace for several more minutes before we get out of bed.

We're sitting in the kitchen, and I'm playing with the fork in the omelet Ethan made. The pictures aren't in the newspapers, but it's too late. Everyone has already seen it.

He finishes eating and checks messages on his phone. "Your parents scheduled an appointment with Dr. Sullivan in an hour. Get ready. I'll take you."

"So now they're talking to me through you?" I don't know why, but it makes me angry. He smiles, and that makes me angrier, so I get up and leave the kitchen.

"Angry is good," he calls after me.

The familiar gray sofa was replaced by a brown one, and for a moment, it confuses me. It throws me off balance.

"It was time for a new couch," Dr. Sullivan notes when he sees my hesitation. "How are you?"

"I'm not sure," I answer honestly. "Yesterday was a hard day."

"And today?"

"I'm not sure. I'm confused. Yesterday, I wanted to kill myself. I looked at the sleeping pills you gave me, and I wanted to take them all." The tears come again, and he hands me the tissue box. I can no longer count how many times he's handed me this box.

"Why didn't you?"

"I've been practicing what we talked about. Not acting in the heat of the moment. Waiting. Talking to someone."

"And you talked to someone?"

I shake my head. "I couldn't. But I waited for the morning."

He nods. "And in the morning, did you still feel like taking those pills?"

"Ethan came back."

Dr. Sullivan looks at me, and I explain what happened.

"He flew to New York and returned within a day?"

I nod. And the doctor writes something in his notebook.

"And you think your improvement has something to do with him?"

"Yes."

"Where were you when you heard about the story?"

"At the office. I saw the pictures on Claire's computer." I take a deep breath. "When I realized what I was seeing, I hid in the bathroom. I stayed there all day." I'm hot, so I take off my coat and put it on the couch next to me. "You saw the pictures. What do you think? How do you see me now that you've seen that?"

"It doesn't matter what I think. What do you think?"

My smile is filled with bitterness. "I couldn't handle their stares. After everyone left, I drove home."

"And at home, that's when the suicidal thoughts started?"

I nod and blow my nose. "Well, before that, actually. But when the pills were there in front of me, it was the hardest. I didn't think there was any hope of going on."

"But you didn't take them."

"No. I mean, I took two. I thought it would help me sleep."

"So, it was your decision, on your own, not to take the entire bottle."

I consider what he's saying. Yes. I dealt with it without talking to anyone, without knowing that Ethan was already on his way back to me.

"So maybe you're not as weak as you thought?"

CHAPTER 30

Ethan

I t's been two days since we rushed our plans and got back to
New York. Improvement is slow but happening. Ayala still
stays in the bedroom a lot and has not yet left the apartment. She does video sessions with her therapist, but it doesn't
feel enough to me. I don't know what to do. How to improve the
situation.

I hover around her all day, trying to help, but I feel like I'm
just messing things up.

"You have to stop, *Kýria* Wolf." Madeleine looks at me with
knowing eyes.

"Stop what?"

"Asking her every moment how she's doing and how she feels.
You treat her like she's made of glass. She needs you to show her
how strong she is."

"I am."

"You two have been through a lot. I saw the pictures." She
shakes her head. "I wish I hadn't. I can't believe she survived such
horror. She's not fragile. Ayala is the strongest there is." Tears
flood Madeleine's eyes, and her voice trembles. "Show her that

nothing has changed. That you still see her as before. That she's still your love."

"I'm trying. I don't know what else to do."

"Try harder." She smiles. "Do what you would have done if it hadn't happened."

My phone rings, interrupting our conversation. "Yes?"

"I found who leaked your flight details to Summers," Jess says.

"Who?" I jump up, ready to kill whoever it is.

"Looks like your secretary told him."

"What? How could that happen?" I yell into the phone as if that would help.

"It seems it was a simple mistake. Their lawyer called her to ask for a meeting with you, and she told him you had a booked flight. She didn't realize it was Mr. Summers's lawyer."

Fucking hell. "I want you to coordinate a briefing for all my employees. Something like this must never happen again." I want to fire her. I want to blame someone. It would be better for my mood if it was her fault, and I could take my anger out on her, but I can't.

Summers wins this round.

"Ayala, I want to go buy a tree," I say to her during lunch.

Christmas is a week away, and it's clear to me we won't be celebrating. But every year, I put up a tree and decorate it with Anna's favorite ornaments, which I've kept ever since.

Those blue eyes are so full of pain that I cringe a little. I want to kiss Ayala until this pain goes away, but I can't.

"It was Anna's favorite holiday," I explain. "Every year, I buy a tree for her and decorate it with her ornaments."

Ayala is still silent.

I sigh. "I'll call Olive to come and stay with you while I'm out." I get up from my seat.

"I want to come with you."

"Come with me?" I turn to her, and my heart flutters.

"If you want me to." She shrugs.

"Very much." I can't believe she's agreed to come with me.

She dresses in jeans and a red sweater, and the long white coat I bought her. She looks to me like the most beautiful woman in the world.

We walk around the tree lot, looking for the perfect tree. Light snow falls and joins the piles already on the ground. There is no one here but us. I don't know if it's because of the cold or because it's already so close to the holiday.

"Maybe this one?" She points to a huge one, much too tall.

"How the hell do we get it into the apartment?"

She continues to search, rubbing her hands together and blowing on them.

"Didn't you bring gloves?"

"I didn't know it would be so cold."

I forget she's not used to snow. "Take mine." I watch as she puts them on and holds her hands up for me to see. They are huge on her, and it's so cute. I laugh, and she smiles. A real smile.

God, she's so gorgeous when she smiles. I've missed it.

I take some snow in my hand, ignoring the fact that I'm without gloves now, and throw it at her.

She squeals and looks at me in astonishment as it hits her in the center of her body. For a moment, I think I may have gone too far, but then playfulness appears in her eyes, and she bends down into the snow.

I turn and start running.

She knows how to aim. I'm hit with a snowball in the back, then another straight in the face as I turn to throw another.

I shake my head, trying to get the snow out of my hair. She

looks at me, amused, and I throw another ball at her, hitting her shoulder.

The snowballs are fired in succession while we dodge between the fir trees. I enjoy hearing her squeal with happiness. When I finally catch her in my arms and spin her in the snow, her blue eyes sparkle, and I can't help but kiss her.

We just stand there, hugging, the snow falling on us, and we sink into each other, blind to the world. For a moment, I don't even feel the cold.

As the magic ends, we go back to searching for that perfect tree. She chooses our tree and insists that we take it home ourselves. I can't refuse anything she asks.

It takes an hour and a half. The tree falls twice on the way, and my arms are sore and red, but I'm not complaining because she finally looks like my Bambi. I'm prepared to carry twenty trees to see her like this, to see the hope and joy in her eyes.

After we put the tree in the living room corner, I bring the boxes of ornaments from the closet and the small box with Anna's bird. The hummingbird she once asked our mother to order when she was obsessed with it. The one I hang every year at the top of the tree.

Ayala gently takes it out of the box. "It's beautiful, Ethan. Can I hang it up for her?"

She climbs the ladder, stretching herself up to reach the top. I can't take my eyes off the bare piece of skin between her shirt and jeans.

How terrible is it that I get a kick out of it? Shit. I shift uncomfortably just as she turns to me with questions in her eyes.

"Sorry. I'm just horny. Don't pay attention to me." I try to laugh it off and stir the conversation away.

She comes down from the ladder and stands in front of me. "You may be horny, but you're my horny... I'm sorry. I was too absorbed in myself. I didn't think how you must be feeling."

"No," I say. "What you went through—"

"You're going through it, too. We were both there. And you're also being accused of murder."

"I—" A ring from my pocket interrupts us. Ugh. I want her to know it will be okay.

"Yes, Ryan?"

"You should look out the window, Wolf. There's a protest outside your building."

"Outside my building?"

"Yes. The public seems to like you. Take a look."

I hang up and glance at the headline in the link he's sent me.

"What's going on?" Ayala asks, her eyes big and wide.

"It turns out the civil case is gaining momentum online."

She flinches when I say this.

"It's not what you think. There's a growing movement that demands dismissal of the case."

"What?"

"Looks like posting those photos is making noise, but not the kind Summers planned for. The Summers only intended to post Michael's photo. They wanted to shock. Make me look like a cold-blooded killer. Make you nothing more than a cheating wife. They want to destroy my reputation and my businesses with it. Your photos were published by mistake. I know you didn't want it, but it benefitted us. The public is calling the Summers family murderers and you the hero. The public is taking your side. Ours."

She looks surprised. "I don't want them to take my side. I want it to go away."

"I know. But we can't go back in time, and this is the way it is. Ryan says they've organized a protest near the building. A show of support for us."

I get up and go look out the window. There are more than I expected. Crowds of people gather outside, carrying large signs.

"Michael Summers is a murderer!" "Ayala, we are behind you!" "Dismiss the case!"

Ayala comes and stands next to me. Her jaw drops as she sees the crowds.

"They're actually here for us," she says in shock. "I want to see what they've written about me."

"Are you sure?" I don't think this is a good idea. She still hasn't recovered from the story a few days ago.

"I need to know." She goes to the room to get her phone, comes back, and sinks onto the couch.

As she reads, I follow her expression with growing anxiety.

"They're calling for the Summers to dismiss the case against us. They hate Michael's parents."

She sounds... I can't decide. Amazed?

"Are you alright?"

She shakes her head. "They call me a hero. I'm not a hero."

"Yes, you are."

"I laid there helpless. You saved me."

A snort escapes me. "I was dying on the floor, and you were fighting him. *You* saved *me*."

She comes closer to me and puts her arms around my waist. "If you hadn't come, I'd still be locked to that bed."

I close my eyes, and she kisses me, her lips soft on mine. A gentle, caressing kiss.

"Okay, so we saved each other."

———

Ayala behaves strangely over the following days. As if she's daydreaming, I often find her deep in thought. She's busy writing all kinds of notes to herself with a determined look on her face. It's better than the depressed mood from before, but it bothers me that she doesn't share with me what she's thinking. I don't know if I should be worried or happy.

At noon Ayala bursts into my home office. "I just talked to Dr. Sullivan."

"Okay?"

"Do you remember our conversation? The one where you told me that when you were at your lowest, Ryan told you that this is not how Anna would want you to remember her? And then you got up and started Savee?"

I nod. It's not a thing you forget.

"So I thought a lot about that conversation, about the desire to do something with my life. Dr. Sullivan told me I can control my thoughts, but I can't control what others think of me. If the public has decided that I'm the hero of the story, then so be it. If I'm a hero in their eyes, then I want to take advantage of this sudden status I've received for the benefit of women like me."

"Do you want to start a company?" I ask.

"No. I want a job in Savee."

"I don't know..." That's a turn I didn't expect.

"You told me I could choose any job I want. Remember?"

"I know what I said. That's not the point. Until a few days ago, you didn't want to leave the room, and now you want to be a public figure? Are you sure?"

"Yes. That's exactly what I want. I want to help. And I can do it because I was there. The role is bigger than me, and I want to use the momentum to raise funds. To have an impact. To do campaigns against violence. Maybe we'll pass some new laws. Maybe we'll be able to get the authorities to intervene more in cases like mine."

She speaks passionately, her cheeks flushed. She's gorgeous. Her enthusiasm is contagious. I can understand that. She sounds just like I did when I started Savee. This insight...the understanding that you can use your personal pain to help others. It's an uplifting feeling.

"Okay. After the holidays, I'll introduce you to Paul Sheridan."

Ayala nods and practically bounces out of the room. She's enthusiastic, and I'm worried. I mean, it's better to see her enthusiastic and full of motivation, but the change is too fast, and I'm afraid she's in too much of a hurry.

The ringing of the phone interrupts my thoughts.

"Yes, Ryan? What now?" I'm ready for any scenario. Every conversation we've had recently drops a bomb on me. On us.

"We're on our way to the hospital!" Ryan shouts.

"What? What's happened? Was someone injured?"

"No, you idiot. Maya's in labor!" his voice trembles. "Now."

"Ryan. Oh, wow," I shout back. "Which hospital? I'm on my way."

"We're going to the Village. I'm texting you the address." He hangs up.

"Ayala!" I scream, and she comes running. I am so excited that I think if I was giving birth myself, I would have been calmer. She looks startled by my behavior, and I try to take a deep breath before I speak.

"Maya is in labor," I inform her. "I'm going to the hospital."

"Oh my gosh. Can I come too?"

I nod and scan the room, looking for my sneakers.

"What are you looking for?" She tries to stop me.

"Shoes." I continue rummaging through the closet, throwing things out as she grabs my shoulders.

"Those shoes?" She points to the white sneakers sitting right in front of me, next to the closet door. "Maybe I should drive?" A big smile takes over her face.

We wait in a tiny waiting room for what seems like hours until Ryan walks into the room, a big smile on his face.

"Well?"

"I'm a dad!" he calls out. "You know, I was scared to hope after last time. I can't believe he's here." Ryan beams.

I hug him, patting him on the back. "Congratulations, dear brother."

"Come on." He calls us to enter the room after him.

Ryan's parents are already inside, sitting by the side of the bed. They get up when they see us enter, and I approach them for a hug.

"Ayala, these are Ryan's parents, Jennifer and James Blake." She says a polite hello. "Maya's parents are on their way. They live in Miami."

Maya is sitting in bed, her hair wild around her face. She's pale and looks exhausted, but a happy and tired smile adorns her face.

In her arms, I see a small package wrapped in a blanket. A small face peeks out, and I move closer to take a look.

This is the cutest and crinkliest thing I've ever seen. I stare at the tiny face. I have never seen a newborn baby. He's just so tiny.

"Want to hold him?" she asks, and I flinch. What do I know about babies?

She smiles. "Don't worry, he won't break."

My hands are almost shaking as she hands me the small package, and I hold him tightly in my arms. He certainly looks fragile.

The first thing I notice is the smell. An unfamiliar smell, a smell that I have no other way to define than the smell of a new person.

The baby's eyes are closed, and he makes tiny sounds. I don't hold back and run a finger over his cheek. The skin is soft and delicate, like fine paper. I don't know why, but the emotions rise in me at the sight of the tiny baby.

What if he was mine? I imagine a tiny face with huge blue eyes like Ayala's. I can imagine a baby with her. Our own family.

I glance at her. She stands there, her eyes wide and glistening. This is surprising to me. I thought she would be at least as excited as I was. Well, maybe a little less than me. Ryan is like a brother to me. But still, how can you not be enthusiastic about this incredibly cute baby?

I return him to his mother's arms. We say goodbye, giving the exhausted mother rest and time with her baby.

"Are you okay?" I ask Ayala when we reach the street outside. She hasn't spoken since we arrived.

Her mouth opens, then closes again. Like she's afraid to tell me something. I stop and take hold of her arm. "What?"

"You looked...happy." She looks down at the ground. "You looked amazing. A man holding a baby, soft and loving. That perfect moment. That's what you looked like. Perfect. And me? I'm broken. I can't ever be a mother."

"Ayala..." I pull her into my arms and kiss the top of her head. "We haven't talked about children. And I didn't ask you for a child tomorrow."

She takes a step back. "You don't understand."

"Let's talk about it at home? This is not a conversation to have on the street."

The drive home passes in silence. I dare not start this conversation on the way. Instead, it's better to use the time to think about what to say.

It felt good to hold that baby, but it's not like I ever gave it a thought before. I didn't even believe I could be in a relationship with someone, let alone want children. So this whole situation catches me by surprise.

Do I even want children? I think I'll want them someday. But not right now. So what does that mean? All these thoughts confuse me.

Ayala plays with her fingers next to me. It's bad. She always analyzes a situation and comes to the wrong conclusions. I just know she's doing it again.

When we get home, I make chamomile tea for both of us. We both need something soothing.

She sits on a stool at the kitchen island, waiting for me to start.

"I saw that the whole situation stressed you today. But there's no point in worrying. I wasn't even thinking about children this soon, and I don't think there's anything to talk about right now."

"Yes, we should," she protests. "You'll want children someday. Do you want to waste years of your life on a relationship that will lead nowhere?"

"Yes, I want! It's not a waste if I'm with the one I love." My voice rises. "I never had a serious relationship before you. I didn't think I would ever have one."

"You didn't think you would, but now you know what it's like. You can fall in love again. You can have it with someone else. Someone who is less broken than me. Someone who will give you what you want."

"I don't want anyone else," I mumble and run a hand through my hair. How do I explain this to her?

"There's something I didn't tell you," she says in a quiet voice. Her expression concerns me.

"I lost our child."

I feel like someone has punched me in the chest. What did she say? I get up and pace away from her. "What?"

"I was pregnant when Michael kidnapped me," she says with a lowered head. "I didn't know until they told me at the hospital after I lost the baby."

"You were pregnant? From me? How?"

"Probably from the time we had sex without a condom."

"But I bought you the pill. I saw you take it."

"It doesn't always work, as it turns out."

"Why didn't you tell me that you were pregnant?"

"I didn't know. And then, when I called you, you told me it was over and not to call again. I didn't think there was anything to talk about after that."

Fuck. I messed up in so many ways. "Was the miscarriage because of what happened?"

She nods. "The beatings caused a placental separation, the doctor said And they don't think I'll be able to get pregnant again because of the trauma to my uterus." Tears stream down her cheeks. "I can never give you children."

I rub my face with my hands. I could have had a baby, and now I never will? "Maya also had a miscarriage. And look at her now. She has a child."

"Maya didn't get kicked in the stomach over and over and repeatedly raped," Ayala says in a weak voice. "My body is broken."

I close my eyes. I can't imagine my life without her. It's not an option. "Can't you see I'm broken, too? I never thought I'd have someone to love before I met you. Someone who loved me. You're the only one I've ever wanted. I love you and your sharp broken corners. I need nothing else if I have you."

She sniffles. "You compromise too much for me."

"I don't compromise on anything. You're everything I need."

She stands and comes to me. "I don't want you to regret this decision in a few years."

"I won't regret a single day I have with you." I pull her to me, and our lips connect for a kiss.

CHAPTER 31

Ethan

I had no intention of going to my parents' house for the New Year's party. No intention whatsoever. But they sent an invitation, just like they do every year, and Ayala decided we should go. And so, here I am, in their house, greeting the guests. This time at least, I have Ayala to back me up.

I hold on to her like a lifeline every time my parents try to talk to me privately. They won't dare confront me in public, and I won't give them the opportunity to find me alone.

The rest of the guests stream in, most of them family members and some of them friends, reaching out to me from time to time to say hello. I like most of them, and we chat briefly.

Ayala tugs on my arm as she sees Olive and her parents come through the door. What are they doing here? Ah. I always forget that I met Olive through my mother, and our parents are friends. I go with her to the door to greet them and join Olive.

"Ayala." Olive hugs her when she sees us. How did it happen that I became second place? "Ethan, I didn't expect you'd be here."

"Ayala convinced me to accept the invitation," I mutter, and Olive rolls her eyes at me.

"This is your only family. You need to reconcile." She scolds me again.

"It's a lost cause. They hate me, and it will never change." I turn to Olive and change the subject. "So, Olive, how were the sales before the holiday? I didn't get your report this week."

"You got it all right. I sent it to you yesterday. There were a lot of deliveries this week. But I didn't want to talk about business in the middle of the part—" Her gaze freezes on something behind me, and I turn my head to look.

"No! Don't look." She pulls my arm. "She can't know I'm staring."

"Who?"

"The woman in the white suit," Olive whispers.

I bend down to tie my shoe and tilt my head back to see. A woman in a tailored white suit, with a precise haircut and a glass of champagne in her hand, is standing not far behind me. She's beautiful, and I don't remember seeing her before. Weird. My parents usually invite the same friends and family every year.

"I don't know her," I tell Olive after I'm done bending over the falsely loose laces. "Do you want me to go over there and see if she's interested?"

"No! are you insane? I'm not even sure if she's into women. I think so, but I'll bury myself in the ground if I'm wrong."

"I'm going to check." I ignore her faint protests and walk toward the mysterious woman.

"Hey." I shamelessly intrude on the woman's conversation with one of my cousins, extending my hand to her. "Ethan Wolf."

She shakes my hand, and a smile lights up her face. "I know who you are."

"I don't remember seeing you before."

"You surprise me, Wolf." There is an amused glint in her eyes. "We know each other."

"Really? I think I would remember someone who looks like you."

She laughs out loud. "I'm Amber."

I keep staring, my brain refusing to make the connection.

"Amber Wolf," she says.

My eyes widen. She's a Wolf? "Amber Wolf? Carol's daughter? The cute little cousin who came to stay with us when we were little?"

She nods. "Yeah, I guess I've grown a little."

"Wow! You look amazing. Where have you been hiding until now?"

"My parents sent me to school in Paris. I returned to New York recently."

"And you intend to stay in New York?"

"I haven't decided what I'll do. Sorry, I think I disappointed you. You tried to hit on me, didn't you."

"Oh, no. That wasn't my intention at all. I'm completely taken."

"Don't be embarrassed. I prefer women anyway."

I smile. "Actually, you just made my day. I have a stunning female friend who wanted to know if you were available."

She looks interested. "Stunning, you say? So who's your gorgeous friend?"

I nod toward Olive and Ayala with their heads bent together, whispering at the side of the room. "The woman in the blue dress."

"Introduce me," Amber says.

"Olive," I call her to come to us and introduce them. Within a minute, they're engrossed in lively conversation, and I return to Ayala.

"Well, I did my good deed for the day," I tell her.

"I haven't done mine yet," she replies. "I want you to make up with your parents."

"I've told you. That's a lost cause."

"I disagree. They're your only family. You still love them, or you wouldn't have come. And they still love you, or they wouldn't keep inviting you." She takes my hand. "Your father loves you too," she adds after I open my mouth to protest.

"We're in the middle of a holiday party."

"Well?"

"So I won't ruin the party by causing a scene."

"We won't ruin anything. We're just going to talk, not fight. Besides, what better place and time? They won't want a scene in the middle of their party either. So they'll respond in moderation."

"Ayala..."

"You know my parents messed up too. Big time. And I forgave them. They're human. They make mistakes. They didn't mean to do me harm. I'm sure yours didn't either."

"Okay, fine. But we'll wait for the party to end."

Ayala sits down at one of the side tables and drinks some champagne. I go straight to the whiskey and use the time to chat with the guests. I haven't seen some of them for a long time, and it's quite nice to catch up. It amazes me that most people don't ask about the incident. I wonder if they're just being polite or simply not interested. I assume polite. Although the incident didn't explode in New York with the same intensity as in San Francisco, those who know me have surely read the details. Two or three dared to ask about it, and I explained with as few words as possible. I also mentioned that Ayala will be working at Savee soon and would promote the app. Everyone expressed support and stated that they would be happy to help.

A light touch on my arm startles me. I turn around with a smile, sure that it's Ayala, only to discover my parents.

"Ethan," Mom says, nodding her head. "How are you?"

"Well, I'm sure you follow all the news, so you know I'm being sued." I don't like these pretenses.

"Ethan." She grasps my arm again. "It's not just a lawsuit. They say you murdered him."

"And you believe what they say?" I glance at my father, who's standing behind her with no expression on his face. "Or he does? You'll believe anything about me, right? I'm capable of anything. After all, I killed my sister, so what's one more person?"

"That's not what I said."

"That's exactly what you're saying. In your eyes, in his eyes. I can see what you think of me."

"That's not true. You're our son, and we love you."

I scoff. "I don't believe you."

"Maybe you'll go back to Olive again? You were such a beautiful couple. Stay away from this woman who got you in trouble. It will help. It will benefit you in court if they see you're staying away from her and you're leading an orderly life."

"I don't believe you just said that. And after you already know that Olive is gay." Mom cringes a little as I raise my voice, but I'm enjoying this. I want them to be embarrassed.

"Well, it's just a phase. She'll get over it. You were lovely together, and she suited you so well."

"A phase? You cross every line. Mom, Olive and I are friends, and that's what we'll always be. I never slept with her. Do you understand that? I love Ayala."

Dad scowls and steps closer. "That woman only brings trouble. You need to stay away from her. Ever since you met, trouble has been chasing you. You almost died because of her, and now you're accused of murder. So you think you're in love. It will pass. Move on. She's not right for you."

"You really need to take that back," I say in a threatening tone.

Ayala finds this moment to come to stand by my side. She's

had a confrontation with them before, but her condition right now isn't stable, and I'm worried.

"Mr. and Mrs. Wolf," she says. "I wanted Ethan to reconcile with you because I believe there's only one family. I was sure he was just exaggerating when he claimed you wouldn't forgive him, but I heard what you just said, and I'm no longer sure I want him to reconcile with you. I love him, and we're a couple, whether or not you like it. The only one who can tell me to go is Ethan." She looks between the two of them, then fixes her blue eyes on mine before turning back to them. "You'll have to accept me or neither of us."

I see her love for me reflected in her eyes. How can she not see how strong she is?

I interlace her fingers with mine, and she pulls me away from them.

CHAPTER 32

Ayala

T oday is my first day at Savee.
The conversation with Paul Sheridan was wonderful. We met right after Christmas, and I liked him right away. His passion for helping and his dedication to making the world better amazes me.

I presented him with several ideas, and my fear that Ethan was prompting him to like whatever I suggested evaporated. Paul has been direct and honest. He has no problem rejecting anything he doesn't like and being enthusiastic about what he does.

Right after the briefing with Paul, I sit down and start planning. One of my first tasks is to plan a large recruitment campaign.

There isn't enough money. I go through the reports that Paul shared with me, and that's the first thing I realize there are a lot of good ideas here, but not enough revenue to put them into action.

"What are these?" I point and turn the screen to Paul so he can see what I'm talking about.

"Transfers of money into the company."

"Yes, I can see that. What I meant to ask is, why is the name of the donor not mentioned? These are transfers of millions every month."

"Ah. These are transfers from Ethan Wolf."

"Wow. That's a lot of money."

"Yes." Paul catches my eye. "You probably know the story. When Ethan founded the company, he quickly realized that to make Savee a reality, he needed more money. He hired me to manage Savee so he could build his business empire to fund it. Every month he transfers a large part of his income here as a donation. That's how he makes sure we can keep expanding all the time. We started as a application for people considering suicide, and now we handle almost every issue—from domestic abuse to neighbor disputes."

I nod. I knew the story. I just didn't think it was of such magnitude.

"After I finish with this recruitment campaign, the first issue I want to promote is the closest to my heart. Family abuse. Support for abused women, and especially early detection of men with the potential for violence."

Paul looks at me with interest. "What do you mean, early detection?"

"Men don't start beating their wives just like that. There are early signs. There are patterns of behavior. We can come up with a program to detect them, even before they enter a relationship, and treat them. We can teach them."

"That's an interesting idea."

"I believe that if we detect them at an early age, such as in high school, they'll cooperate willingly to learn how to conduct themselves in a relationship. We'll carry out tests to identify those at the highest risk, and they can receive psychological support along the way."

I drift into my speech. "My husband, Michael, didn't start as an abusive partner either. The signs were there, but I didn't know how to read them. We need to teach women that. We should hold free workshops for women on these early signs. What to expect.

What to do. The police won't get involved if a woman comes in and claims her husband is preventing her from seeing friends, but that's a bright red sign. They need a place where they can turn to and get help."

"I like this direction. Sit with our creative team and design a campaign. Let's see where it goes and run it."

"And the recruitment campaign?"

"Can you run both at the same time?"

I nod and sink into the work. I enjoyed working at the magazine, but here, there's a sense of a mission. I feel good knowing I'm influencing and contributing.

Deep into the morning, I raise my head to a knock on the door. A messenger stands at the door of my office, holding a huge bouquet in front of his face. A smile spreads across mine. It's probably from Ethan.

"Can you put them on the desk?" I ask.

"I was hoping to get a thank you, too," the messenger says, and my eyes widen.

"Ethan!" I leap up from my seat into his arms. "What are you doing here?"

"You know this is my company, right?" He laughs. "Did you think I wouldn't check in to see how you're doing on your first day?" He raises an eyebrow and examines me.

I kiss him, and the center of my body awakens. My body clings to him more without me even realizing it.

He moans into my mouth. "You're starting something that you can't finish."

"Who said I can't finish? I thought this was your company..." I bite his lower lip teasingly.

"It's lunchtime now, and you need a break." His tongue teases back. "Come on." He takes off with quick steps, and I follow him to the other side of the floor. On the door of a corner office is a sign, "Ethan Wolf, CEO," and he opens the door and goes inside.

"Is this your office?" I look around. There's a large desk with a desktop computer, two chairs in front of the desk and another chair behind it, plus a library of books spread along the entire length of the wall. On the side of the room is a cart filled with bottles of alcohol and glasses that look expensive and a black corner sofa.

"This room looks like something from a TV series and not like an office where people work." I admire the pictures of New York hanging on the walls.

"I'm not here much. I normally work out of the Wolf Industries headquarters. But do you really want to talk about the office now?"

No. I don't want to. The pulse between my legs increases, reminding me of what I really want. He locks the door, closes the curtain to give us privacy, and approaches me with predatory steps. His eyes never leave mine.

He swings me up and places me on the desk, then stands between my knees.

I feel strong today, and that strength fills me with courage. My hand goes to the waistband of his pants, and I open it, roll down his pants, and release his cock.

I get off the desk and kneel in front of him.

"Ayala." He lifts my head. "What are you doing?"

"I thought you'd figure it out on your own."

"I don't want to do something you're not ready for."

"Don't ruin it," I tell him. He makes me doubt myself, and it's not good for me right now. I want to stay brave. He falls silent.

I curl my fist around his hard cock. The skin is smooth and warm to the touch, and I slide my hand from the base to the tip.

I take a deep breath, and my tongue licks the tip. He's panting. His breathing gets louder, and that encourages me. My hand continues to complete the action, gently wrapping and pressing.

I put him in my mouth, wrap my lips around him, and suck.

I'm surprised to find that I like it. It feels good to please him. I put him deep into my mouth, being careful not to trigger the gag reflex. I want nothing to bring back memories I want to forget.

His moans of pleasure cause the throbbing between my legs and the wetness in my underwear to increase. I pin my legs together, and the pressure only rises.

He doesn't touch me at all. His hands drop to his sides, and I can tell he's afraid of doing something wrong. Can I come without him touching me? My hips press together harder as I draw him deeper into my mouth and suck.

"Ayala," he whispers through the moans. "I'm close." He pulls me away from him. "I don't want to come in your mouth."

My cheeks are hot, and I try to cool them with my hands. God, he's so beautiful like that, with his eyes half closed with desire.

He lifts me back to the desk. Luckily I wore a skirt today. Within seconds, he rolls it up my thighs, and his fingers are roaming my flesh. I throw my head back as he finds my sensitive spot and massages it.

"Ouch." Something sharp stabs me as I lean back. Ethan reaches behind me and moves the objects aside. Some things fall noisily to the floor. Not quite the tidy office from television anymore.

"Now," I demand. I need him inside me now, strong and fast. And that's exactly what he does. The panties come off, and he's inside me.

"Oh, yes," I blurt out in a voice that is a little too loud. "Shit, someone's going to hear us."

"I don't care," he wheezes out with a heavy breath.

Happiness fills me that he's no longer gentle with me, no longer afraid to hurt me. I feel normal.

It's going to be quick for both of us. The arousal is building inside me at breakneck speed. Ethan picks up the pace, his head buried in my neck and his hot breaths flowing over me.

"I'm going to come," I call out as my body tightens around him. I push his shoulders, trying to push him away because it's coming too strong. I can't bear it.

"Wait," I call, as I try to get the shaking in my body to cease, but he doesn't stop, and I'm carried up and up and smash into him again.

"Fuck, I can feel you coming around me. It's so strong," he whispers in my ear. "It's amazing." He moans one last time before I feel him fill me with his hot liquid.

We lay panting on the desk. "I think I came twice," I say in amazement.

He laughs. "Next time, we'll go for three."

Suddenly, it embarrasses me a little. I let myself get carried away on the first day of work. Sex on the desk? Damn it. But it was so good. So...normal.

"Are you okay with what we did?" He studies my face. "I see you're not. Shit. I knew I should have stopped you."

Reading my thoughts as always. "No, I'm perfectly fine. I'm not sorry. I enjoyed pleasing you. It's just that this is my first day at the office..."

"The boss approved," he says with a smile. "You fulfilled a long-awaited fantasy for me. Sex in the office."

"You haven't had sex at work before?"

"I don't bring women I go out with to the office, and I've never slept with someone who works for me. I mean, until now. So the answer is no." He thinks about it for a moment. "Looks like we both broke the rules today."

He straightens my skirt, tucking strands of hair behind my ears. "I have a feeling I'll be working from this office more often in the near future."

My first campaign is about to be released, and today I'm giving a presentation to the management. I asked Ethan not to come. I don't want anyone to be afraid to speak their mind just because he's in the room. I know that his presence intimidates some employees.

"The campaign will focus on television commercials, ads on the internet, and lectures for teenagers," I say. "I'm trying something different, and we've secured lecturers and talents who are leaders of public opinion on various social media platforms."

One manager raises his hand. "I think it's better to use someone who is professional and not a model or a singer." I expected some objections, and I sigh internally.

"We want to create a buzz. We want youth to want to come to these lectures, even if it's just to see their favorite icon, but along the way, they'll also pick up some of our topics. I don't care if he or she is an amazing lecturer or not. I want our topics to reach as many ears as possible. I'm looking for exposure. Taking a model with a million followers on TikTok will bring us more audience than the best lecturer in the field at these ages," I insist and show them the key topics in the lecture.

"We created an internet test designed to identify at-risk teenagers of both sexes. We will do the test during the lecture. And you can do it through the app from anywhere. I hope that with the help of the lectures, we can convince them to install Savee, take the test, and also use the application."

"And what if the test reveals that the boy or girl is at risk?"

"This is where the bulk of our budget will be invested," I explain. "We want to provide workshops and treatment to those whom the tests find to be at risk. Anger management workshops, relationship counselors, treatment, and psychological monitoring, either through us or within the community. For free. The bigger the budget, the more options we can offer."

"And if the boy doesn't want to go?" someone asks.

I shake my head. "We can't force anyone. It's not a punishment. We can only try to convince them. We'll explain why it's important and hope they'll want to treat themselves. Even if we reach just twenty percent of the identified youth, that's still a twenty percent success rate." I see nods at the table.

"What are the costs?"

I present the numbers and the expansion plan. "We'll start with a pilot program in New York. We'll see the responsiveness of the youth community and what needs to be improved. What the youth respond to better. Then we'll revise the program. I hope it will be so successful that we'll receive budgets from the government to continue."

A murmur rises in the room, and I raise my hands to silence everyone. "I know it's a big budget for a pilot. Mr. Wolf agreed to contribute a large portion of the amount. I plan to raise the rest through the recruitment campaign, which I presented earlier, and which will go up at the same time."

I sip from my glass of water. "In addition, we'll hold a fundraising party, which will be held soon." I smile and get a few in return from those before me.

"The entire budget will be raised from scratch and will not subtract from existing projects." I know it's important that I use new money for the project. No one will want to give up a running project for something experimental. I see the nods and know I've succeeded. The voting begins, and I find out I was right.

"Ayala." Paul catches me on my way back to my office.

"You have permission to run the campaigns," he says. "I just wanted to tell you, you did a great job. The committee was very impressed with your skills."

I thank him with a smile and enter my office, closing the door behind me.

"Yes!" I shoot my hands in the air in victory. There is nothing like being able to make an impression with the first campaign in the company. I only hope it will also bring the desired results.

I click on the green button, and the advertising campaign starts.

CHAPTER 33

Ethan

Another article about Savee's campaign is in the newspaper this morning, this time with a picture of Ayala. She's making waves. I skim through the text quickly.

You must have heard about the new campaign that calls on teenagers to come to lectures on spousal violence. Many celebrities from the youth world, and on behalf of the Savee company, owned by Wolf Industries, will be conducting the lectures. The company has been working against violence since its inception and treats rape victims. During the lectures, the participants will be asked to take a test that assesses their level of risk. Those diagnosed with a high-risk level are entitled to free workshops and support. Savee hopes for a high response rate.

Ayala Beckett, who leads this important and innovative campaign, is herself a victim of domestic violence and knows the issue intimately.

"I hope youth will understand that they can help themselves and help others. I was a victim of severe violence, and I would have been thrilled if I had a place like Savee to turn to."

"Why would the youth share private information with you? You can report them to the police."

"All the information shared in the application is protected under a confidentiality agreement and will not be shared with anyone. Our goal is not to arrest anyone. We are not aiming this campaign at people who are already in a violent situation. There are other solutions for that. What we are trying to do, for the first time, is to prevent cases in advance. I believe no one wants to be a victim, or worse than that, violent. With proper treatment and proper guidance, we can prevent many of these cases. We offer our solutions free of charge and in confidence. No one needs to know you are being treated."

Ayala enters the kitchen just as I finish reading, and I hand her the newspaper.

"This campaign is amazing. Innovative," I tell her as she skims over the article.

"We still lack a lot of the funds needed to support it. I need to make more noise."

"You don't understand how big this is." She has been so engrossed in work for the past two weeks that I hardly see her. I press the TV remote, switch to one of the news channels, and rewind. She looks at me with a puzzled expression. "Have a little patience. You'll see soon." I wait in front of the screen for a few minutes until the piece I wanted begins, then press Play.

I just watch her, saying nothing, while she stares at the screen and slowly realizes what it's about.

A crowd of people raids Michael's parents' property. Demonstrations continued for days and only got bigger and bigger. The protestors are calling them criminals and murderers and asking for the case against us to be dropped.

They hold additional demonstrations at the doors of the courthouse, also calling for the judge to dismiss the case. *"Disgrace,"*

one protestor calls out. "It's a disgrace, the killer blames the victim,
and the court system allows it."

The article goes on and on, and I click on mute. "Not enough
noise?"

"I didn't know there were still protests about the civil case.
What does Ryan say about that?"

"He thinks it works in our favor. People aren't blind. And the
Summers hear the talk on the street. He thinks it will tilt the case
in our favor."

"The continued hearing on our motion is next month, and
I've been so immersed in work, I think I suppressed it. What if
you get convicted of a murder you didn't commit?"

"Ayala. Remember, this is not a criminal case. And the authorities haven't reopened the matter or charged me with anything.
The Summers just want to destroy me."

"But they could succeed. The Wolf name will get destroyed if
you are convicted."

"I won't be. There's no evidence to support their version
except for my fabricated confession." That confession could bring
me down, but there's no way I'm telling her that. I wanted to save
her when I gave that statement, and I don't regret it.

"Tomorrow is the weekend," I say, "and I'm looking forward
to spending time with you. I can't remember what you look like
anymore. You've become busier than me."

She laughs. "I'm in doubt of that. But I'm having fun. I enjoy
thinking that I might have a positive influence in this world." She
takes a step in my direction. "And thank you for agreeing to
donate all the money to my project."

"When the idea is good, it's good." I kiss her one last time
before we leave for the office. "And how are you going to thank
me?" I give her a playful smile.

She smiles back, and my cock hardens. We leave the building
together, and Ayala gets into the back seat of the car. I'm about to

go in right after her, but then I see someone standing on the sidewalk as if waiting for me.

"Sorry, I just remembered I need to do something," I say to Ayala and close the door. I wait until my driver drives off, leaving me on the sidewalk.

"Lena Castle."

"Ethan Wolf," she says in a sarcastic tone, and I tilt my head.

"How can I help you?"

"Can we go up to talk in private?"

"I'm on my way to the office, and I'm running late. Say what you have to say."

"I think it's better if we do it in private," she insists.

I don't move an inch, and she gives in and sighs. "I'm pregnant."

Fucking hell. No way. "Okay, what does this have to do with me?" The mask of indifference comes over my face.

"It's yours."

"It can't be mine. I used a condom. I always use a condom."

"Condoms are not always reliable. I only slept with you." The look on her face is as cold as mine.

"You're a liar. I don't know what you're trying to get from me, but you won't succeed. Do a paternity test first. Until then, don't come here again." An offended expression comes over her face. I think there are even tears. For a slight moment, I feel sorry for her, but then I remind myself she's known to be a conniving liar. She slept with someone else because it can't be mine.

"Send me the test results." I turn around and go back to the parking garage to get one of my cars. I clench my hand into a fist, the nails digging into the flesh, but I keep my emotions concealed.

Only when the car door closes behind me, do I allow myself to let it out.

"Fuck!" I scream, pounding the steering wheel with my fists.

Why did she turn up? It can't be mine. Just can't be. I'll make her take a test, and that'll be it. She'll have to crawl back into the hole she came out of and leave me alone. No one needs to know about it.

I shake off the emotions from the unexpected encounter and set off.

How did I think I wanted children if the idea of this woman being pregnant turns my stomach?

I imagine Ayala holding a baby with blue eyes. Not repugnant at all. It's just Lena. I only want Ayala, with or without children. I don't need anyone else.

And I decide to make another stop on the way.

CHAPTER 3

Ayala

"Hey, Ryan," I answer. He rarely calls me directly.

"Good morning. Do you know where Ethan is? I called, and he didn't answer. Is he with you, by any chance?"

"No. We were supposed to drive to the office together, but he forgot something and went back." Should I be worried? He always answers Ryan.

"Well, I wanted to tell you both at the same time, but I'll tell you first. It's his problem if he didn't answer," Ryan says. "The Summers dropped the lawsuit against you."

"What?" I almost shout, and all heads in the office turn to me. "What do you mean?"

"All the demonstrations helped more than expected. They couldn't leave their house for several days because of the crowds of protestors. They were afraid. I'd say, in the end, the desire to destroy Ethan wasn't worth the hate they got from the public. Everyone's screaming about them knowing their son was an abuser while they did nothing. There's even a rumor his father got fired."

215

"Ryan, this is amazing! You don't know how happy you've made me. I was so scared."

"I know. That's why I'm telling you, even though Ethan himself hasn't heard it yet. Look, that doesn't guarantee they won't decide to sue again in a few years. But at least for now, you're out of the storm."

"It's a gigantic relief." It's like I have new air to breathe. "And how is Maya? And Dean? We haven't seen you for some time."

"Dean is adorable. He doesn't let us sleep much, but he's too cute to care. Maya is amazing with him. She has so much patience. I just adore her."

"I love how you speak of her. It's so beautiful."

"I'm tough on the outside but a romantic at heart." He laughs.

I thank him and hang up. Great news.

Time goes by crazy fast, and my mood is uplifted after this morning's news. I'm briefing the employees about the initial results we got from the first lectures. All the numbers are good. There was a high response from the celebrity lecturers, as I predicted, but not enough teens filled out the questionnaires.

I'm showing the team some ideas on how to improve on that and letting them make their own suggestions when a secretary knocks on the conference room door.

"Miss Beckett, someone is waiting for you at reception."

"Who?"

"She didn't give a name. She insists on talking to you."

"Be right there." I show the last slide in the presentation before I let everyone go back to work. Who could be looking for me here in the office? A journalist trying to ambush me? Maybe they heard about the case being dropped. I've done a few interviews recently, but they're always pre-arranged. I'm not doing surprise interviews. Determined to kick her out of here, I stride to the entrance.

At the reception, standing with her back to me, is a woman with long blonde hair dressed in a dark blue suit. She doesn't look familiar. I approach, and she turns to me.

She looks at me with narrowed eyes. She is a beautiful young woman. Her face looks vaguely familiar, but I'm pretty sure we haven't met. Is she some famous personality? I'm not big on celebrities.

"Hi, I'm Ayala Beckett. How can I help you?"

"I know who you are," she says in a bitter tone. "Can we talk in private?" She tilts her head. "Unless you're like Ethan and want to talk here, in front of everyone. I don't care either way. I have nothing to lose."

What does Ethan have to do with her? Tension builds in my muscles. "Let's go to my office." I gesture with my hand toward the hallway, and she follows.

After I close the door, I face her. "So what do you want to tell me that you would take the trouble to come all the way here, Miss...?" What could she want?

"Castle. My name is Lena Castle," she says in a high-pitched tone and looks at me as if the name should tell me exactly who she is. The name means nothing to me. I look at her blankly.

"He didn't tell you about me? Why am I not surprised?" She paces the room, muttering to herself. "Two months ago, Ethan was at a fundraising event for children. You know, the one with the vice president in attendance?"

I narrow my eyes. If she's trying to impress me, it won't work.

"Ethan was alone, and he hit on me. Couldn't keep his hands off me." Her gushing tone makes me sick. "I slept with him. And now I'm carrying his child." She smiles and caresses her nonexistent pregnant belly.

My world starts spinning.

She's the blonde from the party. The pain I felt when I saw her picture then is nothing compared to what I feel now. She's pregnant. She'll give him a child. The only thing I can't give him. I want to curl up into a ball and hide under the desk. But I'll be damned if I let her see my pain.

"What do you want from me? I'm not Ethan."

"You're dating him. I just wanted to give you a heads-up. He was happy when I told him that he's going to have a child soon. You should look for another sugar daddy."

"Sugar Daddy?" My plan to remain indifferent crumbles as the anger seeps through the cracks.

She looks around as if examining the place. "Do you live with him? Do you work for him? He designed your life. Looks like you made a good deal. You open your legs for all of this."

"Get out of here," I can't help demanding and raise my voice. "Whatever it is you want, go get it from someone else."

She leaves my office, a satisfied smile on her face. I break down. She got what she wanted.

How long has he known about this? Why didn't he tell me? Fuck. Why is everything so hard all the time?

I shake my head. She came here to play with my mind. To make me doubt our relationship. I won't give it to her. Not before I talk to him.

I call him, but he doesn't answer. It's not that uncommon that he doesn't answer during business hours, but it still frustrates me. It's better if we talk face to face.

For a moment, I consider leaving and going to his office, but a look at my busy schedule proves that it's not possible. I have work to do. I won't let one delusional woman ruin my day. It will just have to wait for this evening.

CHAPTER 35

Ethan

"**D**o you have anything more special?" I ask the saleswoman, who's already bringing out the fourth tray of rings. Nothing here looks like what I'm looking for. They're too ordinary, not suitable for someone like her.

"Sotheby's is having an auction this week. They have some special rings. You should check them out." She sees my troubled expression and offers me an idea she probably shouldn't have offered.

My hand goes to my pocket to take out the phone, but it's not there. I probably forgot it in the car. Shit.

I thank the woman who might get fired for the tip she just gave me and reward her generously before I leave.

I find the phone in my car and see that both Ryan and Ayala tried to reach me. I'll have to deal with it later.

I look through the items for sale at Sotheby's, and one ring catches my attention.

It's a ring with a square blue diamond, weighing three point twenty-four carats, accompanied by two smaller diamonds with a drop polish. The price is estimated at a couple of million dollars.

High price. But the ring is exactly what I was looking for. Special. The bluish color reminds me of her eyes. She deserves something special. She deserves the universe.

I call the gallery and make a higher offer if they sell me the ring now and send it to my home. I'm not a patient man.

After the ring issue is out of the way, I send Ayala a message that I'm in meetings and won't be available for a few more hours. I don't want her to worry but also not to suspect that I've been out of the office, looking at rings.

Then I call Ryan to check what he needs from me. After he updates me with the good news, I drive to the office. I have a lot of work to do. The news that the lawsuit has been dropped could not have come at a better time. Although I pretended I was fine and wasn't worried, the possibility of being formally charged concerned me and occupied a large part of my thoughts during the day.

Now I can propose to Ayala with a clear head. We can celebrate twice—the case being dropped and the engagement.

If she agrees.

What if she refuses? Maybe I should take her somewhere fancy and propose there? My idea to propose to her in our home seems lame to me. Should I put out candles? Decorate?

It's just nervous butterflies. It will be fine. Ayala doesn't like pomp and splendor but intimacy. That's part of what I love about her so much. She'll say yes, and everything will be fine.

When the evening comes, I'm sitting on the sofa waiting for her, my legs bouncing with nervous energy. I avoided her all day because I knew she would read me like an open book. But the serious expression on her face when she walks in has me holding off on my plans. I expected that after Ryan's update, she would be on top of the world. She was more stressed about this lawsuit than I was. But there's no happiness in her posture or her face. She's as serious as the winter outside.

"Hi," I say hesitantly.

"Hi." She tosses her handbag on the counter and takes a bottle of water from the fridge, not looking at me.

I get up to approach her.

"Something happened?"

"You tell me." She looks at me with no smile on her face. She raises the bottle to her lips and sips.

I want to put my ring on her finger, then kiss and fuck her unconscious. But I begin to understand that today that won't be happening.

"They dropped the case," I say, trying to figure out what's going on here. "I thought you'd be happy."

"I am. It's the best news I've heard in a while."

"So why don't you seem happy to me?"

"Oh, I don't know. Do you have something else to tell me?"

Could it be that she found out about the ring? But how? And why does she look angry? "I wanted us to celebrate the good news." I point to the bottle of champagne waiting in an ice bucket in the living room. *And also our engagement.*

"So, everything is normal?"

"Yes," I say, not sure what she expects to hear from me.

"I can't believe I'm saying this, but I'm going to sleep in the apartment downstairs. Call me when you decide to tell the truth." She collects her bag and keys and turns to leave. I hurry to catch her.

"Don't walk out on me. Explain to me what's happened. How can I respond if I don't know what the hell is wrong?"

She breaks free from my grip and narrows her eyes. "You're so unwilling to tell me about it you don't even understand what I'm talking about?" She tilts her head, waiting for an answer from me, but I still don't understand. "A blonde named Lena Castle came to visit me today. Ring a bell?"

Fucking Lena. I will kill that woman. How did she get to Ayala?

"What did she tell you? Whatever it is, it's all lies."

"She said she's pregnant, and it's from you."

"I don't know if she's pregnant, but it can't be from me. She's trying to dump it on me. She has all kinds of false hopes. I threw her out."

"But you slept with her?"

Is she going to make me say that? I nod reluctantly. "Once. After the party, when I was trying to prove to everyone and myself that I was fine and could live without you."

"You also slept with me once without a condom, and I got pregnant."

"I used a condom with her." And I didn't come either, but I don't tell her that.

"You forgot it with me. Maybe it happened to you with her too?"

"No. There was a condom, and she's not pregnant by me."

"And what if she is? What if the condom broke and you didn't notice? She'll give you the child you want." Ayala's voice is quiet now.

"I want nothing from her except for her to stay away from me!"

"I don't understand. You want children. Children, you won't get from me. This is your chance."

"I don't want a child. Not just any child. I want *your* child. Don't you understand? You're the one I want. If it can't happen, then I'm okay with it. I still won't want a child from someone other than you."

"But you are going to have a child with her. Are you planning to deny the child?"

"No. If the child is mine, he or she will get everything they need from me, and I will be the child's father. But I want nothing to do with her."

Ayala lowers her head. "You meant to hide it from me."

"No, I didn't think there was anything to hide, and I still don't. She'll do a test, and if she's even pregnant, the child won't be mine, and the matter will be over. Why do you have to obsess over it before it's necessary?"

"It doesn't matter if it's yours or not," she cries. "The thing is, you didn't mean to share this with me! You don't see me as a partner. You don't share with me what's going on in your life."

She storms toward the bedroom. "I need to be alone. I don't want to stay here right now."

Shit. When we moved to New York in a hurry, I forgot about the whole second apartment thing. I didn't think she would ever ask to sleep away from me, and I didn't prepare the apartment as I promised. "Don't go," I call, and she raises an eyebrow at me. "I'll go. Stay."

Please ask me to stay. I try to convey my thoughts to her as if she can hear them. But she says nothing as I collect my keys and coat and leave.

How can she think I don't see her? I see only her. She floods my thoughts every day, all day. I want to share my life with her. I want to protect her and keep her safe. My hand touches the small box in my pocket. She must be mine.

I want to go out drinking with Ryan right now, but he's consumed with Maya and the baby, and I don't want to bother him. After a short deliberation with myself, I decide not to go to the pub alone either. Instead, I buy a bottle of whiskey and sit on a bench in Central Park, deliberately choosing a dark area so as not to attract attention. People pass by me. Some glance at the strange guy sitting on the bench at night in the middle of winter, and some hurry past, afraid to make eye contact.

An hour later, I no longer feel the cold. I'm warm and

comfortable, but I know it's not good. The heat is an illusion. I get up and decide to rent a room at the nearest hotel before I lose my fingers to frostbite.

"I'm sorry, sir, but without a means of payment, I can't give you a room," the clerk insists.

"Call the manager. They know me here." Why the hell did my phone have to die?

"Again, I'm sorry, sir, but it's late. I can't wake up the manager in the middle of the night. If you don't have a credit card, I'll have to ask you to leave."

I see how he looks at me. He can smell the alcohol and thinks I'm a homeless drunk. Not far from the truth, though. I have nowhere to go, and I am drunk.

"I'll make sure this hotel goes out of business." I raise my voice, and one worker turns his head to me. Damn, I'm drunk and losing control. I need to leave before the situation gets worse and something happens that I'll regret tomorrow.

I only have my keys and a dead phone. I stare at the keys.

The keys.

I can sleep in the office.

CHAPTER 36

Ayala

T he world looks different after a night without him. I miss him and have to remind myself why I wanted him gone yesterday. His phone is off, and I assume the battery must be dead. I decide to go down to the apartment below and talk to him.

The sign hanging on the apartment door reads "Benson," and that confuses me. Am I on the wrong floor? I knock, and an unknown man opens the door.

"May I help you?"

"Oh, I think I'm confused," I say. "Do you live here?"

"For about a year," he answers. "Why are you asking?"

"I thought the apartment would be empty."

"Ah." A look of understanding comes over his face. "Did you come to see the apartment? I'm sorry, but it's irrelevant. The owner told me he wanted to end the lease at the end of the year, but he didn't send the cancellation notice, and I renewed it. So I have another year here."

He closes the door behind him, and I break down. Go to hell, Ethan! There is no apartment? What else did you lie to me about?

Maybe it's all been one big pretense. I can't handle all this now. I don't even have anywhere to go.

I call my only friend here. "Olive."

"Ayala. Come on. I love you, but why on Saturday morning? Let me sleep," she moans in a hoarse voice. "This is the only day I don't need to get up early."

"Can I come to stay with you for a while?" I ask, my voice shaking as I try to hold back the tears.

"What's happened? Are you okay?"

"I'm okay, but I need somewhere to stay until I find my own place."

"You're always welcome here, but what happened with Ethan?"

"I'll tell you when I get there." I hang up and rush to pack some things in a large suitcase. My closet is quite full. So different than my days at Lunis. There are dresses, shoes, blouses, pants, and even jewelry Ethan bought me. I only take enough clothes for a few days. If I take more, it will be final.

I still have hope.

"Ayala." Olive hugs me tightly in the doorway of her apartment. "Come in."

I drop my bag at the entrance and flop down on her couch. "So, how's things with Amber going?"

"You know, slow but steady. Is this an attempt to distract me from what's going on with you?"

Yes. "No," I reply. "I'm fine."

"If everything is so fine, what are you doing in my apartment, in the morning, with a suitcase? Where's Ethan?"

"I don't know where he is," I answer honestly. "He didn't bother to tell me after I found out he lied to me. Twice."

"Okay." She gets up from the sofa slowly. "I think this calls for some alcohol, but since it's so early in the morning, we'll settle for hot chocolate."

I watch her go to the kitchen and prepare the drinks. She has an amazing home, huge by New York standards. I have visited here several times, and I'm still impressed every time. There is always something new, new curtains, a new rug, a new something. Olive is constantly redecorating. She designed the apartment down to the last detail. And I know that unlike Ethan's penthouse, which was decorated by some master designer, Olive's house has been designed only by her hands. She is so talented.

I take a few minutes to compose myself before she returns and serves me the hot drink.

"Come on, spill."

I hesitate because it's all so personal. And she is Ethan's friend, after all. But I can't expect her to welcome me without telling her anything about what happened.

"Do you remember when I was in San Francisco, and Ethan was seen at a party with a blonde woman?"

"Yes. Lena Castle. I know her."

"She visited me yesterday morning."

"Bitch. I told Ethan that was a huge mistake and that it was going to hurt you and bite him in the ass. She only brings trouble." Olive puts her hand on my thigh. "But really, there was nothing between them. He never stopped loving you."

"They slept together," I point out.

Olive frowns in response. "What did she want? To tell you how much he prefers her over you? Because that's clearly not true."

"No. She wanted to tell me she was pregnant with his child."

Olive covers her mouth with her hand. "No!"

"Yes. At least that's what she claims."

"So you left him?"

"I... Yes. No." I don't want to leave him. "I waited for him to tell me about it. But he preferred to leave me out of the loop and hide it."

"It's difficult to tell the woman you love such a thing," she says. "I'm sure he regrets sleeping with her."

"He said he didn't tell me because he was sure it wasn't his. He sent her to do a paternity test."

"Okay. That's good. If it's not his, you'll continue as usual, won't you?"

"You don't understand. I knew he slept with her. It hurts, but I can live with it. After all, we weren't together. If she's pregnant by him, we'll deal with it. But he wasn't going to tell me. Something that has the potential to change our entire lives, and he didn't think I had the right to know."

"He's very protective of you."

"If protecting me means he doesn't see me as an equal, then I don't want it. This woman said he was my sugar daddy. And I think there might be something to what she said." A tear runs down my cheek, and I wipe it away.

"Sugar daddy? Where do you get this nonsense?"

"Look at us! He gives me money, a place to live, a job. And in return, I sleep with him. Isn't that the definition of a sugar daddy?"

"You're a couple! It's not the same."

"We aren't a couple if I'm not equal to him. If he lies to me and hides things from me. A couple shares things with each other."

"What else did he lie to you about?"

I tell her about the tenant I found in the apartment below. "He never kept the apartment for me. The guy who lives there continued the lease for another year."

"Ugh, Ethan," she grumbles. "I apologize on his behalf. I don't know what's going on with him. I have no excuses."

"You don't need to make excuses on his behalf. That's not why I'm here." I smile at her. "I wanted a place to gather my thoughts, and it turns out I don't have an apartment to do that."

She twists her mouth again. "Well, you can stay here as long as you want. What are you going to do?"

"I don't know what to do, Olive." My voice breaks.

"Do you want to be with him?"

I nod. "I love him. From the moment we met."

"He loves you. I'm sure of it. I can see it in everything he does. He's crazy about you."

"But maybe love isn't enough."

She shakes her head. "I don't believe that. A love like yours must be enough. Otherwise, what's left for us in this world?" She leans in and gives me a hug. "I going to call him," she says.

"I already tried. His phone is dead. I don't know where he is."

"Okay, so we'll let him come to us. He can't be without you for long." She laughs.

This is true. I can't be without him, either.

We put a chick flick on the TV, and I try to dismiss the thoughts that scare me so much. That maybe it's over between us

CHAPTER 37

Ethan

"Ayala! No!!" I scream when I see her lifeless body under another man.

Blood.

There's blood everywhere. It flows from her onto the floor and out of the room. I follow it down the hall to the bathroom.

No. Not the bathroom... The door opens slowly, making a terrifying squeaking sound as I approach.

Drip. Drip. The sound of running water makes me shiver. I want to turn and run away, not see what's inside, but my legs carry me on their own. I can't stop staring at the red puddle of water and blood.

The dead woman in the bathtub opens her big blue eyes.

I scream.

My lashes flicker, and my eyes open, but I squint as I try to get used to the dim light in the room and regulate my heavy breathing.

Luckily it's Saturday, and no one can see the big boss crying like a baby on the couch in the office.

How did I get into this situation? Why am I here instead of in my bed? I can't sleep without her.

Oh yes, I stuck my cock into another woman. Why did I have to do that? Fuck. It was a mistake from the first moment, and now this mistake could cost me the love of my life. I can't lose Ayala. I just can't. I tried to let her go, let her find someone less screwed up than me. I tried not to hurt her but failed even this.

I go back to our apartment, hoping we can talk and work things out. I open the door, waiting to see her beautiful face, but she's not here. Super fuck. I have to talk to her. Explain. She's my whole life.

On the way out, the mirror calls me to stop. I can't go out like this. My hair is messy and wild, and my clothes are wrinkled. Dark circles show my lack of sleep. Why would she want me when I look like this?

I take a quick shower and dress in clean clothes, shave and run my hand over my smooth face. I can't remember the last time I had a clean, shaved face. This is strange. But girls love it.

There is nothing to be done about the red eyes. I take the ring out of my pocket and look at it. Now is not the time to propose to her. And my idea to do it in the privacy of our home is no longer an option. After everything that's happened, I need something big. Huge. I need to knock her off her feet. I push the ring deep into the closet. There it will stay until I decide what to do.

But where am I even going? I have no idea where she is.

I check my phone and realize it's still turned off. Fucking hell. I forgot to charge it at the office. I plug it into the charger and wait a minute for it to turn on.

"Answer... Answer... Answer..." I mumble at the ringing sound.

"Hey." Her voice is the most beautiful thing I've ever heard.

"Ayala..." My voice cracks.

"Ethan? Are you okay? Did something happen to you?" She sounds worried. Even now, after a strange woman told Ayala I fucked her and got her pregnant.

"Yes. I..." My voice trails off. What can I say? That I have nightmares when she's not with me? That I want her back? She knows that. It won't convince her of anything.

"Can we meet and talk? Please."

"Yes. Should we meet at my place, where you slept last night?" Her tone is sarcastic.

"You know," I state as a fact.

"I wanted to talk to you, so I went there to look for you."

I clench my teeth. "Let me explain. It's not what you think."

"What else did you lie to me about, Ethan? I can't believe anything you say anymore."

"No, I didn't lie to you. Please, just let me explain. You can't get me out of your life without at least letting me explain," I beg.

"Okay," she says after a long silence.

I sigh in relief.

"I'm at Olive's."

So Olive knows too. Brilliant. "I'm on my way."

Olive opens the door for me. She's dressed in pajamas and has an angry look on her face.

"Not now, Olive," I mutter. I need to concentrate, not start a fight with her too. But it seems she has other plans,, and has no intention of letting me get away easily.

"Yes, now." She blocks my entrance. "How could you be so stupid, Ethan? You are my best friend, and I always thought you were exceptionally smart, and in the simplest things, that's where you fall? I don't get it."

I rub my temples. "Please, let me talk to her. I have to explain to her what happened."

"You should have me on your side, too. It could help you."

"I know. But first, I must see her."

Olive clears the way for me at last, and I go inside. Ayala is sitting on the couch, wrapped in a blanket and looking thoughtful. She knows I'm here, but she doesn't turn to me. Olive disappears from view, giving us privacy.

"What do you want, Ethan?" she says, still not looking at me.

"You."

"You had me."

"I hope I still do." I whisper. "At no point did I mean to hurt you or lie to you."

She turns to me. Her blue eyes are sad, and it hurts like a blow to the heart.

"I made a mistake not telling you about Lena. She caught me by surprise just that morning. I wasn't ready, and I didn't handle it well. I'm not used to being in a relationship. And besides, I'm sure it's not my child, and in any case, I don't want a child from her."

Ayala is silent for a moment. "And if it is your child?"

"It's not."

"How can you be so sure?"

"Because I didn't come." There. I said it. "I couldn't fucking come."

"What do you mean?"

"The whole time I saw you in front of my eyes. I felt like I was cheating on you, even though we weren't together. I could barely get it up."

"And she doesn't know that?" I see I surprised Ayala with my confession.

"No. Of course not. I pretended I did because it was too humiliating." There is no other way but the truth now.

"It affects both of us, no matter the result," she says. "And you didn't feel comfortable sharing it with me. You keep me outside. Do you know what she told me?"

I shake my head. What did that bitch say to her? I never

thought it would be such a big mistake. Huge. And all because I wanted to show how much of a man I am. One hell of a man.

"She said I'd better find another sugar daddy because you'll be busy soon."

I smirk, then realize she's not kidding. "You didn't take her nonsense seriously, did you? She's just trying to freak you out."

"I know. I didn't think too much about it until after I realized you weren't going to tell me. That you were hiding things from me. Now I think she was right."

"No." I grab Ayala's arms, but she shakes me off.

"I don't share your life. I'm just someone who warms your bed. Just like she said."

"Never. I've never felt the way I feel with you. I'm willing to give up everything I have for you. I want to marry you, damn it!"

She smiles a sad smile. "Yeah, right. Marry a doll? Someone who will wait for you at home and not cause problems? So that you can continue to lead your life like before?"

"You are the love of my life, and I've shared more with you than I have ever shared with anyone. You know the hardest things about me. Things no one knows. How can you say that? How can you think that?" I told her about my terrible past, and not only did she not run away, but she also stood up to my parents and defended me. Twice.

"Why didn't you tell me there was no apartment? You let me think I had my own place if I needed it. You made me feel stupid when I went looking for you there."

"The apartment is just a stupid mistake. I planned to cancel the lease while I waited for you to arrive from San Francisco. Then the pictures were published, and I flew back to you, and I forgot the whole matter. I didn't mean to. It just happened. I'd been worrying about you, and I just missed the deadline. I simply completely forgot about it."

She shakes her head. "I would have understood. It makes

sense. If only you'd bothered to explain it to me. But you chose not to share with me. Again."

"I'm just a man. I make mistakes. When I remembered about it, it was too late. And you didn't mention the apartment either. I thought we were doing fine, that we would live together. And yesterday, I was just a coward. I didn't want you to find out and get even angrier with me. Like now. I'll rent you an apartment. I kneel and rest my head on her lap.

"I don't want an apartment, nor anything else. I want a partner. Someone I can tell everything to and someone who will tell me everything back. Even the hard things." Her gaze is fixed on my eyes.

"I can be your partner. I can get better. Give me a chance. I make a lot of mistakes, I know, but I'll learn. You're my first real girlfriend. There's a learning curve." I smile crookedly. What else can I say? How can I convince her? I rest my head on her lap in despair.

I feel a slight flutter in my hair, then deeper, as she runs her fingers through it, and I surrender to the touch.

"I want to believe you," she whispers. "I really, really want to."

"Then say yes." I'm begging on my knees. What else should I do?

"I'm staying with Olive today."

"No, I need you to come back," I beg again.

She looks at me. "You shaved," she notes in a quiet voice. "And your eyes are red. Have you slept?"

"No."

"Are you having nightmares again?"

"Always when you're not with me." And especially when I'm worried about you.

She places a warm hand on my cheek. "Your skin is so smooth like this. I've never seen you without the stubble. You look so young."

I have no idea where her thoughts wander, but I don't risk saying something out of place.

"I want to believe you. But the burden of proof is on you. Let me into your life. Tell me about the mistakes, the things that will make me angry. No more hiding."

I nod vigorously. "I'm an open book. Anything you want."

"I need you to give me time."

The last thing I wanted was to leave without her. But I had no choice. I have to trust her to come back to me. I call Olive from the road.

"Keep her safe," I ask.

"She doesn't need to be looked after. She does a good job by herself."

"You're right. She does a much better job than me. After what happened with Anna, I was on a journey of self-destruction. If I didn't have Ryan and his family to pull me out of the black hole I was in, I wouldn't be here today. I'd either be in prison or dead."

"You know, you never told me what happened to Anna," Olive says in a quiet voice. "I know she's dead. I know her death affected you a lot, but I don't know what happened."

I bite my bottom lip. "Really? Somehow I thought it had already come up, or Ryan had told you."

"Ryan would never betray your trust. He won't tell me anything about you. And I tried. I tried to get embarrassing stories from your childhood out of him. He wouldn't give in."

"Haha." I grin. "How lucky I am he's watching over me. You would make my life miserable if you knew all my dirty secrets."

"Do you trust me?" she asks.

"Sure."

"So tell me what happened?"

"Someday," I say. "It's not a light conversation."

"Okay." She's silent for a moment. "Don't worry. Ayala is fine here with me. Give her some time. I'll convince her to forgive you."

"Thanks, Olive." I hang up.

I crawl through the heavy traffic of Manhattan, lost in thought. I need to tell Olive about Anna. She's a genuine friend. She needs to know.

Fuck.

Fucking hell.

Clifford's words from the party hit my ears like drums.

Even Olive doesn't know that Anna was raped. No one knows. Only my parents, Ryan, and now also Ayala. They didn't tell anyone, and certainly not that son of a bitch. So how does he know?

My whole body contracts in pain, and my fists tighten on the steering wheel. He's going to die.

I press the Call button. "It was Clifford."

"What?" Ryan doesn't understand, and I forget he's not in my head.

"He told me at the New Year's Eve party that even after Anna was *raped* and I got into trouble and didn't finish school, his father still preferred me to him."

"Well, he's screwed in the head. Who cares what his father thinks—"

"No one knows that Anna was raped, Ryan. No one."

A loud silence falls when he realizes what I'm saying. "Fuck."

I growl loudly. "I'm going to kill him."

"Don't go there."

"Do you think I can sit quietly while I know that son of a bitch raped and killed my sister?" My fists close tightly on the steering wheel until my knuckles turn white, and I step harder on the gas.

"You should go to the police and report it. Let them take care of him."

"They won't do anything. She's dead, and I have no proof. My parents never reported what happened. He got away with it. I can't let him get away with it, Ryan." Rage consumes me, breaking all the barriers. All these years, our parents have been friends, invited to the same parties. They stand and smile at me, asking to see me. I even hired that shit as a favor to them. If he hadn't tried to destroy my company, he would still be working for me. I hired the person who raped my sister. I press hard on the brakes, ignoring the beeps and honks from the cars behind me, and pull over, get out of the car and throw up on the ground, unable to bear the thought.

It's not a faceless boy anymore. This is someone I know. Someone who studied with me did this to her.

I hear a voice from inside the car and realize that I didn't disconnect the call.

"Ethan!" Ryan shouts.

I get back into the car and lean my face on the steering wheel. "I'm here."

"Don't do it. Don't ruin your life because of him. Everything you've built, all the women and men you've helped, everything will go to waste."

"He already ruined my life." I hang up.

I close my eyes and open them again. He's going to pay.

CHAPTER 38

Ayala

I need this distance, even though it feels like I'm punishing both of us right now. I realize Ethan's has nightmares and that he's not sleeping. I know how it feels because I've experienced it, too. He also admitted everything right away when I asked. He is trying.

But it's hard not to compare him with Michael. He apologized, and I forgave him. Over and over again. I let my guard down, and evil slipped in. I woke up when it was too late. How can I trust the same thing is not happening now?

Because it's Ethan.

He would never do to me what Michael did. Ethan's not trying to hold me back, imprison me, or separate me from my friends. He was patient with me, waiting for me every step of the way until I was ready for him. I have to at least give him the same patience I got from him. Now it's time to talk.

"Hey Ryan," I answer the call with a smile, ready for the lecture that will surely come now. Ethan's sent his best friend to convince me to return to him. Luckily, I have already decided.

"Ayala, I need you to come with me," he says.

"What's happened?" I rise to my feet.

"He's going to kill him. You must come with me. Help me stop him."

"Slow down. What's happened? I don't understand."

"Ethan believes Clifford Nightingale is the one who raped Anna, and I think he's right."

"What?" I scream. "How?"

"Clifford made a slip-of-the-tongue during their last meeting. He said something he wasn't supposed to know. Ethan is on his way there, and I think he's going to kill him. Ethan's life will be over if he does that."

"I'm at Olive's. Can you pick me up?"

"On my way to you."

I get dressed as fast as I can and go downstairs, shifting weight from foot to foot until Ryan's Mercedes pulls up next to me. What if it's too late? What if we don't arrive in time?

We race to the address. Ryan runs red lights and almost has an accident, but nothing stops him. As soon as he parks, I burst out of the car and run to the house. Ethan's Porsche is there, parked on the street. Shit, he's already here.

"Ayala?" The Porsche door opens.

I stop running and turn back. Ethan's tormented face appears before my eyes.

I run into his arms, collapsing on his lap, tears flooding my eyes. He's here. He's okay.

"I want him to pay for what he did to her. I want him to suffer," he mumbles.

"We'll make sure he pays." Ryan appears beside me. "I'll help with what I can to bring him to justice."

Ethan closes his eyes. "I planned to go in and kill him. I was ready to give up everything I have, my businesses, Savee... I was willing to sit in jail to make him pay for what he did."

"And why didn't you do it?" I ask.

"Because of you. I promised I'd be there for you. I promised not to leave you again."

After we file an official report, and the police promise to summon Clifford for questioning, we get into the Porsche and drive home.

Ethan hasn't spoken since we left Clifford's house, and I'm debating whether I should try to talk to him or let him be quiet. But he surprises me and starts talking by himself.

"I didn't expect we'd ever find out who did it," he says. "After all, more than a decade has passed. In the beginning, I drove myself crazy trying to learn who did that to her. I used my resources to find the criminal, to confront him. But I failed. In my dreams, the police would throw him in prison for the rest of his life, and he'd be raped over and over while there, just like he raped Anna. Poetic justice." Ethan looks at me.

I nod. "Didn't the police try to learn who it was?"

"My parents never filed a report about the rape. So no."

"They didn't file a report? Why?"

"Family honor, or something stupid like that. They said nothing would bring her back, so there was no point. They didn't want anyone to know what happened, not to tarnish her name. As if it was her fault that she was raped."

"I'm so sorry."

"Do you think they knew what happened before the suicide and tried to hide it to protect themselves?" he asks.

I shake my head. "No. There's no way they would do that. At least, I can't believe they would. I'm sure that, like my parents, they simply made a mistake in their judgment when they found her. You saw what happened to me when the pictures got published. It's difficult. They didn't want to go through all that. They didn't want *you* to go through all that."

"I needed that closure. I wanted to see whoever was responsible taken to court. Instead, I got years of torture. I let him work for me, damn it!" He pulls over onto the side of the road and puts his head on the wheel.

I want to comfort him. I put a hand on his shoulder, and he leans into my embrace. We sit, hugging each other for long minutes, then he starts the car and gets back on the road.

We go back to his apartment, and I restlessly pace the floor.

I still think of it as his apartment. That's part of the problem. It doesn't feel like our home. I'm still a guest here. But there's no point in renting a place for myself. I won't use it. I hadn't felt the need for it until yesterday, and there's no point in paying for it.

"What?" Ethan looks up at me from his laptop. He's quiet and has been working on something since we got back but doesn't miss my mood.

"I was thinking about the apartment," I explain.

"I told you. That was a terrible mistake. I'll rent you another one."

"I'm thinking I don't want one."

"Really?" He arches an eyebrow.

"It's unnecessary to spend so much money on an apartment that I'll never use. You won't do anything to make me leave again, right?"

He nods.

"But this apartment... I don't feel like I belong here. I'm a guest here."

"Tell me how I can help."

"I want Olive to redecorate it. I love her style." How did I not think of this before? I adore her house.

"Ayala... Olive's very busy with the store. She has no time for such things. And I would know because I help her run the business."

"Right. So you know how much to pay her for her to agree." I see him take a deep breath, but he doesn't refuse.

He seems distant, and that worries me. "I know you've had a rough morning, but it's Saturday. Maybe we can do something together?"

He gets up and closes the laptop. "Sure, what do you want to do? I'm ready to spend the rest of the day in bed."

"That's not what I meant." I give him a fake, sullen look.

He laughs. "Okay, okay... So, first, we'll go out, then bed?"

I smack him in the arm. "How about skating at the Rockefeller?"

"No way."

"Why not?"

"Because I don't feel like breaking anything. I've seen enough hospitals for the next few years."

"Wait a moment. You don't know how to skate, do you? How is that possible? You grew up here."

"Have you seen my parents? Do you think they took us skating?"

No. Probably not. "I'll teach you. It's not that hard." I laugh.

"Okay, let's go. But you're not allowed to laugh at me or mention it later. And if I break something, you'll have to take care of me." He grins.

Okay. He asked me not to mention it. But he said nothing about pictures...

We rent skates and enter the rink. I have to hold back from laughing when I see him step on the ice, looking terrified. He's so out of his element. His hands are stretched out in front of him, and his legs are shaking. A powerful man, afraid to land on his ass. I'm glad I skated a lot as a girl and can support him.

I tease him a bit, swirling around him, poking him. Taking the opportunity to remove all the evil air that has blown in the last few days. I want to feel like a normal couple, just hanging out and having fun. Not two people who have gone through unspeakable things. Today we are just Ethan and Ayala. Two ordinary people.

He makes an angry face, but I can see he is amused by me. I haven't had this much fun since I was a girl. It's fun to skate with the chilly wind on my face.

He moves forward, and I decide it's time to help him. I slide next to him and give him a hand. We glide, hand in hand, foot by foot. He sways and loses his balance, causing me to wobble and struggle to steady both of us. So I decide to stand in front of him, take both of his hands, and skate backward.

"Tell me if I'm going to bump into someone," I warn him, hoping he notices because his gaze is fixed on me, and he doesn't seem to be aware of his surroundings.

"Ethan!" I have to repeat his name twice before he shakes it off and answers me.

"I need you to look ahead, or we'll both fall." He looks up and directs me while I hold his hands, keeping him steady, and we slide together. This is a pleasant feeling, his hands in mine. I can watch him without feeling like I'm staring. I can check out his beautiful features. His strong jaw, the full lips, his golden eyes...

The idea of Ethan and me getting into bed and not coming out doesn't sound so bad to me right now.

After he gains some confidence, I let go of him so he can try on his own to stay upright. It just takes a minute before he's as excited as a little boy who's just discovered there's no monster under the bed. He succeeds, and we glide side by side, still close to the railing. Ethan doesn't dare to get far yet.

I haven't skated in years, but I was good as a girl. Let's see what I remember.

I move away from him, gain some speed, and glide around,

being careful not to collide with the dozens of other skaters. A little swing, and I spin on the ice. Yay! I did it!

I turn to glide back and try a tiny jump. My landing is bad, and I only keep my balance at the last second. Well, I'm too rusty for jumps. I turn back to see where Ethan is and find him standing rooted to the same spot and looking at me in amazement.

With a broad smile, I slide toward him and break in front of him. "What?"

"How do you know how to do that? You're a professional."

"I used to skate a lot as a girl, but I'm far from professional. I raise my head to kiss him, and he grasps my hips and pulls me closer.

We skate some more, side by side, circling the rink. Two squealing children pass us with great speed. Ethan tries to stop but gets knocked down.

Shit.

"Are you okay?" I hurry to bend down to the ice. He smiles at me and doesn't seem hurt. Laughing, I take my phone out of my pocket and take a picture of him.

"Hey!" he protests. "I'm laid out here on the ice, and you're taking a picture? Where's the help? Where's the loving treatment?"

"Okay." I reach out to him to help him up. He takes my hand and pulls.

I fall on his chest, and now we're both lying on the ice, laughing.

I want to stay like this, in our own little private world, where we're both happy and not thinking about our troubles.

"Is everything all right, ma'am? Mister? Need help?" I look up to see a rink employee standing above us.

Ethan shakes his head. "It's all right. We're getting up." I stand, pulling Ethan with me, and he plops down again, then tries to get up carefully. The employee helps Ethan to his feet.

As soon as the guy pulls away, Ethan tells me, "I think I broke my ass," and a giggle escapes me. "But it's worth it to hear you laugh like that today," he adds. We slide together to the exit. "Thank you for taking me here, for helping me forget a little."

It's funny to me how this day has flipped since this morning. I had planned to stay on Olive's couch and bawl my eyes out. Then I raced after him in a panic to keep him from going to jail, and now we're both laughing and embracing after a day out.

There's something in what I feel with him, this safety and security. The comfort. It's as if I am finally home. Something I didn't have even when I *was* home.

It doesn't matter which apartment we are in. I feel at home when I'm with him.

He takes off his coat and rubs his tailbone.

"Hurts?"

"A little. I told you I'd break something." He smiles. "And now you have to heal me. And I know exactly how."

CHAPTER 39

Ayala

"I'm sorry, but I have to finish something. Give me a couple of hours." Ethan insists on continuing to work on the laptop, even though it's the weekend.

I decide to use the time to video call my parents. I miss them. "Hey, Mom."

"Sweetie! How are you? All is well? Are you still seeing Dr. S—"

"Yes, yes, I'm fine. Have you seen my campaign?"

"Yes. I saw," Mom says, and Dad's face pops onto the screen. "We're proud of you, sweetie."

"How's Ethan?" they ask. It's code for "how's your relationship doing." Since the dinner at their place, they're more interested in him than in me. How did he conquer them like that?

Same as he conquered me.

"We're fine. He needs to get some work done, so I thought we'd talk." We chat some more before I hang up.

I check on him again and see that Ethan is still working. But I'm bored.

Missing my parents reminds me of the fragile relationship between Ethan and his parents. I provoked a confrontation between them at the party and instead created a bigger rift between them just because they don't like me.

His parents are important to him. He never cut contact with them, despite what happened. He always hoped that someday they would accept him back, and I ruined it.

I need to fix it.

"I'm going out for a bit," I say, grabbing the Jeep keys and slipping out the door before he can question me.

What if they don't let me in? I barely know them, and they don't like me. But I know if I had called to announce myself ahead of time, they would lock the door and not agree to talk to me. Using the element of surprise, I still have a chance.

I knock on their door. And then louder when no one answers. Maybe they're not at home? Shit. Why didn't I think to check?

I raise my hand to knock again, and the door opens, leaving my hand in mid-air.

"Mrs. Wolf." I nod to Ethan's mother.

Her eyes widen as she takes a moment to speak. "Yes?"

"Can I talk to you?"

She's blocking the door with her body as if I'll burst in and cause a commotion. Then she moves aside and gestures with her hand for me to come inside. I got in.

Mr. Wolf is sitting on the couch, and I guess he didn't hear it was me because he almost leaps from his seat when he sees me.

"What is she doing here?" he asks his wife.

She shrugs. "I don't know. She asked to talk."

"Thank you for agreeing to speak with me." I thank her and wait for her to sit down as well. "First, I wanted to apologize." I see the surprised looks on their faces. This is not what they expected to hear from me.

"I understand you don't like me, and you have a reason for that. I got Ethan into a lot of trouble." Lots. "But I love him, and as long as he wants me by his side, I have no intention of leaving."

I declare my intentions, pausing for a moment for the message to sink in.

"It was a mistake on my part to keep him away from you because I know how important parents can be. I know how important you are to Ethan. And he needs you in his life despite everything, even though I don't think he deserves the treatment he receives from you." Looking at their shocked faces, I remain silent for a moment.

"I wanted you to know that I intend to encourage him to renew the relationship and come here. I'll stay at home so as not to cause conflict, and I'll not stand between you anymore. If he decides not to be in contact with you, that will be his decision alone."

"Do you love him?" Laura asks me.

I nod vigorously. "Deeply. I didn't plan on it. I wanted to build a life here on my own, but he kept coming, again and again, until I gave in and fell in love with him." When I recall our encounters, I smile. I even smacked him in the head, and still, he kept coming.

"He can be stubborn, our son," his father, Gabriel, says in a soft voice.

"He's stubborn," I agree. "Stubborn, beautiful, and noble and the best person I know."

Laura shakes her head. "I don't know how to reach him. He never agrees to share anything with us. He's completely cut us off. He didn't even allow us to visit him after that horrible incident." Tears come to her eyes. "He's our only son, the only child we have left."

"You made him feel guilty for his sister's death. He can't shake it off. He can't get over it. And every time you talk to him, you only reinforce that belief."

Gabriel scoffs. "We took him for treatment for years. All he did was destroy everything he touched. Do you know how hard it was when he was a teenager? How much trouble he got into? He broke into stores just to show he could. Every day I would worry about what I would have to do to get him out of trouble. He was almost killed once. Did he tell you about that? It's a miracle he's alive and well and not in jail."

Does this man truly not understand? How can he not see what is so obvious?

"Ethan didn't break into shops to show he could. He broke into stores because he wanted your attention. Because he was crying out for your love. A psychologist cannot give him the forgiveness he needs from you."

"Excuse me?" Laura asks.

"Did either of you ever tell him he wasn't to blame for what happened to Anna? That she didn't kill herself because of him?"

"But it's obvious," Laura says. "It's obvious he's not guilty. He didn't do it."

"It's not obvious to him! He thinks you blame him for the party and for her death. All you did was send him to more and more therapists. You never talked to him about what happened. About how he found her. Do you know what a trauma it is to see such a thing?"

"Do you think it's easy for us to talk about this?" Gabriel raises his voice, and I panic and take a step back. He lowers his tone. "Do you think it was easy to come home and see our daughter lying in a pool of blood?" His voice breaks.

"No. I think it was terrible. That it was terrible for all of you. And especially for a seventeen-year-old boy who thinks that everything rests on his shoulders."

Gabriel shakes his head in disbelief. "No."

"And now, today, I find out that you didn't even file a report with the police. Ethan couldn't even get the closure he needed."

"We didn't file a report because Laura couldn't withstand it. You weren't here. You didn't see. We were broken. Laura was living on sedatives. If we had opened it to the public, we wouldn't have survived."

"But Ethan was broken, too! Do you know he still has nightmares? Over ten years have passed, and he still has nightmares. Everything he does is for her in some way."

"I didn't think—"

"Yes. And he became such an amazing person. Everything he does, the company he built. It looks so simple from the outside, but now that I'm working there... Do you know he donates most of his income to keep Savee alive?"

"No." Laura shakes her head. "What do you mean?"

"Savee is not a profitable company. Ethan invests private money into it. In big numbers."

"I didn't know that," Gabriel murmurs.

"You don't know many things. But what he did when he was a teenager...? That's not who he is now. The fact that he could come to his senses and organize his life as it is today without your help is a miracle in my eyes. I know that without my parents, I wouldn't have been able to get out of the black hole I sank into. Ethan did it alone."

Gabriel looks at Laura with wet eyes. I might have started some wheels turning.

"I don't know why Clifford Nightingale did what he did, but I hope they convict him and you all finally get some peace. I know Ethan needs it."

His parents nod. I see tears glistening in his mother's eyes. "We pushed Clifford on Ethan all these years. His parents wanted them to be friends, and we agreed. Only it never worked. We always thought Ethan was to blame, that he didn't accept Clifford as a friend, but it was Clifford. He was too jealous of Ethan for it to work. His parents and the two of us are guilty of his hatred. Everything that happened was because of us. I can't believe we were friends with this family."

"Don't blame yourself or Ethan. Clifford is the only one to blame. I also blamed myself for a long time for what happened to me. I thought I was in the wrong, that I brought the beatings and abuse on myself. But the victim is not the guilty party. Just a victim."

They nod.

"Invite him again," I say. "I'll make sure he comes. Without me."

"No." Ethan's father surprises me. All of this, and he still isn't ready to forgive?

"We want you to come with him." He exchanges a look with Laura, and she nods.

"We should apologize," he says. "We were also unfair to you. We blamed you for things you had no control over. You're good for him. I've never seen him as happy as he is with you."

Tears come to my eyes.

"Maybe we can turn a new page," Gabriel says.

His mother adds, "When you were away from him, he faded away. Even in the brief times I saw him, it wasn't the Ethan I knew. It was as if the joy of life had disappeared from him. At first, I blamed the terrible experience he went through, the injury, and the police investigation. But time passed, and he didn't get any better. He only came back to life when he reunited with you. Even the lawsuit didn't concern him once you came back. I was blind not to have seen it sooner," Laura says, standing and approaching me.

She reaches out to me, and I decide to go for it and hug her. I can feel the automatic reluctance, but then she softens and gives in to the embrace, and we break away.

I don't think anyone has hugged her in a very long time.

A tear runs down her cheek.

"I hope we can be on good terms," I say. "But even if not, it's okay. I won't stand in the way. But if you hurt him again, I will protect him. I will always protect him."

"I wouldn't expect any less," Gabriel tells me, his eyes glistening with unshed tears. "I understand what he sees in you. You are a fighter."

We say goodbye, and tears of joy fill my eyes. I can't believe what just happened. I got approval from Ethan's parents.

I got a fucking hug from the ice queen. Well, I took one anyway. I get in the car and take the phone out of my handbag.

Shit.

Sixteen missed calls from Ethan.

I call him immediately. "Hey."

"Fuck, Ayala." His voice trembles.

"Sorry, the phone was in my handbag. I didn't notice. Are you mad?"

"No. I'm dying of worry. You left without saying where you were going, and it's been several hours. Where did you go?"

"It doesn't matter. I'm on my way back."

"Where are you?" His tone is low.

I squirm. "Uh…"

"We said no more secrets," he scolds. "It works for both sides."

He's right. And it's not that I have anything to hide, but not sure how he'll take it, I prefer he didn't know that I messed with his affairs.

"Tell me where you are now," he demands in a cold tone, and for a moment, I feel like hanging up on him and running away. But he sounds upset. Really upset, so I resist the urge and answer him.

"At your parents' house." I close my eyes.

"Come home."

I don't know what to expect as I walk in. What will he say? What will he do? Is he angry at me?

I find him sitting on the sofa, his head between his hands. He doesn't look up, and the worry nibbles at me. When he finally looks up, there's pain in his eyes. He reaches out and pulls me into his arms.

"Please don't do that again. Don't disappear like that. You know what goes through my mind."

I shake my head. "What?"

"Come on. You disappeared from me twice. What am I supposed to think?"

"The only reason I ran away no longer exists." I take his face in my hands. "I'm not running away anymore. But you're right. It wasn't wise for me to disappear without explaining where I was going and not answering my phone. I'm sorry."

He hugs me tighter. "What did you do at my parents' house?"

"I went to tell them I won't interfere with your relationship with them. I regretted that evening."

"Ayala..."

"But the conversation developed in directions I didn't expect, so it took some time."

He shakes his head, looking stressed.

"It's not what you think. We came to an understanding. About many things. You could even say we've made up," I hasten to say.

His eyes widen. "What do you mean 'we made up?'"

"We didn't become good friends, but I think they no longer object to my presence in your life," I explain. I hope they also apologize to Ethan, but we'll have to wait and see.

An expression of disbelief crosses his face.

"Don't be so faithless. I have powers of persuasion."

"Oh, I'm sure of it." His lips crush mine.

CHAPTER 40

Ethan

M y parents invited us to dinner and specifically mentioned that both Ayala and I were invited.

I don't understand how she did it. She must be a magician if she could soften someone like my father.

"Ethan," my mother says as we sit down, "I'm so glad you came. We want to know what's going on with you." She glances at Ayala.

Ayala squeezes my palm, but I just don't know how to answer that. How do you reconnect after such a long time? Shall we talk about Clifford's arrest? I'm not sure this is an appropriate topic of conversation right now.

Silence falls.

"Ethan is helping a lot with my new Savee campaign," Ayala says, trying to save the conversation. "Have you heard of it?"

They nod and start talking to Ayala while I watch her. She's excited and speaks enthusiastically, sweeping everyone into her sphere. How can anyone resist her? Her gaze is radiant as she explains the subject close to her heart. I watch my parents. They are captivated. It seems they've learned to appreciate her.

"What do you think, Ethan?" Ayala turns to me, interrupting my wandering thoughts.

"What?" I have no idea what they said.

"Your mother suggested organizing a fundraiser for Savee. To help my project expand. What do you think?" she asks again.

"Yes, that sounds like a great idea," I say.

"I understand you donate quite a bit to Savee," my dad points out, and I nod. "I didn't know that. Too bad you didn't tell us. We'll be happy to help, to contribute as well."

"I don't need hel—"

Ayala kicks me under the table.

"And he'll accept with pleasure," Ayala answers, and my father looks pleased. Since when is he satisfied with giving me something?

We finish eating and move to the living room. My mother puts a pot of tea in the center of the coffee table.

"We owe you an apology," she says. "More than an apology," she clarifies, throwing a meaningful look at my father. I don't understand what she's talking about. But it seems everyone else does.

"Ayala helped us to realize we wronged you many years ago. That we didn't make it clear enough that you're not to blame for what happened with Anna. We never blamed you, Ethan. It was so hard for us to bring up the subject, and it was easier to avoid it, but that was a mistake. We needed to talk to you. To let you know it was not your fault." Her eyes glisten with tears.

Dad clears his throat. "We didn't do it then, but we'll do it now, and hopefully, it's not too late to repair the damage done. We're sorry for what happened. It wasn't your fault. It was never your fault. You just threw a party, which any normal seventeen-year-old would have done. As her parents, it was our responsibility to pay attention to what was happening with Anna. I wish you hadn't been the one to find her like that. I wish I could take it all away from you, make you forget the sight. It wasn't your fault."

I can't breathe. The tears begin to flow. I can't hold it back. I just can't. I get up and leave the living room.

"Ethan!" I hear my mother calling after me, but I don't stop. My legs lead me to my old room. I stop at the entrance, and my eyes widen. It looks the same as when I left. They changed nothing. I close the door and sit on the bed. I need air.

Not a minute passes, and there's a knock on the door.

"Give me a minute," I ask, not wanting them to see me like this, but the door opens. I open my mouth, ready to ask them to go away, but my gaze finds Ayala. Her blue eyes are full of understanding.

And that's it. I can't hold back any longer, and the tears pour down my face.

She doesn't say anything. She walks up to me and takes me in her arms. I'm a total mess. This couldn't happen to me at a more inappropriate time.

"I'm sorry," I say to her after I gather myself.

"You're not the one who needs to apologize for anything. They had to, and that's exactly what they did."

"I love you so much," I say, tightening my hold on her. I can never let her go.

I planned everything. Every little detail. And now all that remains is to execute.

I walk through the gallery where I met Ayala for the first time and give instructions to the employees who are tidying up the place for me. It must be perfect.

"Ethan, stop," Olive scolds me. "You're confusing everyone.

You asked me to do this. Let me do my job." She pushes me out of the way.

It's better this way. I'm too nervous. I'd better go get ready before I lose my shit. There's not much time left.

When I return to the gallery later, wearing a new suit, I look around, amazed.

Olive did a crazy job here. The place doesn't look at all like before. The walls are black to create a dark and romantic atmosphere. Coal bulbs hang from the ceiling, illuminating the place with a golden light. A huge glass sculpture of a humming-bird stands in the middle of the gallery on a small platform.

"I know you're here, little sister, watching over me," I whisper to the statue. "You would have loved Ayala."

The vegetation that was here the first time we met was brought back, also illuminated. Small tables are scattered around the space. At my request, Olive also organized a small dance floor, and next to it is a stage with all the band's equipment. The place looks magical.

I'll have to thank Olive later, as she went to get Ayala. The guests I invited are arriving, and I have to welcome them.

Everybody's here. Ayala's parents, my parents, Madeleine, Amber, Ryan, Maya, and the baby. All the employees from Savee. I even invited the team that worked with her at Lunis.

Olive
Five minutes to arrival.

"She's coming!" I yell, sending everybody to stand in their places. My heart is beating so hard that I think everyone here can hear it.

I stand in the center, and as soon as we hear the car pull up outside, I signal the band to start.

They play "Every Breath You Take." The song I sang to her for our first date. I'm on my knees.

The door opens.

I look only at her eyes, looking for that blue sparkle, for the love in her eyes that gives me strength every day.

I see the initial shock, her mouth falling open, and the glimmer of tears when she sees me kneeling. Then her gaze leaves me, and she sees everyone who came for her. So many people who have come to love and care about her in such a short time.

"Ayala Beckett," I say as she approaches. "You appeared in my life like a tropical storm. A storm that changed my life. You poured champagne on me, hit me in the head, and knocked me to the floor. Literally." I hear laughter in the background. "But no matter what you do, you won't be able to keep me away from you. Because from the moment I saw you for the first time, I knew you had to be mine. You changed me and brought me back to life. Now I understand what it is to truly live." I stop and take the box out of my pocket.

Tears run down her cheeks, and she inhales deeply as her eyes land on the blue box.

"Ayala, I don't want to go through another day without you. I don't want to fear that you won't be mine. I love you like I didn't know it was possible to love. You broke me and rebuilt me. I'm yours forever. Will you agree to be mine?"

I open the box and extend my hand to her.

She's crying and doesn't answer, and for a moment, my soul sinks. She falls to her knees in front of me, nodding, tears flowing down her cheeks. "Yes, Ethan. I'm yours. Always have been."

I take out the ring, and it sparkles under the lights, just like the sparkle in her eyes, and I put it on her finger.

I stand, and she falls into my arms, kissing me. Everything and everyone around us disappears. I don't even notice the applause of those around us as I turn to them and scream, "She said yes!"

They come from everywhere to hug us, to hug her.

"You deserve to be happy," Dana says as she also gives Ayala a big hug. "When I saw you for the first time, I knew you were special and strong, and you proved it in a big way." She turns to me. "Take care of her."

I nod.

Nicky is next to congratulate Ayala. "I can't believe you're going to get married! All the dates I arranged for you, and in the end, you marry this guy." She looks at me and winks.

"Hey," I protest with a smile. "I'm one of the most wanted bachelors. I'm quite a bargain."

Ayala and Nicky laugh. The band plays another song, and I pull Ayala to me and spin her around in my arms. We dance, surrounded by our loved ones. That's all I ever wanted.

CHAPTER 41

Ayala

"**H**e's not mine." Ethan turns to me, a big smile on his face after he hangs up the phone.

"What?" I look away from the TV, where I've been sitting curled up for the last half hour. I don't feel so good.

"Lena's baby. It's not mine. I got the test results. Her lawyer sent the papers. There's no match. I told you it wasn't mine. That woman is going to have to crawl back into the hole she came out of."

I can't help but release a sigh of relief. I'm glad that woman will be out of our lives forever.

"How terrible am I that I'm happy?" I ask him.

"Of course, you're happy. I'm happy too. I don't want a child from a one-time mistake I made." He sits down next to me on the couch, and I curl up under his arm, lifting my hand to take his, the blue stone on my finger shimmering. Reminding me of what I agreed to do just a few days ago.

I never would have believed that I would get married again so soon after what happened, but when I look at Ethan next to me, and my heart expands with happiness, I know I'm in the right place. With him, I feel safe. Loved.

A wave of nausea rises in my throat, and I gag.

"What's wrong?" Ethan looks worried. "Again?"

I raise a finger and run to the bathroom, just in time to reach the toilet and throw up. Ethan comes after me and holds up my hair. I groan as the spasms in my stomach subside, then I sit on the floor. "This virus has been bugging me for two days."

Ethan's eyes widen. He opens his mouth to speak and closes it again without saying a word.

"What?"

"I'll be right back," he says and hurries out.

I close my eyes, exhausted. Where did he go? Is the sky going to fall on us again? Life has thrown us every obstacle possible, and we've survived. "Come on, throw everything you have." I look up with narrowed eyes. "Can you hear me? Nothing will break us!"

I freshen up and go back to sitting on the couch, leaning my head back. I feel so weak.

Where the hell did he go? I want him here.

Half an hour passes, and finally, Ethan returns, holding a bag. I look at him with interest. "What did you bring? Something for my nausea? I'm not sure it will help. I'll just wait a few days for it to pass."

"I think you'll have to wait more than a few days," he says, pulling a box out of the bag. "I think you're pregnant."

My mouth falls open. "No."

He nods. "You need to test."

I take the box he hands me with trembling hands. It can't be. They told me I couldn't... "What if I am?"

"Then we'll raise him or her together, with love." He kisses the top of my head. "I can't wait to have a child with you. A big blue-eyed baby."

I get up and go to the bathroom, Ethan on my heels, holding my hand. I look at his loving eyes and exhale. "Nothing will break us."

The End.

Afterword

If you liked Ayala and Ethan, and you want to read a little more about how their story continues, head to the link below for a bonus **FREE** epilogue.

By registering at this link, you will also be joining my newsletter, where you will be the first to know about new releases, bonus content, reveals, and giveaways.

subscribepage.io/shattered

If you enjoyed *Shattered Secrets,* help me reach more readers by leaving a review on Amazon — it would be greatly appreciated — even a few words are a huge help.

https://www.amazon.com/review/create-review/?&asin= 965930451X

Write a review for Shattered Hope:

https://www.amazon.com/review/create-review/?&asin= 9659304501

On a Personal Note...

When I was seven or maybe eight, I lived in a small building in the city with my family. I had a friend who lived on the floor above us with her extended family. I used to go there to play with her, stay at her house, and sometimes eat with them. I trusted them. Just like most children trust the adults who surround them. As any normal child should be able to do.

One day, when I was playing outside, a member of her family approached me and asked if I liked sweets. He offered me candy.

I took it.

The next day, he bought me a marshmallow and gave it to me.

I liked it. I felt special. Out of all the kids in the building, he bought it for me. Only me.

The next day he told me he had bought me sweets again, but they were in the building's basement, so he invited me to come with him.

My parents taught me not to go with strangers, but he wasn't a stranger, right? He was a neighbor. I knew him. I had been in his house many times.

So I went with him.

He sat me on his lap. He told me I was beautiful.

He tried to unbutton my pants. I didn't want to. I tried to stop him, but he was persistent. He kept trying to put his hand in my panties.

I knew it was wrong. It didn't feel right. I was terrified and couldn't move. I didn't understand what he was doing. What he wanted from me. I just knew I didn't want him to touch me there.

Today I know he must have touched himself behind my back while he was trying to touch me.

I didn't tell anyone about this. I was so ashamed, even though I did nothing wrong. And although nothing too severe happened to me, and I got out of there before anything else happened, this memory from so many years ago is still imprinted in my mind.

Sometimes, even those we trust the most can betray us. Sometimes it can even be the person we love. It is not your fault. You have nothing to be ashamed of.

Even though this book is a work of fiction, I hope that my words will touch hearts. I hope that maybe, just maybe, my words can give someone the strength to get up and walk away.

The signs of abuse can be diverse. It doesn't have to be physical abuse. It can be sexual, mental, or emotional abuse. If you know someone in that kind of relationship, reach out. Offer help.

If your partner puts you down, if he's extremely jealous, if he forces you to do things you're not comfortable with, if he isolates you from your family or friends, if he doesn't allow you to work or to have money of your own, if he tries to control you, please seek help.

About the Author

Author Karin Winter was a software engineer who used to write code but decided she loved to write books even more. She writes steamy contemporary romances about strong women and broken men.

She lives with her husband, their four children, and a dog and dreams of traveling the world.

For new release updates and other fun goodies, sign up for her mailing list:

https://subscribepage.io/karinwinter

You can connect with her on:

https://linktr.ee/karinwinter

Join the Facebook group and discuss the book:

facebook.com/groups/1060206537985717

facebook.com/AuthorKarinWinter

tiktok.com/@karinwinterauthor

amazon.com/Karin-Winter/e/B0BL1JC8WV

goodreads.com/karinwinter

Also by Karin Winter

Read on how Ethan's story begins in the short story UNWORTHY

Grab your FREE Copy

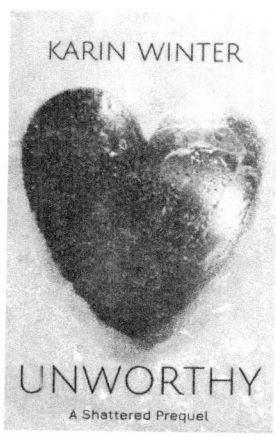